UP FOR GRABS

"Where are you from?" Kenlyn asked sweetly.

"Los Angeles," Travis replied pleasantly.

"What type of work are you engaged in...I mean...if you're at liberty to discuss your job?"

He glanced at her in confusion. Why wouldn't he be at liberty to discuss the fact that he was a meat inspector? "I'm a meat inspector," he said out loud.

A *what*? She fumed silently. How stupid did he think she was?

HOT ON HIS TRAIL

"While we're on the subject, Mr. Hayden, are *you* seeing other women?"

"Of course I'm not. I'm not that type of guy."

"Meaning that I *am* that type of woman?"

"How should I know? That's what I just asked you," he retorted heatedly.

"Then, no, I'm not seeing anyone but you. Is that what you want me to say?"

"Yes, but only if that's the truth," he said.

"Well, whether I'm telling the truth is something you'll have to decide for yourself!"

Other *Leisure Books* by Lori Copeland:

PLAYING FOR KEEPS/A TEMPTING STRANGER
OUT OF CONTROL/A WINNING COMBINATION
OUT OF THIS WORLD/FOREVER AFTER

UP FOR GRABS
—— & ——
HOT
ON HIS TRAIL

The Best Of
Lori Copeland

LEISURE BOOKS   NEW YORK CITY

A LEISURE BOOK®

October 1991

Published by

Dorchester Publishing Co., Inc.
276 Fifth Avenue
New York, NY 10001

To four very special couples at the lake,
The White Rock Partnership:
Junior and Shirley Hart, Tom and Rita Ratliff
Rodney and Lee Ann Morgan, and
John and Cathy Smart.

UP FOR GRABS

CHAPTER ONE

Kenlyn Grant pecked out the last paragraph on the keys of the aging IBM typewriter and let out a sigh of relief.

True, there wasn't a whole lot of news to report. Not much out of the ordinary ever happened in the small desert town of Isabel, Arizona, but when it did, the Isabel *Gazette* was right on top of it. The family-owned and -operated newspaper was only published once a week, so by the time its limited number of copies hit the local stands, most folks had already talked to death any news it contained anyway. But that had never stopped Kenlyn's determination to produce the best stories she was capable of pounding out.

The Isabel *Gazette* was a far cry from the Phoenix *Herald,* and it wasn't exactly the Yuma *Daily Sun,* either. But it didn't really matter to Kenlyn that she wasn't sitting behind some fancy desk in a bustling newsroom, breezing through her assignments with the aid of an expensive, high-tech computer.

Come to think of it—she snickered—an apple did sound good right now. Especially one of those big, juicy Red Delicious variety she had eyed earlier this morning over at Petersen's Grocery Store. The grumbling of her empty stomach agreed as she wished lunchtime would hurry up and get there.

Ever since she could remember, Kenlyn had dreamed of becoming a reporter. Like her father and his father before him, she was perfectly content in her dedication to filling the blank pieces of paper that would comprise the pages of the Isabel *Gazette*. As Grandpa Grant often said, "A good newspaper is what makes a town."

Sometimes an interesting story was hard to come by. Still, a story of *some* kind could always be found. Most of the town's population of five hundred citizens, give or take a tongue or two, were more than eager to supply a headline here and there.

And, besides, Kenlyn had been born with a nose for news. She could sniff out a hot scoop right with the best of them in the competitive field of journalism. The competition in Isabel wasn't exactly a dog-eat-dog situation, though. And she had to admit Tom Brokaw was never seen stalking the back streets of Isabel in hot pursuit of juicy tidbits. But she was satisfied with her station in life.

With a flick of the paper-release lever, she freed her latest journalistic contribution from the confines of the electric typewriter. The hot item this week was the surprise marriage that had taken place between Marcella Staples and Otis Clever. Critical, violet-blue eyes proficiently scanned the page as she made a final editing before handing in the article for publication. With professional pride, she glanced through the sentences that contained the coverage of Isabel's most recent and surely most talked about wedding.

A smile of accomplishment parted her lips as she read the details of the fashionable ceremony. The event was certain to have tongues wagging for months to come. Maybe it hadn't been as elaborate as Prince Andrew's wedding to Fergie, but it had been big enough for the entire community to be in attendance for the uniting of the local middle-aged couple. And, in honesty, could the Royal couple boast such a turnout for their home town, the article pointed out proudly.

Kenlyn's smile widened as she recalled how the wedding had taken the town completely unaware. That was a miracle in itself for Isabel. *Everyone* knew everyone else's business, but Marcella and Otis had managed to pull off the secret relationship without the town suspecting a thing.

Who would ever have thought that anyone would have proposed marriage (much less followed through with it) to homely Marcella Staples? Kenlyn sighed again. Guess a person would just have to meet the groom, Otis Clever, to ever believe it. She chuckled as she thought of Marcella's crispy, curled, mousey-brown hair that always looked fried to a cinder from too many home permanents. Maybe it was the Coke bottle-lensed glasses that prevented skinny Otis from noticing the strange orange glow her gums emitted when she grinned. But, bless her good old soul, Marcella *was* always grinning, and Kenlyn felt a warm affection for the newlyweds and wished them many long years of happiness.

Satisfied with the accuracy of her report and the absence of any glaring grammatical errors, she leaned back in her chair and lazily stretched her petite frame. Seconds later she grabbed her copy and headed for the desk of the *Gazette*'s editor and publisher—her father, Kenneth Grant.

The close-fitting jeans she was wearing clung to her small frame in all the right places, and her stylish leather boots made a rhythmic clicking sound as she walked across the polished hardwood floor. Ask any male in Isabel, sixteen to sixty, about Kenlyn Grant, and they'd be quick to point out the fact that she was a real "looker." The Western cut of her lavender and pale blue plaid shirt accentuated her slender waist and the full form of her breasts. Today the muted colors she was wearing made her eyes the Elizabeth Taylor violet that sent men's pulses racing.

And the nice thing about it all, the town would happily relay to all who cared to listen, Kenlyn Grant didn't seem to be aware of her unusual good looks. She was bright, infectiously happy, and totally unaffected by what nature had so richly blessed her with.

Kenneth Grant, a distinguished fiftyish-looking man with a slight frosting of gray sprinkled throughout his temples, was deeply engrossed in the composition of the weekly specials at Petersen's Grocery as Kenlyn triumphantly tossed the crisp copy of her assignment into the metal tray on his desk. "All finished, Pop!" Propping herself up on the corner of his massive desk, she grinned at him affectionately. "Wait till you read it. You'll envy ole Otis to death."

14

Mr. Grant peered back at her over the rim of his reading glasses, the familiar yellow pencil resting behind his ear. "I doubt that."

"Oh, you will," she teased. "If I do say so myself, I have done a marvelous job reporting *the* biggest social event of the year."

"Oh? I thought you were covering Marcella and Otis's wedding," he remarked dryly.

"I am! Don't you consider the uniting of Miss Marcella Staples to Mr. Otis Clever in the bonds of holy matrimony a stupendous event yet to be rivaled in the annals of history?"

"No."

"Oh . . . well, neither do I, but it'll make good reading."

Her father grinned indulgently as he proceeded to proof his daughter's material. Kenlyn leaned across the desk and picked up the piece he was working on and absently began to check his work.

"Dad," she scolded, the tone of her voice interrupting his reading.

"Yes?"

Pointing a well-manicured nail to the statement in question, she clucked her tongue shamefully. "Mr. Petersen's ad should read, 'Snickers—three for a dollar'—not 'Sneakers—three for a dollar.' "

"What? Let me see that!" His face reddened in disbelief that he could have made such a blunder.

As he reached for the list his daughter was waving in front of him, she laughed and hopped off the desk to plant a kiss on his receding hairline. "Just teasing, Pop."

15

"You young whippersnapper," he grumbled, but she noticed he was still grinning as he said it. "Haven't you got anything better to do than hang around and torment the prune-and-bran flake generation?"

The sign proudly boasted, *Isabel—6 Miles*, with a large white arrow pointing north. Travis Richmond veered the white sedan sharply to the right, leaving the comfort of the highway's smooth pavement and consenting to the potholes in the blacktop road. His mind was intent on finding a place where he could eat and rest for a while. He had been driving since the crack of dawn and he was badly in need of stretching his legs.

Keeping his speed at a reduced level to accommodate the bumps, he glanced out his window searching for a glimpse of a town, a house, a service station— anything that might be inhabited by something other than a Gila monster.

Nothing! Unless you were looking for a vast desert plain generously peppered with saguaro and organ-pipe cactus, broken only by the short mountain chains far in the distance. From all indications, it looked as though the path he had taken would lead him absolutely smack dab to the middle of nowhere.

The small green sign with its peeling white letters had promised a town called Isabel, he reminded himself. And he knew for certain that had he stayed on the main stretch of highway, the next town was still another seventy miles away. Although the digital clock on his car's dash told him it was another hour before it was officially lunchtime, his stomach pleaded a severe case of the empties. He had skipped breakfast this morning because of a last-minute meeting. After the meeting, he had still not eaten, thinking he'd get an early start home. Now he was feeling the consequences of his neglect.

It was assignments like the one Travis had just finished in Phoenix that made his otherwise repetitious job as a federal meat inspector worthwhile. When he could stop unscrupulous distribution practices, he felt the ultimate satisfaction from his occupation.

To think anyone would stick big bucks in their pockets from knowingly selling tainted meat products was detestable. And when the unsuspecting recipient was an entire school system—well, that was just too much. What really ignited his temper was when the culprits were given a legal slap on the hands and allowed to go right back to their scavenging. Fortunately, in this instance there had been more than enough proof to sustain a strong case against the suppliers and ensure proper punishment.

Just as he was giving serious thought to quitting what seemed like a wild-goose chase, he caught sight of the town of Isabel.

There sure wasn't much to it, he thought as he continued to drive in a northerly direction. But they should at least have a café. The way his stomach felt at the moment, he would even settle for a hot dog stand.

Several heads turned as the unfamiliar white sedan cruised the narrow main street. Travis immediately spotted the red brick building that housed the local diner. Braking, he swung the car into the curb directly in front of Leroy's Bean and Burger. The café was small, but neatly kept. Its starched red-and-white gingham curtains hung proudly in the yellow-lettered window. If outward appearances were any indication, and they usually were, it looked like a decent place to grab a quick bite to eat.

He didn't think the local patrons would mind if he was not decked out for the occasion. He had tolerated the burgundy tie that complimented his dark gray suit about as long as he could. In his opinion ties were nothing more than a fashionable nuisance, and it was long past time for his to go. He made quick work of taking it off before he left his car.

The brass bell above the door jingled as the tall stranger entered the small diner and took the first empty booth closest to the gingham-curtained window. The worn red plastic made a slight crackling sound beneath the weight of his muscular six-foot build.

The lunch crowd was just beginning to trickle in and several sets of curious eyes turned in his direction. A few stole a quick, cursory glance, while others stared more boldly, their eyes filled with growing curiosity.

The jukebox was belting out a tearjerker. Some heartbroken woman with a thick country drawl was singing about some man doin' her wrong and not havin' enough money to pay the rent.

At the end of the counter, a heavyset, middle-aged woman with curlers wound tightly in her hair pushed back her empty plate and lit another cigarette to accompany her second cup of coffee. Travis thought from the taut look of her face that she seemed to know exactly how the voice on the forty-five rpm felt. Her eyes maintained a faraway look as her foot tapped to the music's rhythm on the chrome ring of her stool.

His eyes located the plastic-covered menu, its single page propped upright between the salt and pepper shakers. The next few minutes he spent pondering the culinary options, trying to decide if he'd live dangerously and go for the blue plate special or play it safe and order a cheeseburger and a bowl of chili.

From his vantage point in the steamy kitchen, Leroy Blankenship, proprietor, cook, cashier, and chief bottle washer of Leroy's Bean and Burger, peeped his balding head out of the pickup window when he had heard the clanging of the diner's brass bell. It didn't take a moment before his perceptive blue eyes spotted the stranger's car bearing a government license plate.

Leroy focused his attention on the dark gray, expensive-looking suit the man was wearing and his eyes narrowed. No one in Isabel dressed like that. No one he knew in Isabel *knew* anyone who dressed like that. And he knew everyone.

With mounting curiosity, he hurriedly wiped his stubby little fingers on the stiff muslin material of his bibbed apron. Yes-sir-ree, Bob! He was anxious to check out this situation and find out what had taken the stranger so far off the beaten path. And if anyone could do it, ole Leroy would be just the person who could find out what this "foreigner" was doin' in their midst, he thought smugly.

He felt his adrenaline surge with heady anticipation. It had been a while since any outsiders had drifted into the diner. Not many folks were willing to leave the main highway to take in the sights of Isabel. Oh, once in a blue moon you'd have some tourist with time on his hands who'd drop by for something cold to drink—that was about it. And Leroy could count on one hand how often that had happened and still have plenty of fingers left over.

Not wanting to appear too eager, he slowed his steps. Anyway, he reasoned, he only wanted to snoop out the man's business, not scare him to death.

He stepped behind the counter to scoop up a red plastic glass full of crushed ice. Hitting the tap on the dispenser, he sprayed a stream of water on the frozen crystals and waited until the container filled.

Ceremony dispensed with, he scurried to the man's table. "Howdy!"

The thick rubber soles of his black mason shoes had enabled Leroy to descend upon the booth undetected by the stranger.

With a start, the man jumped at the abrupt sound of the gravelly voice in his ear. "Uh . . . yeah . . . howdy." Travis's dark brown eyes uneasily surveyed the dingy grease line on the apron that encircled the man's pudgy stomach.

Leroy hadn't missed the man's jumpy reaction to his simple greeting. Sure was fidgety, he thought as he fished a pudgy hand into the pocket of his apron and brought out his pen and order pad.

The stranger continued to study the menu as Leroy peered over his shoulder and tried to guess how much the suit had set the man back. A bundle. He would bet his reputation on that. He drummed his Bic pen impatiently on the green pages of his order pad and waited.

"You're not from around these parts, are you?"

Travis raised a dark brow, amused by the man's question. It was obvious from the unrelenting stares he had been receiving that the locals could pinpoint an unfamiliar face a mile away. And unless he missed his bet, he was sure this was no exception. "No, I'm not."

Disappointed with the stranger's lack of ready information, Leroy silently plotted his next line of strategy as he waited for his order. A few moments later he shifted his weight to the other foot and ventured, "You decide what you want yet?"

"Well, I think I will have the cheeseburger and bowl of chili," Travis decided. "Lettuce, tomato, and onion on the cheeseburger . . . light on the mustard, and chili with beans." His stomach was already rolling with protest, but he knew he had a package of Rolaids handy in the glove compartment of the sedan.

"Easy on the mustard." Leroy scratched on the pad, pretending to be totally absorbed with his task at hand. "Want a side of fries with that?"

"No, that should do it," Travis said pleasantly.

"Shouldn't take but a minute," Leroy assured. "You visitin' relatives here in Isabel?"

21

"No, just passing through." Travis carefully replaced the menu between the salt and pepper shakers.
"Oh?"

Travis nodded politely, then diverted his attention to stare out the gingham-covered window.

"You want anything to drink with this?"

"Oh . . . yes, a large glass of iced tea with lemon."

"Sure thing. Just passin' through, huh?"

"Yes, just passing through." Travis was getting a little annoyed at the man's obvious try to keep the conversation going. He didn't want to be rude to the friendly waiter, but he was hungry. "Make that burger well done," he added, his tone showing a discreet dismissal.

Leroy reluctantly took the hint. Drats, he fumed as he hurried back to the kitchen. In all the years he had been slinging hash, there had yet to be a single stranger passing through town who'd made it this far without Leroy knowing most of their life's history. There was no doubt about it—this one was sneaky.

Taking his place at the grill, he consoled his disappointment with the reminder he still had plenty of time to crack the stranger.

Ten minutes later he returned to the man's table carrying a metal tray heavily laden with the appetizing lunch. Leroy lifted the bowl of spicy chili and placed it in front of Travis, then the sizzling cheeseburger and frosty glass of iced tea.

"Just noticing your suit there. Sure is nice material," Leroy complimented. "Looks like it might of came from New York or Callyforniee . . . or somewhere big like that."

Travis was preoccupied with trying to decide what to eat first. "Thanks. Can I bother you for a bottle of ketchup?"

"Ketchup? Oh, yeah." The request had taken him by surprise because he had been waiting for him to say where he had bought the suit. "Here you go." Leroy handed him a bottle of ketchup he absentmindedly confiscated out of the hands of the surprised customer sitting in the next booth.

It was obvious he was not going to get any information out of the man until his appetite had been appeased. He might just as well give up and try again in a few minutes.

"If you need anything, just give me a holler."

Travis nodded as he sampled the cheeseburger, relieved the man was going to leave him alone for a while. Strange little town, he mused, still aware of the indiscreet glances that were still coming his way. In a few moments the waiter and other customers were forgotten as he devoted himself to the tasty meal.

Leroy had been keeping a watchful eye as he scurried about taking care of the lunch crowd. But the small diner was getting so full, it was becoming increasingly difficult to devote his attention to the stranger. He was right in the middle of taking Elmo Wilson's order when he saw the stranger wipe his mouth on a napkin, then slide out of the booth.

"And I'll have a . . ." Elmo didn't get a chance to

finish his order as Leroy suddenly pivoted on one foot and started to the register.

"Hey, Leroy!" Elmo complained.

Leroy stopped long enough to flash Elmo an irritable frown. "Keep your shirt on, Elmo! I'll be right back."

Elmo wasn't any too happy about the shabby treatment, but he had little choice if he wanted lunch.

"How was your lunch?" Leroy grinned as Travis approached the register to pay his check.

"Just fine. What do I owe you?" The room suddenly felt very warm to him.

"Now let me see." Leroy rifled through the green pad, trying to stall for time. "I've got it here somewhere. You gonna be in town long?"

Travis tugged uneasily at his collar, feeling as though it was suddenly hard to breathe. The small diner was extremely stuffy and he needed a breath of fresh air. "Could you speed that up a bit?"

"Sure thing . . . uh . . . let's see . . . looks like you owe me about three dollars and a nickel."

Travis hurriedly paid the bill, taking time to walk back to the table and leave a generous tip beside his empty plate. As he started to walk away, he felt the floor gently move beneath his feet.

Hell! I hope I haven't gotten a case of salmonella poisoning, he thought as he felt his stomach roll again. He quickly made his way to the door and jerked it open.

"Say, if you're looking for a place to stay the night—" Leroy called.

"For heaven's sakes, Leroy! A man could starve to

death around here," Elmo shouted. "You gonna take my order or not?"

"Pipe down! I'm a-comin', I'm a-comin' . . ."

Travis shut the door as the two men's voices grew louder. He stood out on the sidewalk, sucking in huge gulps of fresh air. He felt lightheaded and extremely nauseated.

Suddenly, a sharp stabbing pain, seemed to rip right through his middle as he leaned against the parking meter and fought down the urge to empty his stomach in one of the diner's large potted plants. Thinking he'd feel better if he sat down for a moment, he headed for his car. With each step his blood seemed to pulsate in throbbing sensations in his head.

He made it to the car, where he realized that was about as far as he'd get. Feeling as though the strength had suddenly been vacuumed out of him, he sagged against the hood as beads of sweat popped out on his forehead.

He couldn't remember ever feeling so sick, so unexpectedly.

And he wasn't sure which hurt worse—his pounding head or the steel hand relentlessly gripping his insides.

Kenlyn grabbed her purse and headed out the front door of the *Gazette*. With an unlimited supply of energy, she went about everything she tackled in full force. And that included her lunch. Especially today—she was starved.

"Pop, I'm going to Leroy's now. Can I bring you back anything?" she offered, aware that sometimes her father became so involved with his work he forgot to eat.

"Not today, honey. Mom said she'd stop by later with a couple of sandwiches. Thanks anyway."

"Okay. See you later."

Kenlyn hadn't much bolted out the door than she spotted the unfamiliar sedan with the tall man leaning against the side of its door. From where she stood, the stranger looked terribly ill.

Hurriedly glancing down both ends of the street—why, she didn't know—she quickly walked to the other side. One good thing about Isabel—there wasn't a string of cars to dart through when crossing the nearly deserted streets.

Her footsteps slowed as she walked up to the stranger. Again she noted how pale and unsteady on his feet he looked.

"Hi . . . you okay?"

Travis carefully lifted his head at the sound of her voice. He tried to focus his blurred vision on the lovely apparition that had suddenly appeared out of nowhere, but it was difficult.

The harsh noonday sun reflected soft highlights on the raven-haired, violet-eyed girl who stood looking at him worriedly.

Even in his extreme state of illness, his appreciation for such unusual beauty wasn't totally lost. If he was dying and Saint Peter had sent someone this good-looking to make the trip easier, then he was properly grateful.

"I think . . . I've been poisoned . . ." he rasped

weakly, before his head slumped back down on the hood of the car.

"Poisoned?"

"Yes . . . over there . . . I think it was the chili. . . ." He managed to point a feeble accusing finger in the direction of Leroy's Bean and Burger.

"In Leroy's?"

He nodded again sickly.

Kenlyn laughed, instantly ashamed of her thoughtlessness. The poor man was turning almost green, and she could see he was very ill. "Oh, Leroy's chili will make you belch fire, but he's never poisoned anyone," she comforted.

"Is there a doctor in town?" Travis managed between stomach spasms.

"Sure." She stepped closer and wrapped her arm around his broad back. "Here, I'll help you to his office."

Travis lifted his head, his dark eyes questioning whether he could make it that far.

Reading his thoughts, she smiled. "It's just across the street. Lean on me." It would be a pleasure to escort such an attractive man, she thought pleasantly.

"Thanks."

A few minutes later Kenlyn had deposited the stranger in the waiting room of Doctor Bakker's office. She had filled in Thelma Whitlock, Doctor Bakker's nurse, on what little information she knew, and Thelma had promised they would see to the stranger's needs. Probably a flu bug of some sort. There was a lot of that going around, Thelma had assured.

Kneeling down beside the chair he was slumped in, Kenlyn patted the man's arm reassuringly. "Want me to wait out here while the Doc takes a look at you?"

"No, I don't think that'll be necessary." He struggled to sit up straighter in the chair. "I appreciate your help, though."

"No problem. And I'd be happy to wait if you want me to."

"No, I don't want to keep you. I'll be fine, really." Again he was aware of her light floral smell and the unusual color of her eyes.

"Well . . . I do have a five o'clock deadline, and I want to get a bowl of chili at Leroy's . . ." Her voice trailed off lamely as she saw a shudder of repulsion ripple through him with the memory of his own lunch.

She patted his shoulder again, then stood and smiled at Thelma. "Take good care of him and let me know if it's anything serious."

"I will."

A few moments later Travis Richmond's angel of mercy had slipped out the door and he wilted miserably lower in his chair.

CHAPTER TWO

Kenlyn found her thoughts still lingering on the handsome stranger she'd assisted at lunchtime. For the last hour she had been working on an article about Biddy Maxwell's annual Christmas bazaar, but she couldn't concentrate. She hadn't thought to ask the man's name, but she supposed it really didn't matter.

The shrill ringing of the phone brought her out of her reverie and she expelled a slight, irritated breath at the unwelcome interruption. It never failed, she thought, reaching for the screaming black box. Somebody was always interrupting her daydreams!

"Isabel *Gazette*," she answered as politely as possible into the demanding little gadget.

"Kenlyn?" Leroy Blankenship's rough voice came over the line, his excitement barely under control.

"Yes?" Kenlyn was almost hesitant to respond to her name. She'd known Leroy long enough to know when he was up to something, and from the breathy, secretive tone he was using, Leroy was up to something again.

"This here's Leroy! Listen, you've got to get yourself over here immediately!" he ordered. He hadn't wasted a minute contacting the newspaper once he'd figured out what was going on.

That stranger's car had sat out there in front of the diner for more than an hour, and the more he'd thought about those government-issued license plates on the front, the more excited he'd become.

Tumblin' weeds of Tucson—a G-man! That fella was a fed! Right there in Isabel they had them a real G-man.

The idea was so titillating it had nearly taken his breath away.

"Hi, Leroy." Kenlyn crossed her fingers and held her breath, hoping she was wrong about him being up to something. "What's cookin'?"

Leroy in his excitement did not catch her intended words of humor. "I smell trouble brewin'! *Big* trouble," he predicted.

Kenlyn stifled a groan that begged for escape. Leroy was forever "smellin' " something. And, by all rights, he should. He always had his nose stuck in someone else's business.

"Maybe your chili's burning," she joked.

"Now, Kenlyn! You cut that out! I'm dead serious! There's something really big ready to go down in Isabel!" he scolded.

Kenlyn chose her next words carefully. One word —one false fiber of encouragement, and Leroy would be skipping off to one of his eternal flabbergasting worlds of unreality. "I'm sorry, Leroy. Now, calm down and tell me all about it," she soothed, feeling a little guilty for teasing him.

Leroy bit his lower lip and hesitated for a moment before he spoke again. Considering the possible severity of the situation, maybe it wasn't such a good idea to divulge any pertinent information over the phone. Because the government could have already moved in and tapped his phone line.

"Well, I can't get into the particulars over the telephone," he hedged in an uneasy voice. His voice dropped to a low hush. "You know . . . certain ears might be listening. But, I can tell you this. If you want a shot at what could very well be *the* hottest story to ever hit the pages of the *Gazette,* you'd better get yourself over here. And I mean pronto!"

Kenlyn knew better than to trust Leroy Blankenship's opinion of what was and was not newsworthy. The day he landed a genuine news lead would be the day she'd retire her pad and pen permanently.

Still, she hadn't ever heard him sound quite this excited. Her mind flicked a quick rerun of the last time she'd succumbed to the "hot tip" he'd phoned in. No, he'd been excited then, too.

Then, like now, he'd been rattling on like a madman. She'd barely been able to sift through his excitement as he shouted in her ear some wild account of a raging street fight over on 2nd and Elm. Since raging street fights weren't the norm in Isabel, she had tried to pin him down for more of the facts.

"Who's fighting, Leroy?"

"Don't know—it might be some of those rival motorcycle gangs out of Calleyfornee. Yes-sir-ree! Bet it's one of them gangs come to duel it out right here

31

in the middle of the streets of Isabel!" he'd speculated wildly.

Later Kenlyn had found out old Mildred Dooley had just come from the beauty shop and stopped off at the diner for a piece of pie and coffee on her way home. She happened to mention the fight to Leroy. But she hadn't gone into any specifics . . . and she didn't see all that well. Still, she'd said someone on a motorcycle was over at the bar looking for trouble—and Leroy had jumped on the bandwagon.

He had sounded so sure of his story, he'd even convinced Kenlyn in a moment of weakness. Like an idiot, she'd grabbed her pad and pencil, stopping just long enough to sling the strap of her Nikon across her shoulder—because, a picture was worth a thousand words.

"Got a big one, Pop!" she had shouted as she raced for the front door.

"Slow down or you're going to break your neck," her father had warned in an absent voice.

She had sped off in her bright red Volkswagen, strongly resembling a miniature version of a fire truck on its way to extinguish a citywide inferno. The only things lacking to complete the description were the flashing glare of an emergency light and the screaming wail of a siren.

When she reached the corner of 2nd and Elm, she locked her brakes and came to a jarring halt. She looked around, refusing to believe her eyes. There was no street fight going on.

Her eyes focused on the old motorcycle sitting at the curb of the one and only bar in Isabel, and she groaned as Marge Hopkins came storming out the pub's front door, dragging her husband, Howard, behind her. The big burly woman had a grip on her husband's left ear that was to be envied. And he sure didn't look to be putting up much of a fight as Marge twisted his ear to a bright throbbing red.

Kenlyn couldn't blame him for going peacefully. The Hell's Angels themselves would have hesitated before trying to tangle with Marge "The Malicious" Hopkins.

That's *if* they had been there.

She had sat fuming at her own stupidity. That darn Leroy had done it again. There were no greasy choppers, no leather-clad, chain-draped, tattooed bikers! There wasn't even so much as a Big Wheel in sight, she seethed. Howard Hopkins had simply dropped by the bar for a beer after work, and Marge had gotten wind of it and come after him on her motorcycle.

Darn that Leroy! If she could have gotten her hands on his chubby neck at that moment, no judge would have been able to hold her accountable for her actions.

And now here she was, ready to be suckered in again.

"Well? Are you comin' over or not?" Leroy demanded.

"Oh, Leroy . . . I don't know. I'm up to my ears in work right now," she argued.

If she went running over there it'd be a mistake, but if she didn't and he had something this time . . .

"You mean you're gonna sit there and let the opportunity of a lifetime pass you by?" he challenged.

He didn't believe this woman sometimes! Lordy. Give her first shot at what may very well turn out to be the biggest thing that had ever happened in Isabel, and she had to think about it! He glided a nervous hand across the top of his smooth head.

Kenlyn was debating what to do. Leroy was irritating sometimes, but he was harmless, and she didn't want to hurt his feelings by completely ignoring his summons. But she wasn't exactly crazy about encouraging him either. Besides, she had done her good deed for the day by taking the stranger to Doc Bakker's office, and she wasn't in any mood to go on another wild-goose chase.

"Kenlyn?"

"Yes, Leroy," she said patiently.

"You're gonna come over here . . . aren't you?"

He sounded so pathetically hopeful, she didn't have the heart to tell him no. She could almost see his short legs pacing the tile floor of the diner in his frustration.

Well, she could always get a cold root beer while she was over there. So, she'd give him ten minutes of her time. What could it possibly hurt? Leroy really did try hard, even if he did manage to bungle up more times than he was successful when it came to unraveling these great mysteries his mind was forever inventing.

"Okay, Leroy. I'll be over in a few minutes," she relented, knowing full well what she was letting herself in for. She was a soft touch and everyone knew it.

She replaced the receiver on its hook and promised herself she'd give him no more than ten minutes. Ten minutes—that's all.

"Dad, I'm going to Leroy's," she admitted defeatedly.

From the look of amusement on her father's face, Kenlyn knew he had been listening to her conversation. "I thought you'd already eaten lunch." The slight twinkle in his eye made her suspect he was enjoying the predicament Leroy had her in again.

She blushed. He knew darn well she had already eaten lunch. He was just making the most of her dampened dignity.

"I won't be gone long," she promised.

"No hurry." Kenneth glanced up and grinned. "Who knows? He might have something this time."

"Yeah, maybe. But, I doubt it."

Travis had spent the better part of an hour in the doctor's office. The elderly physician had poked and prodded and mumbled under his breath until he was thoroughly convinced the sudden onslaught was simply a case of flu.

"Lot of it goin' around," he'd said. "Should feel good as new in a couple of days."

He had given Travis a shot and a prescription and told him to drink plenty of liquids and go to bed.

"I'd avoid Leroy's chili, too," he'd added. "Just to be on the safe side."

As Travis had stepped out of the doctor's office, it had occurred to him he'd have to find a place to stay until he could overcome the bug.

He glanced around the main street of Isabel and he felt his spirits sag. Damn. It was bad enough being sick as a dog, but why did it have to happen when he was away from home? The image of the young woman who had assisted him to the doctor's office momentarily surfaced. She was a lovely little thing. Well, maybe the unexpected delay wouldn't be all that bad, he reasoned. With luck, he might be able to become more acquainted with the girl.

Anyway, he couldn't do anything about the delay, so he might as well make the best of a bad situation. First thing he had to do was call Dan and let him know he was going to be held up for a couple of days. He started across the street.

Leroy Blankenship had already informed the local patrons gathered around his counter and tables that a government man was in their midst. A few of the people seemed a bit cloudy about what that could mean, but they knew by the way Leroy was acting that he was all a-twitter about it.

He kept running to the window and peering out at the man's car that was still sitting at the curb. He couldn't figure out where the guy had disappeared to suddenly.

When an hour had passed and the fella hadn't shown up yet, Leroy really began to worry. That's when he had decided there must be something really big ready to go down in Isabel and Kenlyn should be in on it.

He was standing at the window now as Travis approached the diner. "Here he comes," Leroy warned. "Now everyone just act natural."

The patrons scurried back to their booths, and when Travis opened the door to the diner all appeared to be normal.

"Well, howdy," Leroy greeted, coming from behind the counter to greet him. "See you're back."

"Yes. I was wondering if you have a phone I could use?"

"Sure thing. Right back there next to the john."

"Thanks." Travis made his way to the back of the diner, aware all eyes were again centered on him. This town must be starved for visitors, he thought as he dug in his pocket for change.

An uneasy silence descended as he dropped the coins in the phone and punched out his office number. Turning his back to the room, he waited as the circuits made the necessary connections.

The brass bell over the door signaled another arrival as Kenlyn entered the diner. Leroy immediately scurried from behind the counter and took her arm and ushered her to the nearest empty booth.

"It's about time you got here!"

"What is it, Leroy? I haven't got much time to waste."

Leroy's voice dropped to a low whisper. "You notice anything strange?"

Kenlyn glanced around the crowded diner that was unusually subdued. "Everyone's awful quiet."

"Shhh! They're trying to hear what You-know-who's saying."

Kenlyn's eyes slowly traveled the room. "Who's 'You-know-who'?"

37

"Shhh!" Leroy casually motioned with his brows to the back of the room.

Kenlyn finally noticed the stranger she had taken to the doctor's office earlier. "Oh. Why are they trying to hear what he's saying?"

Leroy leaned across the table, cautious to keep from arousing the man's suspicions. "Didn't you notice the plates?"

"The plates?"

It was all Leroy could do to keep from shouting. Lord almighty, this little gal could be dense sometimes! How she'd ever got to be a newspaper reporter was beyond him. Why, if she couldn't sniff out a story this big, then she was in real trouble.

"The plates on his car!" Leroy hissed. "He's with the United States Government."

"Oh?" Her gaze went back to the stranger. She'd thought he was different. He had a certain undefinable air of excitement about him. She'd noticed it immediately.

"Oh! Oh! Is that all you can say?"

Kenlyn eyed him impatiently. "What do you *want* me to say, Leroy?"

"You mean to sit there and tell me you didn't notice those license plates on his car?"

"No, I'm sorry, I didn't. But what's all the fuss about?"

Leroy shook his head in amazement. "Lordy, Lordy, Lordy, you got sawdust for a brain, girl?" He leaned closer and lowered his voice until she could barely hear him. "We got us a G-man in town."

38

The news still did not arouse Kenlyn. "Well, he stopped to eat and came down with the flu—"

"Came down with the flu?"

"Yes, didn't you know? He's been over at Doctor Bakker's since he left here."

"Well, he didn't get sick on *my* food," Leroy snapped.

"No, Thelma thought it might be the flu—"

"So he's gonna try that ole trick, huh? Listen." Leroy leaned even closer. "I think there's something fishy going on here and he's gonna use gettin' sick as an excuse to hang around. Let's ooze on back and slip in that booth next to the phone and listen to what he's sayin'. I'll bet you a dollar to a donut he's making his first contact."

By now Leroy was beginning to get her attention. "You mean you think he's here for a purpose?"

"Of course he's here for a purpose! How often has the government come all the way out here in the desert and gotten sick on a bowl of my chili?"

If it weren't for Leroy Blankenship's watchful eye, anyone who wanted to could just sashay in here and throw this town in a brown paper sack and walk right off with it! Leroy thought irritably.

Kenlyn hated to admit it, but Leroy might have something this time. It *was* unusual for such an intriguing stranger to be in Isabel.

"What do you think he's been sent here to do?"

"Who knows? It could be a lot of things—a lot of very unpleasant things."

"Oh—then what should we do?" she whispered.

"Let's mosey real easylike back there and find out

39

who he's talkin' to. He may slip up and drop a hint on what he's up to."

They both slid out of the booth and nonchalantly made their way back to where the man was still talking on the phone.

Travis glanced up and noticed Kenlyn as she approached. He smiled and gave her a flirty wink, then turned his face to the wall and continued his conversation in a lower tone.

"See how funny he's actin'?" Leroy prompted. "Real edgylike. I noticed that earlier."

Kenlyn's pulse had given an unexpected flutter when the stranger had winked at her, and she didn't view the fact that the man wouldn't necessarily want her and Leroy to hear his conversation as being "edgy." But knowing Leroy's vivid imagination, she declined to voice her opinion.

Slipping quietly into a vacant booth, Leroy bent his head and whispered. "Better take a few notes for future reference. Male, Caucasian, six-one, young— early thirties—dark hair and eyes, handsome—although he's a might pasty-looking."

"I can see that. Good grief, Leroy. You sound like we're going to put him in a police line-up!"

"Shhh! You want him to hear us?"

Unaware that his conversation was now being closely monitored, Travis chatted with his supervisor and close friend, Dan Williams. "No, I hope it won't take more than a couple of days . . . if I'm lucky."

"Take all the time you need. They say that particular strain of flu can knock you for a loop."

"It feels that way."

"Well, just be sure you're over it before you come back to work. I sure don't want the darn thing."

"Don't worry. I'll play it safe."

Kenlyn and Leroy's ears strained nearer as someone put a coin in the jukebox and Eddy Arnold began to sing "Cattle Call."

"You'd better give me the motel where you'll be staying in so I can get in touch with you if I need to," Dan suggested.

"Negative. I have to case the place out first to find one."

Dan chuckled. "You mean the town's that small?"

"You might say that."

"Well, let me know when you get settled in. Surely the room will have a phone. You just concentrate on getting well."

Travis grinned. "I'll do my best."

"Say, Annie and I were talking the other night. Let's take a few days vacation next month and I'll fly us back down to Tijuana. You think Melody might like to go? I know you two haven't been seeing each other, but it might be fun for old times' sake."

Travis winced at the mention of his ex-fiancée. "I don't know, Dan. I'll give it some thought. . . ." He paused, suddenly aware of the owner of the diner leaning out of a booth, straining to hear every word he was saying. "Listen, I can't talk right now. I'll keep in touch."

"Sure, buddy. But think about Tijuana. I'm ready for a little relaxation."

"Right. Tijuana or bust."

"We'll party hardy for four days and end up with

another one of those memorable headaches," Dan chuckled.

"Yes, I imagine it'll be another big one, all right."

"Yeah, but we'll wait until you're back on your feet."

Kenlyn bolted upright in the booth, her eyes widening in disbelief. "Did he say . . . marijuana?" she asked in a hoarse whisper.

"Shore 'nough!" Leroy's eyes grew even rounder. "He must be with the FBI."

She sucked in her breath reverently. "Do you think so? Oh, dear . . . you were right. He *is* up to something!"

"Didn't I tell you?" Leroy gloated.

Merciful heavens. The United States Government was planning a marijuana bust right here in her very own town. A *big* drug raid that would put Isabel, Arizona, on the map.

Kenlyn grabbed her purse and slid out of the booth, nearly knocking over the stranger, who had just replaced the receiver back on the hook.

Travis leaned weakly against the wall where she had shoved him in her haste and watched as she rushed out the front door in a flurry of excitement.

He shook his head wearily. She was good-looking, there was no doubt about that—but maybe he'd better rethink his previous thoughts about getting to know her better.

CHAPTER THREE

Oh, Lordy! He knew it! Leroy, who had never been able to resist the temptation of basking in the limelight, was primed and ready to wallow in the confirmation of his suspicions. But Kenlyn hadn't waited to hear his gloatings. She had sprung to her feet, rattling the condiments as her knee banged into the table's corner. The jolt sent the salt shaker spinning wildly across the Formica top. She had seemed unaware of the disturbance she was causing as she rushed to the diner's front door.

Women! Leroy fumed silently. She could have at least cleaned up her mess before she went charging out of the diner like a crazy woman!

For someone who'd been almost impossible to convince earlier, there was something funny going on. She sure didn't need any pushing now, he had mumbled under his breath.

Kenlyn, completely immersed in her own thoughts, hurried back across the street to the *Gazette*. With each step her imagination raced wildly with the newsworthy possibilities that the stranger's conversation had inadvertently supplied. Her sharp

43

journalistic mind, feverishly explored and exhausted every angle of the coverage she was certain her eavesdropping had exposed.

Shivering at the ripple of excitement that trickled down her spine, she admitted how smart she had been to follow up on Leroy's lead. This time he really had something! And she was going to be the reporter who broke the astounding story first!

Visions of receiving the coveted Pulitzer Prize danced tantalizingly through her mind. She knew she had to work fast, before wind of the story hit the other news wires—surely before the CBS news team arrived. With a story of this size, undoubtedly Dan Rather would be more than determined to fight her tooth and nail for a chance at the story.

Kenlyn darted across the deserted street. With her anticipation mounting, any thoughts of glancing in either direction for oncoming vehicles had completely escaped her this time.

Claude Grant sat on the porch of the *Gazette* and rocked in a slow easy rhythm in the weathered Boston rocker that had been passed down from one Grant generation to the next. He watched as his granddaughter raced with breathless vigor up the porch steps and skidded to a halt beside his chair. He took a long steady puff from his pipe as he prepared himself for the storm he knew was coming. Kenlyn had been with Leroy. That knowledge alone was enough to let him know something was brewing again.

He wasn't an easily excitable man, but it was hard occasionally not to get caught up in his granddaughter's unending thirst for life. He eyed her, a slight twinkle of his amusement at her frantic manner visible in his faded blue eyes. He didn't have the slightest idea what all the commotion was about today, but he'd bet something was going on.

With violet-blue eyes as big as saucers, Kenlyn fought to compose herself and control her erratic breathing. "Grandpa, you'll never believe what's happening," she gasped.

"Probably not, but try me anyway," he offered with the same calmness he always seemed to possess.

"Well, you simply won't believe it when I tell you!" she declared, expelling a heavy breath. "It's the most exciting thing that's ever happened in Isabel."

"Oh?"

She leaned against the railing of the porch to try to regain her composure. "Listen to this. I got a call from Leroy a little while ago. Well, naturally, at first I figured it was just another one of his crazy 'tips.' But, it wasn't, Grandpa! If I hadn't heard it with my own two ears, I'd never believed it!" she exclaimed, placing a hand to her pounding heart, hoping to slow its thunderous beating.

An amused smile tugged at Claude Grant's lips at the mere mention of Leroy's name. In his earlier newspaper days he'd received a few of those calls himself.

"Leroy thinks he's got another big one, huh?"

"Oh, he does, Grandpa. Believe me, he *does* this time! The stranger . . . you know, the one I took to Doc Bakker's this morning?" She glanced around to see if any nosy ears were listening, then, assured there wasn't, pointed to the car parked in front of the Bean and Burger across the street. "He's with the g-o-v-e-r-n-m-e-n-t," she whispered in a secretive voice.

"The g-o-v-e-r-n-m-e-n-t?"

"Yeah . . ..government," she repeated. She leaned even closer. "What do you think of that?"

Claude took another long pull off his pipe, cautious not to discourage his granddaughter's eagerness to share her scorching feature story. "Well, they're probably good people to work for."

"Oh, no, no, Grandpa. I didn't mean what do you think of his job," she scolded. "I mean, what do you think about a government official eating in Isabel and then pretending to become ill? Don't you think that's strange?"

Claude thought for a moment. "Nope. Seems to me government men can get sick just like anyone else," he reasoned.

He had heard all about how the stranger had been passing through town and decided to stop for a bite to eat, then suddenly gotten ill. Didn't seem strange to him. He'd eaten at Leroy's a few times himself.

Lowering her tone of voice, Kenlyn returned to whispering again. "But, he's more than just your average, run-of-the-mill government man. *We* think he's with the FBI!"

"Is that a fact?" Claude whispered back. "Who's we?"

"Me and Leroy."

"Oh."

"So? What do you think now?"

46

"How did you arrive at this fascinating conclusion?"

"I . . . I told you. I heard it with my own ears," she defended lamely, feeling her face flush.

She knew if she confessed Leroy had been the one to decide the stranger was with the FBI, then the story wouldn't be as plausible.

"So . . . there's an honest-to-goodness FBI agent right here in Isabel," Claude mused thoughtfully. He rubbed his large hand down the front of his white mustache, then continued in a seemingly serious manner. "Well, no doubt there could be a story there . . . if you're sure of your facts."

"That's what I thought!" Kenlyn grinned, relieved to hear he didn't think she was on the wrong track again. "The way we see it, it's not the fact that he's a federal agent that we're worried about." Her eyes glowed with excitement. "I suppose anyone could drive through town and stop for a bite to eat. But because of what me and Leroy . . . uh . . . accidentally overheard a few minutes ago, the real scoop is what he's here to do!"

A swirl of white smoke fogged around her. "You overheard him let that slip out, did you?"

"Yes! That's what I'm trying to tell you! And he's going to do it right here in our town!" Kenlyn exclaimed, satisfied she'd clarified the entire situation, enabling her grandfather to see the potentially worldwide effect of this story.

It was becoming increasingly difficult for the older gentleman to believe there was a story. He had lived long enough to know a government man didn't come to Leroy's Bean and Burger and discuss his plans over a pay telephone. Ordinarily, his granddaughter was a very concise and accurate reporter. But because of what she had just told him, it looked like Leroy had just led her down the path to fantasyland again.

"Okay, honey. Now just slow down and tell me what you think this stranger has got up his sleeve," Claude said gently.

"It's not what I think—it's what I know!" she argued, realizing he still had doubts.

"And that is?"

Her wide eyes quickly scanned the streets, reevaluating their privacy. Leaning across the arm of the old rocking chair, she spoke softly into her grandfather's ear. "He's here . . . to conduct a major marijuana raid! A federal drug bust, right here in Isabel!"

A chuckle almost escaped Claude Grant with the proclamation of her information. Anything this silly *had* to have come from the mouth of Leroy Blankenship.

"Did Leroy tell you this?" he asked bluntly.

"No," Kenlyn denied uneasily, hoping he'd leave it at that. But knowing her grandfather, she knew he wouldn't. She added reluctantly, "I got my information from an anonymous source."

She'd been cautious in her reply, not wanting to admit her eavesdropping and not wanting to be anything less than truthful to him. Well, she *didn't* know the federal man's name. So in a sense he was an anonymous informer, she defended silently. Even if he hadn't meant to inform her personally.

"You and Leroy have been over there eavesdropping on that poor man, now haven't you?" Claude accused sharply, and she felt herself blushing. She had never been able to pull anything over on him and get away with it.

Any further questioning her grandfather might have been ready to undertake was interrupted as Kenneth Grant pushed open the screen door and joined them on the front porch. In moments Kenlyn had retraced every exciting detail of the story to him.

"Now, Pop. Is that a scoop or is that a scoop?" she finished proudly. She eyed her grandfather sternly, hoping he'd keep quiet until her father had expressed his opinion.

"Hogwash." After a few moments of stunned silence, Claude Grant was the first to speak.

Kenlyn threw up her hands in exasperation. It was plain to see he was going to be a real stinker about this! "What do you mean—hogwash? Why, nothing this exciting has ever happened in dull ole Isabel!" she exclaimed, annoyed that her grandfather of all people couldn't see the impact of such an occurrence.

"That's just it! It'd be a heck of a story," Claude agreed. "But have you ever stopped to think where in the world would anyone be growing a big enough marijuana patch in Isabel to warrant such a large-scale invasion?"

It took a few moments for his words to sink in, but when it did, Kenlyn's animated face began to wilt.

Darn! She hadn't stopped to think about that. Where *would* anyone grow marijuana in the desert?

"I'm sorry, honey." Claude reached out and

tweaked his granddaughter's cheek affectionately. "I hate to burst your bubble, but I'm afraid you've misunderstood what you've heard." He winked at her solemnly. "That's what happens to eavesdroppers. No telling what the man was talking about, but I'd bet my last dollar if he's with the FBI he wasn't standing there talking business on a pay phone in a public diner."

She suddenly felt the rapid flow of blood rush to her cheeks in hot throbbing spurts. That rotten Leroy had done it to her again!

She didn't know which made her feel worse—the crushing disappointment in knowing there would be no history-making headline story, no Dan Rather, and positively no Pulitzer Prize or 'the embarrassment of having been gullible enough to believe for one minute there could ever be such an unlikely occurrence as a drug raid in the Arizona desert town of Isabel.

Her grandfather, not being one to rub in the stinging salve of you-should-have-known-better, stretched his lanky legs and politely excused himself as he stepped off the front porch of the *Gazette* for his afternoon walk.

Kenneth Grant smiled apologetically and patted her shoulder. "Well, it *would* have been a dynamite story, puddin'."

"I feel like such a fool," she mumbled.

"Think I'll mosey over to Leroy's and get me a cold soda. Can I bring you back a root beer?"

"No thanks."

Kenlyn sighed as she sank down in her grandfather's vacated chair and began to rock off some of her anger. Darn that Leroy! she simmered silently. She suddenly stood up and pivoted on the point of her fashionable boots and marched to the café. One of these days . . . one of these days she was going to stop listening to his wild ideas! But at the moment she was determined to confront him with the disturbing turn of events—while her blood was still boiling.

As she approached the Bean and Burger, the door suddenly flung open and out walked the tall, attractive federal man. For a moment her heart skipped a beat when he glanced up and smiled at her. She smiled back and thought he still looked a little pale and unsteady on his feet.

"Hi, there. Feeling better?" she asked. She might be mad at Leroy, but she surely wasn't going to take it out on this poor man. He was probably just an innocent bystander.

"Hi." His gaze lingered appreciably on the way the jeans she was wearing hugged her feminine curves so nicely. "I think I'll probably live now," he admitted.

She acknowledged his complimentary regard with a shy smile, immensely grateful he wasn't aware of her eavesdropping and the ridiculous conclusions it had caused.

"You look a little better," she offered, noting that although his coloring was pale, he didn't look quite as green around the gills as he had earlier.

"Thanks. The doctor thinks it's some sort of flu that's been going around. He thinks I'll be back on my feet in twenty-four to forty-eight hours."

"Oh? Then you'll be spending the night in Isabel?" Although he sounded sincere and his story about having a flu bug would surely be easy enough to check out with Doc Bakker, she still had a nagging seed of suspicion where he was concerned.

Maybe he was going to try to fake this illness just so he could stay in town and snoop around—that was possible. She shook her thoughts away with sudden annoyance. Good grief, Kenlyn! You sound just like Leroy!

"Yeah, I guess I will. Maybe a couple of nights." He glanced around the main street and frowned. "I suppose there's a hotel or motel around where I can get a room?" So far, he hadn't seen anything that even closely resembled such an establishment.

Kenlyn couldn't help but laugh at his innocent inquiry. Hotel, motel—a person could refer to it by whatever name they chose. In Isabel, it didn't really matter. It didn't have either one.

The entire inventory of the town was a couple of gas stations, the bank which the citizens proudly boasted had never been robbed (unless you wanted to count the time Harlo Lowmeyer embezzled twenty thousand dollars), a greasy garage, Petersen's Grocery, Perkins' Pharmacy, the *Gazette,* the doctor's office, and Leroy's Bean and Burger—which just might not be in operation too much longer if a certain little troublemaking proprietor didn't quit sticking his nose in where it didn't belong, she simmered, again recalling the reason she was heading back to the diner.

"Did I say something funny?" Travis asked, bringing her wondering thoughts back to his original question.

"Oh, no. It's just that your question struck me that way." She smiled. "I'm afraid we don't have motels or hotels in Isabel."

"You don't?" His forehead creased with concern as he felt himself becoming lightheaded again. No motel meant he'd have to drive on to the next town, and he wasn't sure he could make it the way he was feeling.

Seeing his discomfort, Kenlyn reached out to steady his swaying form. "Oh, don't worry! You can stay with me," she assured brightly.

A slow grin played at the corners of his mouth. "With you?" This illness could turn out to be more interesting than he had imagined.

Realizing how her offer must have sounded, her face flooded with color as she hurriedly clarified her rash invitation. "Oh, no . . . what I meant to say was, on the rare occasions when a visitor decides to stay overnight in Isabel, you see . . . my *parents* have this huge old house and they have a couple of rooms . . . they rent . . . out . . occasionally. . . ."

She really wished he'd stop grinning at her that way!

Feeling another hot flush of embarrassment, she was thankful that her long dark hair adequately hid part of her face. Otherwise, she was certain the bright throbbing of her cheekbones would glow like a pulsating blood-red beet.

"Well, I'd be grateful to find a place to lie down," he acknowledged.

"Good. If you like, I'll take you over there right now," she offered. "I know you probably don't feel up to driving. My father and I can come back later and get your car." Seizing the opportunity to let him know that his government-issued license plates hadn't gone undetected by her, she casually added, "That is, if it's all right for a civilian to drive your car. I noticed you have government plates."

He hadn't realized anyone had taken notice of the plates, or even cared for that matter. Still, he reminded himself, he should have known that the watchful eyes of a small town would be the first to spot what was undoubtably a rare occurrence.

"No, no problem. At least not in this case." Right now all he wanted to do was get off his feet.

Kenlyn caught sight of two leery blue eyes peeping out from behind the gingham curtains of the diner as she and the federal man walked to her red Volkswagen parked across the street in front of the *Gazette.*

She snickered with revenge as she visualized Leroy's mind spinning with frustration. He wouldn't have the slightest idea where she was taking the stranger, and she wasn't planning to let him know. After what he had just pulled, it'd serve him right to have to sweat it out for a while, she thought smugly.

She whirled and waved at the two eyes and the curtain immediately dropped back in place.

Travis turned to look in the direction she had just waved.

She smiled. "Just saying hello to an acquaintance."

Moments later, she sat behind the steering wheel

of the Volkswagen and the stranger climbed wearily in beside her.

She thought he looked funny sitting in the seat beside her with his long legs drawn nearly to his ears. Suddenly it occurred to her she didn't even know his name.

Turning the first of three corners necessary to take them to the Grant residence, she said shyly, "I guess we should introduce ourselves. I'm Kenlyn Grant."

"Travis Richmond," he offered, wishing he felt more like talking to her.

"Travis Richmond." She turned and smiled at him again. "Hi, I'm very pleased to meet you. Although I wish it were under more pleasant circumstances. At least for your sake," she added, thinking that maybe if she could loosen him up a little, he might be inclined to contribute at least an inkling as to why he was in Isabel.

But he wasn't so inclined. He simply smiled and turned his head to assess the small town scenery that passed by his window.

Well, she was almost certain she could rule out his being here to conduct some ludicrous marijuana raid. But Leroy was right about one thing. The man was definitely being secretive about what he was up to.

As the car purred along, the inquisitive fires again began to burn in her mind. She considered the various methods of trying to gain the information she wanted. Not that she *really* believed he was here for any dark, sinister reason. Yet it'd be interesting to know why he had picked Isabel to have lunch.

And if she were nice to him, why, he'd naturally

favor her with the details of the big story—if by some miracle there turned out to be one—before it was to happen.

Anyway, she'd already done him a big favor by helping him to the doctor's office. He almost owed her the right to exclusive coverage, she concluded.

"Where are you from Mr. Richmond?" she asked sweetly.

"Please call me Travis, and I live in Los Angeles," he replied pleasantly.

That was sure easy enough, she complimented herself. It was not going to be so tough getting him to admit that he was, indeed, a secret agent on a mission in Isabel, Arizona. Feeling more confident that he was becoming more at ease with her, she continued. "Gee, Los Angeles. You're still a long way away."

"Yes, I know."

"You'll probably want to call your wife to let her know what's happened." He wasn't wearing a ring—but one never knew anymore.

"I'm not married."

She had no idea why, but she felt a sudden sense of exhilaration at his statement.

"Why did you pick Isabel to stop for lunch?" she continued, unaware of how nosy her questions sounded until she felt his curious gaze upon her. Turning to meet his gaze, she gave him an innocent smile. "I mean, why Isabel? It's so . . . small."

He turned his attention back to the passing scenery, becoming a little annoyed at the interrogations he'd been through since entering the city limits of this strange little town.

"I was on my way home from an assignment in Phoenix when I decided to pull off the main highway and get a bite to eat."

Hmmm, smooth. Still sticking to his original story, she thought sourly. Turning the second corner, she plotted her next move. Realizing she only had a few minutes alone with him before they reached the house, she jumped right in with her next question.

"What type of work are you engaged in . . . I mean . . . if you're at liberty to discuss your job?" She shot him a challenging look. "You do work for the government, don't you?"

He nodded, flinching as his stomach began to cramp and a cold sweat popped out on his forehead. He prayed it wasn't much farther to the house.

Ah-ha! She hadn't failed to miss that strange, almost guilty look that had suddenly come over his face. She had undoubtedly touched a sore spot.

She pressed on. "Well, I'd surely understand if you're not at liberty to discuss what you do. After all, your job might be highly . . . uh . . . secretive." She turned quickly to see if she could catch his reaction to that observation.

He glanced at her in confusion. Why wouldn't he be at liberty to discuss the fact that he was a meat inspector? "I don't think that the government would exactly place a shroud of secrecy around what I do." He removed a handkerchief from his back pocket and wiped at his forehead.

"Oh? Then you're at liberty to discuss it?"

She thought his eyes looked a little shifty. Yes, she was sure of it. They were a beautiful color of brown,

57

but definitely shifty. Strange—she should have noticed it before.

"I'm a meat inspector," he said.

Her smile faded. A *what?* she fumed silently. A meat inspector! How stupid did he think she was?

Well, she should have known. It had been too easy to break him. Feds just didn't break that easy! He couldn't be telling the truth. Of all explanations, he could have used a little more imagination in his obvious try to throw her off track.

Did he honestly think for one minute she'd fall for something so transparently fabricated! A federal meat inspector, my foot!

"A meat inspector?" She forced her voice to remain passive.

"Not very exciting, huh?"

"No . . . I'm sure your job is interesting," she returned curtly, stifling the urge to tell him what it really sounded like—the biggest lie she'd ever heard.

She abruptly braked the Volkswagen to a halt, having reached their destination. The sudden jolt threw him forward and he flung his hands out on the dash to steady himself.

"Sorry." Actually, she wasn't. He deserved a knot on his head the size of a goose egg for lying to her that way.

She got out of the car and slammed the door, while he looked on indecisively. A few moments later he crawled out of the passenger seat and followed her up the walkway.

Kenlyn was already on the massive front porch

talking to an older lady who was setting in a swing reading the latest issue of *McCall's* magazine.

Since there was such a strong resemblance between the two women, Travis knew immediately this had to be her mother.

"Mom, this is Travis Richmond. He would like to rent a room for a couple of days," Kenlyn introduced Travis as he stepped up on the old porch. Her violet eyes flicked over him coolly. "He's a meat inspector." And I'm Nancy Reagan, she added silently.

Removing her dainty reading glasses, Oneida Grant smiled a warm welcome to the newcomer. "Hello, Travis."

"Mrs. Grant." Travis took her hand politely.

The older woman's hair was an attractive salt-and-pepper color, wrapped securely in a bun atop her head. Travis sensed immediately that he was going to like her.

"My husband has been telling me about your unfortunate bout with a bug. I do hope you're feeling better?"

"I think I will be if I can lie down somewhere for a while." His strength was almost drained, and a bed would be a welcome sight even if it were in Isabel.

The petite woman rose to her feet immediately. "Then come along. I have a comfortable old feather bed that I'm sure you're going to find delightful." She turned and motioned for Kenlyn to follow. "While I settle Mr. Richmond in his room, why don't you put on a pot of chicken broth for our guest, dear."

"Okay, Mom."

The old screen door flapped shut and Kenlyn could hear her mother commenting on how pleasant the weather had been for the past few days as they started to climb the carpeted stairway leading to the bedrooms on the second story of the house.

Federal meat inspector, my foot, she thought again irritably, as she opened the door and started for the kitchen.

Travis Richmond must be a real wiseacre!

CHAPTER FOUR

With the guest comfortably settled into the upstairs room, Kenlyn decided to return to the office. She figured she'd made Leroy miserable long enough, and she still had the article to finish.

The proprietor of the diner was still stealing periodic peaks out the windows when she drove into her parking place at the *Gazette*.

Well, let him stew! she thought. But the moment she walked through the doorway, her father handed her the phone.

"Leroy?"

Kenneth nodded.

Laying her purse down on her desk, she sighed and took the receiver. "Hello."

"Where in the cat hair did you disappear to?" Leroy demanded.

"Fine, thank you. And how are you, Leroy?"

"Don't be sassy, little lady. Now tell me what you could worm out of the G-man."

"Nothing. A big, fat zero."

"Nothing!"

"That's right. But I can tell you this." She slid off

61

the desk and braced herself to let him have it. "I seriously doubt there's going to be a drug raid in Isabel."

"Did he say that?"

"No! He didn't say that. I just put two and two together and came up with the idea all alone!"

"Now hold on to your socks, little missy . . ."

"You hold on to yours, Leroy. Now think a minute. Do we or do we not live in the middle of the desert?"

"Well, yeah . . ."

"And don't you think if there was a marijuana patch around big enough to get the government's attention, someone around here might have noticed it, too?"

"Well . . ."

"Case closed."

"But we both heard him say 'marijuana.' How do you explain that?"

"I don't know, but we must have misunderstood. That's what happens to people who eavesdrop."

There was silence on the other end of the line as Leroy tried to digest the bad news.

"Where's the fed right now?"

"Mr. Richmond is probably sitting in my mother's kitchen eating a bowl of chicken broth."

"Probably trying to map out his next move. He's got us all believing he's sick, so now he's got a cover to stick around town for a few days. I tell you, he's up to something."

"I don't think so. Besides, I was able to find out what his job is."

"You was! What'd he say?"

"He said he was a . . . meat inspector." She felt foolish even repeating it.

"Oh, sure!"

It was hard to argue with Leroy's disbelieving tone of voice, especially when Kenlyn found the government man's alleged occupation equally hard to digest.

"Well, that's what he said he was, and I don't think we have any choice but to take his word for it—"

"Well, I don't have to take his word! Why, I'll bet it's even worse than we thought! He's either with the FBI or CIA, and they're smart—real smart," he warned.

"Leroy, you're going to have to get hold of yourself! I really don't think he's with the FBI or the CIA! And I'm almost positive there isn't going to be any large-scale marijuana raid in Isabel—now or ever for that matter—"

"Okay, so it's something bigger than that. Well, that's possible. We'll just have to get our thinkin' caps on and outsmart them bureaucrats."

It was hopeless. She wasn't getting through his thick skull!

The only way to get her point across was to come right out and lay it all on the line for Leroy to pick through.

"Leroy. Listen to me, please. The man's name is Travis Richmond. He's not from Washington, D.C., he's from Los Angeles. He's a federal meat inspector. He isn't with the FBI or CIA."

"So *he* says."

"Well, he should know what he does!"

"Women. They'd believe anything a good-lookin' man told 'em."

"Listen close, Leroy. He's a *federal meat inspector!*" Kenlyn repeated in a tone that made Kenneth's head snap up to look at her.

What few suspicions she'd harbored about Travis Richmond were rapidly diminishing with Leroy's pigheaded refusal to accept what for now seemed to be the logical truth.

"He might have told you that, but I'm not buying it for a minute, little missy."

"Well, you'd better! Think, Leroy. Have you ever heard of the government of the United States descending upon a worthless piece of sunbaked desert to uproot a million-dollar marijuana crop?"

There was dead silence for a moment, then: "Well . . . no." His fading voice answered with a noticeable loss of stamina. "But there has to . . . Wait a minute! wait a minute! That's it!"

"What's it?" Kenlyn groaned, not having the faintest idea of what he was talking about now.

"That would explain what we heard!"

"You mean, what we thought we heard!" she clarified sternly.

"No! You know as well as I do we heard that Richmond fella say, 'marijuana bust,' " he defended. "That's what he said, all right. I'd bet my boots on it."

"But I just told y—"

64

"Don't you get it? Marijuana bust—it's a code name used to cover up the *real* operation!"

She shook her head hopelessly.

"Why on earth would they want to use such an attention-getting code name, for heaven's sake! I thought they used ordinary terms like 'Daisy Mae,' or 'Humpty Dumpty,'" she argued.

"That's just it, Kenlyn," Leroy explained in the most patient voice he could muster up. "Don't you see? All this rigmarole is meant to throw us off the track. What it all boils down to is simple. It's a ploy. One cleverly designed to throw the entire town off guard, while this federal man goes about his devious work free as a lark."

"Leroy, I really think you're way off base this time."

"You go right ahead and think what you want to think! But I'm warning you, I don't plan to sit around and watch our town be overrun by the feds. I'm calling for a town meeting tonight at Perkins' Pharmacy. And believe me, if you care one whit what happens to your town, you'd better be there and so had everybody else!" he threatened, then slammed the phone down angrily in Kenlyn's ear.

Rubbing her throbbing eardrum, she sagged against the corner of her desk and let the phone cord dangle around her feet where she had dropped it.

Boy! All this hullabaloo over a simple meat inspector?

While the last couple of latecomers trickled through the opened door of the pharmacy, Kenlyn

65

sat in the folding metal chair impatiently tapping her foot against the tile floor.

She resented the fact that she was here and not home shampooing her hair. She still fumed when she thought of all the relaxing things she'd given up to be in attendance at this absurd meeting. Luxurious visions stole through her mind—a steaming bubble bath, a tingling facial, followed by a pampering manicure. With resentment mounting, she even found herself thinking that an evening spent with her Water Pik would be more enticing than having to sit through another heated town meeting.

It had been difficult to sit across from Travis Richmond at the dinner table tonight and look him in the eye, knowing full well that immediately after his hosts finished dinner they'd be off and running to a witch hunt that was being held in his unsuspecting honor. She had carefully avoided meeting his gaze, pretending to be engrossed with the piece of liver on her plate. And, oh, how she detested liver! Her stomach churned even now as she recalled how grotesque the main course had smelled, looked, and tasted. But, for the sake of Mr. Richmond's "blood," her mother had insisted on serving it for dinner. It was important to his speedy recovery.

She stifled a laugh when she recalled how Travis had turned that funny shade of green again and had barely been able to excuse himself from the table to make a mad dash for the hall bathroom. Maybe the liver wasn't totally responsible, but he had been green enough to convince her he was ill.

Her thoughts were brought back to the present by

the sound of her father calling the meeting to order. Since Kenneth Grant was the official mayor of Isabel (through no choosing of his own, he was always quick to point out) there was an unspoken agreement that Oneida and Kenlyn would always be in attendance at the meetings. Tonight was no different.

As her father called the meeting to order, a still hush came over the jabbering crowd that had descended upon the makeshift town meeting hall like a small army of ants going to its first picnic of the summer season.

On cue, Marcella Clever stood to read the minutes from the last meeting, which took all of thirty-five seconds.

Kenlyn sat absently studying Marcella's red polyester dress. It was no secret that the new Mrs. Clever strove to be the fashion plate of Isabel, and considering the limited designing insights she had at her disposal, she didn't do all that bad. But somehow Kenlyn could not help think that the Doctor Scholl's exercise sandals Marcella was wearing tonight would have looked more proper with shorts. Or was it the complimentary rhinestone accessories that draped from her ears, neck, wrists, and fingers that was lending the wrong impression? It was impossible to assess which was more stunning, the blinding glare of her twinkling jewels or the high nervous giggle that accompanied every word she said.

Seated among the restless spectators was her adoring groom, Otis. Not once did his love-struck gaze leave Marcella throughout the duration of her report. At any moment Kenlyn was expecting to see his thick-lens glasses steam over, for it was plain to see the Clevers were still on their honeymoon. When Marcella finished her recitation, Otis sprang to his feet with a thunderous ovation.

Leroy was rustling around in his seat, openly anxious to get the meeting under way, as Kenneth rose to his feet again.

"Thank you, Marcella. Now, as far as I know there doesn't seem to be any impending business, so since Leroy has asked for the floor . . ."

Kenlyn sprang to her feet enthusiastically. "I make a motion we use the remaining part of our time to discuss the coming Winter Carnival. It's only a little over a week away and I feel we still have a lot of details to address."

"Thought we had all that stuff taken care of," Elmo Wilson said in a disgruntled voice. He had given up a football game on television to come and hear all this yicyak because Leroy had called while he was eating supper and told him to get himself over here because this meeting was gonna be real important.

"I agree with Kenlyn," Marcella spoke up. "I think we need to talk about my booth at the carnival. Nobody's made any posters as far as I know."

"Has it been definitely decided that a color analysis booth would be the best choice?" Kenlyn asked hesitantly.

Marcella sniffed. "Well, it's not up to me, but it's the going thing in the bigger cities. I've already sent for my *Color Me Beautiful* book." She sniffed again. "But if the ladies of Isabel aren't interested in improving themselves, then I suppose we could always go back to selling Maude Willow's pickled peaches."

"No, you can't!" Maude protested petulantly. "I ain't made no extra jars this year!"

"Well, I think we might need to take another vote," Kenlyn suggested.

"Now wait a cotton-pickin' minute!" Leroy jumped to his feet, no longer able to contain himself. "Winter Carnival, my eye! Kenlyn Grant, you know darn good and well why I've called this meeting! I say we cut through the garbage and get right down to the brass tacks of the business at hand!" he demanded.

All eyes immediately centered on him.

Satisfied he had their full attention, he turned to face the curious gazes of his fellow citizens with a red face. "All those in favor?" he asked meekly.

Since no one was even sure why they were there, no one was inclined to disagree.

"I said! All those in favor?" Leroy demanded again, flashing a daring look of reprisal to anyone who would challenge his sudden authority.

The halfhearted yeas outnumbered the "Shut up and sit down, Leroy's."

Kenneth stood. "Order now. Let's have a little order. Leroy Blankenship now has the floor."

"Well, thanks." Leroy tugged irritably at the sleeves of the sport coat he had outgrown two years ago.

"Just get on with it, Leroy," Elmo pleaded. "I still got time to get home before the second half."

"Where's your civic pride, Elmo? Here we're probably faced with one of the biggest crises ever to hit Isabel, and all you can think about is that stupid football game!"

The crowd perked up at the mention of a crisis.

"What do you mean, Leroy? What crisis?" Henry Perkins challenged.

"I mean that government man who's in town— that's what I mean!"

There was a chorus of disgruntled boos.

"Oh, for heaven's sake, Leroy. Is that what you dragged us down here for? To talk about that stranger who got sick on your food?" Howard Hopkins complained.

"It wasn't my food he got sick on!" Leroy denied heatedly. "Don't you recognize a conspiracy when you see one?"

Conspiracy? Anxious voices rose in the crowd.

"Conspiracy! What in the world are you yakking about this time?" Elmo demanded.

"I'll tell you what I'm yakkin' about. I say there's something funny going on here, and if we know what's good for us we'll get the jump on it and nip it in the bud before it's too late!"

"Before what's too late?" Claude Grant prodded.

"Why, before the federal government comes in here and does whatever they're planning to do. That's what."

"What do you think they're planning to do?" someone in the crowd pressed. "I thought the fella just stopped here for a bite to eat and happened to get the flu."

"Oh, ho! So *he* says. But I pride myself on bein' a

70

whole lot smarter than to fall for something that obvious. I say there's some type of covert action or maybe even some plain old espionage going on here!"

The room suddenly sprang alive with voices raised with indignant protest. A few moments later Kenneth banged the wooden meat mallet Leroy had lent for a gavel and tried to regain order.

"Order! Here . . . I say order! Now hold on Leroy. I think you'd better explain these wild accusations you're throwing around."

That's what Leroy had been waiting for. "I'd be glad to, your mayorship. And I'm not the only one who suspects something strange is going on."

Kenlyn sank lower in her seat, praying he wouldn't involve her in on his wild theory.

"That little lady sittin' right there"—he pointed an accusing finger in Kenlyn's direction—"plainly heard that stranger say there was goin' to be a marijuana bust in Isabel!"

Now the room did explode in a frenzied uproar and it took Kenneth Grant a full five minutes to get it settled back down to normal.

"For heaven's sake, Leroy! Sit down for a minute and let's try to approach this in a reasonable manner!" The mayor turned to his daughter. "Now, Kenlyn. Would you stand and explain exactly what you thought you heard?"

The blood rushed to Kenlyn's face as she slowly stood to face the crowd. "Well . . . Leroy and I were sitting in a booth close to the pay phone in his diner around lunchtime . . ."

Her words faltered. She hated to admit she had

heard what she heard. Travis Richmond seemed like a nice enough man. And he was sick. She was sure of that—or else he was a darn good actor.

"Go ahead, dear," Kenneth prompted.

"But, Pop . . ."

"Tell them what you heard, Kenlyn," Leroy urged.

"Well, as I said, Leroy and I happened to be sitting in the booth next to the pay phone and Travis—the stranger—made a phone call."

"Who'd he call?"

"I don't know. All I heard him say was something about . . . marijuana . . . but I could have been wrong," she hastened to add quickly.

"Holy Moly! Marijuana!" Jim Blanchard jumped to his feet. "Where in the world is anyone growing marijuana around here?"

Kenlyn glanced at her grandfather and her blush deepened. "That's just it. After giving it considerable thought, I'm not sure what I heard was 'marijuana.' It had to be something else."

"Bull manure!"

Kenneth banged his gavel. "Leroy. Must I remind you there are ladies present."

"Well, I apologize, your mayorship, but I'm *sure* that I heard him say marijuana, but if by some strange chance I happened to be wrong, that still doesn't rule out the possibility that he's here for other reasons. A government man just don't come through Isabel and end up staying, unless he's up to something."

"He has the flu," Kenlyn objected.

"So *he* says."

"And he says he's a federal meat inspector," she argued.

"Can you believe that?" Leroy looked to his audience for support. "The man told her he was a *meat* inspector and she falls for it hook, line, and sinker."

Jim Blanchard was on his feet again. "I find it hard to believe the government's in Isabel looking for drugs, but I don't think we can completely rule out what Leroy is saying. Why, who knows what they might be up to?"

Leroy expelled a sigh of relief. At least he had found one comrade. "That's right, folks. After all, wasn't I the one who warned you last year that Harlo Lohmeyer was embezzling that money from the bank?"

No one could dispute that. Leroy had been the one to blow the whistle on Harlo, although no one could ever figure out where he'd gotten his information.

"And wasn't I the one who told you the railroad was thinking about shutting down its service to Isabel?"

He had them again. He had been the one, all right.

"Then why in the world won't you listen to me this time?"

"Because I think we're blowing a very innocent incident completely out of proportion," Kenlyn said, trying again to convince him he was wrong. But by now it was obvious the crowd was beginning to form opinions of their own.

Henry Perkins seized the floor. "Maybe they're trying to throw us off track. Maybe they're not here

73

to uncover anything. Maybe they're here to *bury* something."

The mayor's forehead wrinkled with concern at Henry's puzzling contribution. "Bury something? What?"

"Well, isn't Arizona one of the states they chose to dump all that toxic waste? Now think about it, folks. That fella might be here lookin' for a place to bury that stuff, and it *could* be right here in our own back yards!"

The room came alive again.

"Don't know how the rest of you feel, but I don't want my grandchildren to glow in the dark!" he ended in a grave voice.

You'd have thought the meeting had suddenly turned into a wake, as a deadly hush fell over the crowd.

"Of course, that's it! I don't know why I didn't think of it myself!" Leroy shouted, breaking the silence the room had succumbed to. "They're planning on coming in here and bringing all that crap—probably some of that nuclear stuff from Three Mile Island —and *dumping* it . . . on us!" he added for emphasis.

The crowd's eyes grew wider as the disturbing news began to sink in. Their nervous chattering began again as they discussed the possibilities among themselves.

Marcella fanned herself nervously. "Oh, dearie me. That stuff makes your hair fall out, doesn't it?"

Otis patted her hand. "Sure couldn't do it any good," he had to agree in a worried tone.

Again, Kenneth was forced to call the room to order. "Now let's all calm ourselves for a moment. No one's grandchildren will glow in the dark, and no one's hair will fall out," he tried to assure in a soothing tone. "Henry, where in the world did you get your information about all this approved dumping?"

Henry scratched his thinning gray head as he tried to recall his source. "Um . . . why, on the television, I think."

"You think?" Kenneth questioned, mindful of how Henry was always forgetting or confusing things.

"Well, to be honest, I'm not sure. But, just the other night I was watching the six-o'clock news and Walter Cronkite said . . ."

Shaking his head, Kenneth scolded. "Henry, Mr. Cronkite hasn't been a nightly anchorman for quite some time now."

"Oh." Henry frowned, accepting Kenneth Grant's word without rebuttal. "Then maybe it was Peter Jennings or one of them other young bucks. Anyway, I'm pretty sure I heard it."

Kenlyn lifted her eyes to the ceiling in disbelief, then glanced at her mother, who had been extremely quiet during the whole meeting.

Oneida was crocheting an afghan, but taking in every word.

"I think Mr. Richmond is a very pleasant man," she offered. "He doesn't appear to be up to anything."

"Ha! He's just good at his job," Leroy accused.

"But if the government were looking for a dump

75

site, they wouldn't have to sneak around to do it," Kenlyn pointed out.

"Oh, yes they would! They're sneaky little devils," Leroy contended. "They know we'd raise old billy hell if they come in here and tried to pull that on us."

Kenneth banged the gavel again. "Leroy. The ladies?"

"Oh, yeah." He grinned lamely. "Sorry about my language, ladies."

"Well, what can we do about this?" Elmo asked.

"Now, I'm glad you asked that," Leroy took a deep breath. "I have a plan."

"And what might that be, Leroy?" Kenneth mentally braced himself.

"I think we're gonna have to outfox those devils."

"Yes?"

"I think we're gonna have to sic one of our own on the stranger."

Kenneth raised a brow. "Oh?"

"Yeah. See, the way I figure it, we can do our own detective work. Why, we can find out what the government's planning to do to us and turn the tables on them. Once we find out what they've got up their sleeve, why—*bingo!*—we'll confront 'em with it and throw us a big hissy fit, and chances are we'll scare 'em away."

Kenneth cleared his throat uncomfortably. "I don't know, Leroy. Who would we get to do such a thing . . ."

"It'd have to be a female," Elmo warned.

"Yeah, and a pretty one," Howard added.

All eyes suddenly turned on Kenlyn and she felt her stomach turn queasy. "Now wait a minute . . ."

"She's the only logical choice," Leroy was quick to seize the idea. "She's a real looker, plus a shrewd reporter. She could squeeze the information we want out of this Travis Richmond and he'd never know what hit him."

"I will not!"

"Now just a minute. I resent the fact you think Kenlyn's the only pretty woman in Isabel." The offended voice came from the blonde sitting in the back who had been filing her nails for most of the meeting.

"Oh, no, Sierra. We didn't mean to suggest Kenlyn was the *only* pretty girl in Isabel." Kenneth hurriedly tried to soothe her ruffled feathers.

Sierra Laythrom was eligible and certainly lovely. She just wasn't a reporter. She was a checker at Petersen's Grocery Store.

"I should say not!" Otis denied sharply, incensed that his wife had just been inadvertently insulted. He smiled at Marcella and patted her hand.

"No, I think what Leroy meant to say was, Kenlyn has been trained to sniff out a story and she might be the one most suited here for the job," Kenneth appeased.

"Pop!"

"Yeah, that's what I meant, all right," Leroy agreed.

Kenneth turned to his daughter. "Kenlyn, dear. I know this is quite distasteful, but I think in the name of prudence it's our given duty to explore what is going on," Kenneth apologized. "Don't you, Oneida?"

Kenneth rarely made such serious decisions without consulting his wife. She was known to have a level head.

Oneida shrugged. "Mr. Richmond doesn't appear to be trying to deceive anyone, Kenneth. If he says he's a meat inspector, I'd be inclined to believe him."

"I agree," Kenlyn nodded.

"Well, I don't!"

"Leroy, I think we're all aware of your position." Kenneth turned back to the room full of concerned Isabel citizens. "Since this matter will directly affect all of us, I suggest we use the democratic process and take a vote."

"Don't I have a say in this?" Kenlyn objected. Travis Richmond was a handsome, eligible man, and she didn't want to waste the small amount of time he would be spending in Isabel trying to play detective. She would much prefer to try and get to know him better for reasons of her own.

"Of course, dear. But we know the welfare of your town comes first," Kenneth reminded.

"Yes, and this Richmond fella's gonna be staying right there under your own roof, so you won't even have to go out of your way to pump him," Leroy pointed out.

From what she could hear from the low murmurings, the crowd thought that was the least she could do for her own fair city. She had a terrible sinking feeling she was going to be damned if she did and damned if she didn't.

"But the man only has a simple case of flu. The moment he feels like traveling, he'll be gone," she persisted.

"Then it's up to the town to keep him here until we can find out what he's up to." Leroy tugged at the cuffs of his sports coat again. "We'll just convince him he does look ill and he best stick around a few days longer. He'll be looking for an excuse to stay, so it shouldn't be any problem. Now let's get on with the vote."

The vote only took a minute or so, and in the end Leroy's motion that Kenlyn be used as the town's own gumshoe won by a landslide.

"But, Mom," she protested as the meeting adjourned and they started to walk the two blocks home. "I don't want to do this!"

"I know, dear. But sometimes we all have to set aside our own personal feelings in the name of justice."

"But he says he's a meat inspector," she tried again lamely. She was beginning to feel a certain attraction to Travis Richmond that she was powerless to explain.

"And I firmly believe he is." Oneida paused and smiled encouragingly at her daughter. "And now you've been given the perfect opportunity to prove it."

CHAPTER FIVE

Getting to know Travis Richmond wasn't quiet as easy as Leroy had implied it would be. In fact, getting to know him was about as easy as pulling hen's teeth, she noted glumly as she sat at her desk the third morning and stared out the window.

Against her better judgment, she'd spent the last two days blundering through fruitless tries at getting the government man to slip up, but nothing had worked so far. It seemed she dogged his every step, but he was persistently cautious to reveal very little about his business affairs or his personal life. Kenlyn was becoming increasingly frustrated with her futile endeavors and his tight-lipped attitude.

And it could be he was starting to avoid her.

Take this morning, for instance. He had deliberately turned that funny green and hurriedly excused himself from the table to race to the safety of the bathroom when she had dropped the subtle hint that she was going to have lunch at Leroy's today. No doubt he was beginning to suspect he was being watched, and at this point he couldn't afford even the slightest slip of tongue, so he had again used the excuse of illness to avoid any further questioning.

Well, fine. She had to give him credit for discretion. But it was becoming a matter of pride to see if she could shake him.

And by golly, she would, she suddenly decided. Not for Leroy's, or the town's sake, but for her own. It was getting a little irritating to see the way he was beginning to elude her when they were in the house together.

Picking up the phone, she dialed the diner and waited until Leroy's gravelly voice came over the wire.

"Bean and Burger."

"Leroy, this is Kenlyn—"

"What'd you find out?"

"Nothing. I called to tell you I won't be over for lunch today."

"Why not?"

"I think I'll go home and have a sandwich," she explained, deliberately keeping her voice casual.

"Good thinkin'. Maybe the G-man will eat with you."

"Maybe."

"That why you're going home?"

"Not necessarily," she hedged, although she knew full well that was exactly what she hoped would happen.

"Well, I gotta go. Let me know what you find out." Leroy clicked the receiver down.

Maybe she would and maybe she wouldn't, Kenlyn thought rebelliously. It would depend solely on what she uncovered.

It didn't take long to cover the distance between the *Gazette* and her house. It was her mother's day to play bridge, so the house was quiet when she let herself in. She paused to listen a moment, hoping to catch Travis in the middle of an incriminating phone conversation, but the only sound she could hear was the soft hum of the humidifier.

Walking to the kitchen to prepare a luncheon tray, she thought about the way Leroy had been watching her as she left. Not just Leroy, but the whole town watched every move she made lately. She should save them the eye strain and stick up a score card in the window of her office each morning. Stranger ten, Kenlyn zero.

Lying on the counter was a note in her mother's handwriting addressed to Travis. It explained where his lunch was and instructions on how long to heat the stew in the microwave.

In a few minutes, she had fixed an attractive tray to take to his room. She paused in her preparations to toss down a couple of vitamin C's, E's, and a garlic pill. Garlic was good for blood pressure, and Lord knew she needed that right now. Staring at the bottle in her hand, she shrugged and shook out a couple of capsules on his tray, then replaced the lid. She also shook out some C's and E's.

On second thought, she rummaged around in the cabinet and came up with a bottle of A and two different bottles of vitamin B. She added the capsules to the small pile she already had, then replaced the bottles back in the cabinet. He probably didn't take care of himself the way he should, she excused.

Satisfied the light lunch would be all his nervous system would tolerate, she left the kitchen and started up the stairway.

When she reached the door to his bedroom, she found it closed. Balancing the tray on her knee she had started to knock when she heard his voice, apparently speaking with someone on the phone.

"No, it's going slower than I expected."

She froze and her eyes narrowed.

"I know, but I don't know what else to do right now. I suppose I'll just have to give it a little more time." Then. "Oh, they're nice enough people, but I'll be glad when it's over. I don't like to be like this."

Well, at least he sounded as though he wasn't completely heartless in what he was about to bring upon her poor town.

"Sure, I'll let you know the minute I think it's safe to return to L.A. Maybe in a couple more days."

Oh, Lord. She didn't have much time. She rapped sharply on the door before she lost her nerve.

"Yeah . . . hey, hold on a minute, Dan." Travis covered the mouthpiece of the phone with his hand. "Yes?"

"Hi! It's me. I brought your lunch."

Travis reached down and hurriedly drew the blanket up over his bare legs. "Okay, just a minute." He had barely become decent when the door sprung open and Kenlyn waltzed in.

"Hi, again. I hope you're feeling well enough to eat some lunch."

He smiled lamely, then cupped the mouthpiece and spoke in a hushed voice. "I'll get back with you."

She eyed him sternly, barely able to disguise her feelings, before she swiftly sat the tray on the bedside table.

Replacing the receiver, he suddenly found his pillows being proficiently plumped and the blankets on his bed jerked to a taunt neatness.

"There now, Mr. Richmond. I hope you like beef stew?" She smiled at him coolly. "And vanilla custard."

Leaving no time for reply, the tray was immediately plopped against his chest, and with curt, efficient movements she had shaken out the white linen napkin and placed it under his chin. "Sorry to disturb your phone conversation," she fibbed. "I wasn't aware you were talking until it was too late." She scooped up a large ladle of the stew and held it to his mouth.

Looking a bit uncomfortable, he quickly blocked her hand. "I'm able to feed myself," he complained.

"Oh, sorry." She relinquished the spoon gracefully. "I just thought you might be still feeling ill from this morning."

He carefully blew on the stew and took a cautious sip before he answered. "No, I'm feeling better. The damn bug seems to come and go with irritating unpredictability."

"Well." She slapped her hands against her knees

and pulled up a chair beside his bed. "Then I'll just sit here and chat while you eat."

He sighed inwardly, knowing what came next. She was cute, but worse than a IRS audit when it came to personal questions.

"I'd think that a pretty girl like you would have more to do than sit around a sickroom all afternoon," he observed as he ventured another bite of the stew.

She found herself blushing at the casual compliment. "Thank you."

He glanced up expectantly. "For what?"

"For saying that I am . . . pretty."

"Oh." He smiled. "Well, you are." The more he saw of her, the more attracted he was to her. And when he felt better, he planned to do something about it.

The color in her cheeks rose higher.

For the next ten minutes she chattered about unimportant things and read articles aloud she thought he might find entertaining from last week's *Gazette*.

When he'd finished the stew, his gaze focused suspiciously on the large mound of pills she had placed on the tray.

"What are these?"

She glanced up from the carton of yogurt she was eating and smiled. "They're your vitamins."

"Vitamins." He frowned. "I don't take vitamins."

"That's what I thought," she scolded. "Well, you should, and while you're in my care, you'll have them every day."

"But I don't want them," he argued.

"But they're good for you," she coaxed. Sitting her near-empty yogurt carton on his tray, she scooped the capsules up and motioned for him to open his hand.

With a slight hesitation, he finally conceded, but she could tell he still wasn't very happy about it.

"Now, vitamin A is for growth, color/night vision, healthy tissue, skin, and hair, plus resistance to infection." As she talked, she dropped the capsules one by one into the palm of his hand. "C is for the immune system—which, I might point out, you're in bad need of—resistance to colds and infections, healthy gums, skin and blood vessels, and, oh, just lots of good things."

He listened to her recitation with a sinking sensation in the pit of his stomach. He'd *never* get all those capsules down.

"And B's are marvelous for stress." Her violet-blue eyes penetrated his sharply to see what his reaction would be to that little piece of information, but when he did not appear overly guilty, she hurriedly moved on. "And everyone should take a couple of garlic pills a day."

"Garlic?" She noticed he was beginning to fake that peculiar green color again. Boy, was he getting good at that!

"Yes, garlic is marvelous for lowering the blood pressure, among other things."

Why was she so hung up on my blood pressure? "There's nothing wrong with my blood pressure."

"Great! We caught it in time." She brought his hand to his mouth and he was forced to open and swallow. "You need to take fish oil, too. It's good for the heart."

Grasping for the glass of water on his tray, he managed to get the capsules swallowed.

"Holy Moses! That was enough to choke a horse!"

"You'll be fine." She patted his back soothingly. "Now, if you're through with your tray, I'll just set it over here on the table."

It was more than all right with him. After taking all those capsules, he couldn't eat the custard anyway. While she dispensed with the tray, Travis self-consciously readjusted the sheet.

"Mr. Richmond—"

"Please, any woman who feeds me garlic pills should be on a first-name basis, don't you think?" He grinned at her and she could not help wishing they had met under different circumstances. There was something about Travis Richmond she could really like.

"Oh, yes . . . I suppose so." She smiled back and her eyes seemed determined to focus on the wide expanse of his bare chest. It was an exciting, manly chest. "I've been thinking. Would you care if I interviewed you for an article in next week's *Gazette?*" It was a simple request, one designed to cleverly delve into his shadowy background.

"Me?" He laughed. "Why on earth would anyone be interested in reading about me. I'm afraid I'd bore your readers to death."

"No, you wouldn't!" she insisted, almost too eagerly. If he only knew just how much they'd drool over such a tasty tidbit. "We're a small community where everyone knows everyone, so when a visitor does manage to find his way to Isabel, it makes for interesting copy. You know, it sort of lets us know how the other half lives."

"You're kidding," he chuckled, still finding it highly amusing that she'd want to do a story on him.

"No, I'm not. Really."

"I'm afraid my life would make a very dull story. But thanks anyway. I'm flattered you'd even ask."

"Honestly, you don't understand. It's different in a small town. Our people love reading about other people's lives."

She begin to panic at the realization he might refuse her. She'd never once thought of that obstacle. Most people fell all over themselves to be interviewed for an article in the *Gazette*.

"Besides, it's almost become a town tradition," she pleaded. "It's our way of saying thanks for stopping in."

Travis shifted around uncomfortably. "I didn't exactly mean to stay," he pointed out.

"No, but you're here and that's what counts." A pad and pencil magically appeared in her hand. "Now then, where were you born?"

He shook his head and sighed in resignation. "Los Angeles."

"Mother and father?"

"Yeah, I suppose that's how it worked," he teased.

She felt herself blushing. "No, I mean, *who* were your mother and father?"

"Jack and Ilene Richmond. In fact, they still are," he added with a growing twinkle in his eye. It was plain to see he still wasn't going to take the interview seriously.

"They still are what?"

"My mother and father."

"Oh." She pretended to ignore his questionable humor. "And you're with the United States government. Is that correct?"

"That's correct. I'm a meat inspector."

She bit her lower lip painfully, "Yes . . . a meat inspector. And how long have you been with the government?"

"Oh, let's see. Close to five years now."

She glanced at him and smiled. "You like your job?"

He shrugged. "It's a living."

"I suppose, being with the government, there are times when you sort of . . . oh . . . work undercover," she coaxed.

"No, they rarely go to the trouble to disguise me as another cow," he admitted.

She stared back at him impatiently. "No, I meant, working for the government is probably very exciting. Are you called upon to maybe help in other areas of the government—you know—something outside the realm of . . ." She cleared her throat and forced the words out. ". . . inspecting meat?"

"Oh, yeah." He sat up straighter. "Sometimes I stay in the office and do paperwork. That's always exciting."

The point of her pencil suddenly snapped with suppressed anger and the broken lead fell into his lap. She murmured a muted apology and started to reach for it when her hand rammed into a most embarrassing part of his body.

Her face flamed with suffused color as he flinched, then politely removed the lead himself and handed it to her.

"This is really fun. I hope it's a long interview."

She could have died! He was baiting her and she wasn't planning to fall for it.

Springing to her feet, she marched to the window. "Mr. Richmond! I really think this interview would be far more interesting if you would try to be a little more specific on exactly *what* you're doing in Isabel—" She caught herself before she gave her motive away, then continued in a more rational voice, "I mean, for instance, if you'd want to be more specific . . . oh, not for public knowledge, mind you, but if you'd reveal a tiny tidbit that would make the story more interesting, then I might be able to phrase it in a way that the reader would be able to understand your exciting job." She smiled knowingly. "Do you know what I mean?"

Surely, he wasn't dense. He had to know that she was onto him. But would he open up?

Travis wrinkled his forehead thoughtfully. He'd never thought of his job as exciting, but it certainly held an unusual fascination for her. Oh, well. If she wanted the boring details . . . "Well, I don't know what I could tell you that I haven't already. You see, I've been over in Phoenix inspecting meat—" He jumped as he heard her slam the pad shut she had been writing in.

"Thank you for your time, Mr. Richmond—"

"Please, call me Travis." He winked at her playfully and her stomach turned over.

"Yes . . . Travis," she said obediently. "I think that will be all for today. I wouldn't want to tire you unnecessarily."

It was clear he was well honed in his work. He wasn't ready to break—at least not today.

A whole hour wasted and not one inkling of incriminating evidence to show for her suffering. Great balls of fire! she agonized mentally as she scooped up the dinner tray and prepared to leave. I'm beginning to *believe* the man's cock-and-bull story! There had been no hints of espionage—no romps with the CIA, the FBI, or even the EPA. Even a job behind the desk of a one-person FHA office would be more exciting than Travis Richmond's job!

"Thanks for bringing my lunch."

"It was no trouble. I'll see you at dinner this evening."

She slipped hurriedly out of the room as Travis folded his arms behind his head and settled back against the pillow. He lay for a moment staring at the ceiling, the memory of his ex-fiancée surfacing to his mind. He wished Melody had been more like Kenlyn Grant. Kenlyn had an honesty and a freshness about her that was beginning to intrigue him.

Whoa, man, he cautioned. You've just come out of a long, frustrating relationship, and you shouldn't be thinking so much about Kenlyn Grant. Yet he wasn't soured against women. On the contrary, he was looking for the type of woman he could love and respect.

If only Melody had been a more caring and sincere person. He'd have married her in a minute.

The thought only served to dredge up painful memories. Melody had always been such a conniving person—one of the very reason's why he'd suddenly found the courage a few months ago to break the engagement. He'd decided he didn't want to spend his life with a woman who tried to manipulate him. And she was cold—sometimes downright callous in her dealings with other people—and he hated that.

No, it'd be hard not to be attracted by a woman as attractive—or as whimsically appealing—as Kenlyn. He rolled over on his side and the scent of her perfume still lingered in the room.

He closed his eyes and recalled how disappointed his parents had been when he'd told them of his decision. They had hand picked Melody Winslow, and they thought he was being a fool. Well, maybe so. But it was his choice.

He suddenly burped, and he cringed as he tasted garlic. Did he have to be punished this way?

CHAPTER SIX

"I don't know, Grandpa. It all seems so silly." Kenlyn was sitting with her grandfather on the porch of the *Gazette* the following morning. Travis Richmond had been in town four days and rumors still flew like a sleet storm in Anchorage.

Leaning to knock the ashes out of his pipe, Claude tried to remember what it was like to be young and have so many confounded troubles. One thing nice about growing older—life's everyday problems never seemed as bad as they once did.

Sitting back in his chair, he begin to scrape the bowl crusted with layers of smoked tobacco. "The situation seems to be getting a bit blown out of proportion," he agreed.

"If you ask me, I think the whole town has gone nuts."

"Looks that way."

Again, he leaned over the banister and emptied the bowl of the pipe. It was common knowledge the routine discussions around every dinner table lately revolved solely around one subject: Travis Richmond. Over pork chops and chicken that usually grew cold, the residents of Isabel continued to ask the repetitious questions to one another. Who *is* this stranger and what is he planning to spring on us?

"You know, Grandpa, I think he's a pretty nice man, no matter what he's here to do," Kenlyn confessed.

Claude noticed how her face would automatically soften when she spoke of the stranger. Too bad those two younguns' hadn't met under different circumstances, he thought. " 'Pears to be. Didn't I see the two of you takin' a walk last night?"

Kenlyn smiled as she thought about the stroll she and Travis had taken after dinner the night before. He'd said he felt strong enough to take some fresh air, and they had meandered up and down the street in front of the house. They'd spent the time talking about various, unimportant things, but she'd enjoyed the evening immensely. She'd enjoyed herself so much, she'd completely forgotten her appointed civic duty.

"Lemon pie's my favorite," he'd revealed as they paused to sit on an old rock wall covered with trailing vines.

"It is? I love cherry," she confessed.

"You're an only child?"

"Yes. How about you?"

"No, I have a brother and a sister."

"Oh, that's nice. I always wanted a brother."

"You date anyone steady?"

She blushed. "No. Not steady. How about you?"

He smiled and reached over to take her hand.

94

"Not anymore. I was engaged for a couple of years, but it didn't work out."

"Oh . . . I'm sorry." She wasn't really. "What happened?"

"We found out we had made a mistake."

"I'm sure that was very painful. What was her name?"

"Melody Winslow."

"Was she pretty?"

He leaned over and touched his mouth to hers. "Not as pretty as you."

For a brief moment, Kenlyn had felt a twinge of pain for Melody Winslow. What would it be like to be in love with a man as vital and as blatantly male as Travis Richmond and then lose him?

Brought back to the present, she glanced at her grandfather, fearful for a moment he might be able to read her irrational thoughts. Satisfied he was lost in his own meanderings, she decided to examine those thoughts more closely.

What was there about Travis that she found so intriguing? It wasn't his job, that was for sure. Because if it were his job with the government that was causing all this interest, then she should be ashamed of herself. If he were snooping around in Isabel on a mission that would bring the town harm, then she'd be nothing but a traitor with these puzzling new fantasies she was beginning to have about him.

When they'd accidentally brush against one another, or she'd catch him looking at her in a way that would send her pulse racing—well, she had to wonder what had gotten into her. Here was a man who had a questionable intent in Isabel, and *she* was going all starry-eyed over him? Her feelings were beginning to worry her.

As each day passed, she found herself seeking him out at every opportunity—and not just in hopes of questioning him. She honestly enjoyed his company, and there were times when she dreaded the thought of his supposed recovery. For then he'd be leaving, and she had gotten used to his being around.

And the way the townspeople treated him! She was mortified. If he hadn't noticed all the icy stares and hushed whispers that accompanied any public outing he had briefly undertaken, then he had to be blind. Why, just last night, Marcella and Otis had been taking a walk also, and when Travis had made an effort to be cordial, the newlyweds had scurried away like frightened children about to have their candy taken away from them.

"Has my deodorant failed?" Travis had turned to her and deadpanned.

"No, not at all." Kenlyn watched the hastily retreating backs of the middle-aged couple, trying to control her tongue. "Some people are just rude!"

"I suppose you'll be at the meetin' tonight?" Her grandfather's voice snapped her back to the present.

"Oh . . . yes. I'm head of the committee this year."

Plans for the Winter Carnival had been shoved to the background since the government man had arrived, but a planning session was scheduled for tonight. The Winter Carnival was an important annual event in Isabel, since it supplied most of the funds for the local fire department.

"Well"—a puff of cherry smelling smoke completely engulfed Claude as he coaxed his pipe back into life—"I was gonna come, but my bunion's been actin' up again. I think I'll just stay home and soak it this evenin'."

"I'm sorry. I thought maybe I'd let you buy me a hot fudge sundae after the meeting," she teased.

"Nope, couldn't do that. Wouldn't want to get Joe Hensley all riled up."

The expected red flags surfaced on his granddaughter's cheeks. "Oh, Grandpa! You know I don't care one whit about Joe Hensley!"

Claude chuckled, a devilish twinkle coming into his blue eyes. He loved to see her get flustered when he teased her about Joe. Now if Joe had his way, he'd buy Kenlyn a sundae every night of the week, Claude speculated with growing amusement, but somehow Kenlyn just never seemed interested in the shy banker. No, there was only one man who seemed to bring a bloom to her cheeks and a sparkle to her eye these days, and that man was Travis Richmond.

He sure hoped she wasn't heading straight for trouble.

Later that evening, a brilliant orange sunset dipped low on the horizon as Kenlyn stepped out the front door. Dinner had been a pleasant interlude with Kenneth and Travis discussing farming. Claude had joined the family for dinner, then returned to his small apartment over the garage.

She sat down on the steps as the screen door opened again and Travis came out to join her. The air had taken on just a hint of crispness as he pulled the collar of his jacket up closer and glanced to the setting sun.

"Isn't it gorgeous?" Kenlyn sighed, as he sat down beside her on the steps.

"It is."

"You seemed to be feeling better this evening."

"With all those vitamins you've been giving me, how could I miss?" he chided. "I am feeling better. It's a strange bug. It comes and goes."

Actually, he'd felt well enough to start for L.A. yesterday, but for some reason he continued to delay his departure. Isabel was a peaceful town (although the people were a little strange) and he enjoyed their laid-back way of life. And then he couldn't totally say he wasn't enjoying the attention Kenlyn Grant had been showering on him. He found he didn't want to leave her—at least not yet.

They both watched the sunset in contented silence for a moment.

"You know, living in a big city has its advantages, but I think a person tends to forget what a beautiful thing nature is," he admitted, fascinated with the ever-changing colors on the horizon.

"Have you ever seen anything more lovely?" It seemed to Kenlyn that tonight nature was going all out to impress her rapt audience.

"Oh, I don't know." He smiled, thinking of the unsuppressed beauty Kenlyn radiated when her violet-blue eyes sparkled the appreciation she held for such a seemingly simple thing as a sunset.

"What do you mean, I don't know," she bantered softly, enjoying the quiet camaraderie she and Travis had so easily developed over the past few days.

"I mean, it's almost as pretty as an ocean sunset."

"You've seen the ocean?"

"Sure. I live in L.A. Remember?"

"Oh, yes. I'd forgotten for a moment. Of course you've seen the ocean." She leaned back on her elbows and gazed at the evening star that was just beginning to rise. "You're lucky, you know. Yuma is as far away as I've ever been." She glanced over and grinned, feeling a bit foolish since Yuma was less than a hundred miles from Isabel.

"That far, huh?"

He returned her grin and again she noticed what a picture-perfect smile he had. She had no idea why she suddenly felt so good, but she did. He had a way of making her feel that way.

"Well, I wouldn't give up on seeing the ocean yet," he encouraged. "You'll make it someday."

"Oh, I'm not even sure it's all that important that I do," she admitted.

"Really? Why not? It's awesome to feel and experience its power."

"Yes, I'm sure it is. And I'll admit I've thought of moving to somewhere like L.A. and trying to get a job on a big newspaper, but when I think of leaving Mom and Dad and Gramps, I get a little nervous."

"Why?" He was intrigued with her simple honesty.

"I don't know. Maybe because I've never been

away from them before, or maybe because I'm just content living here. Either way, I'll probably just grow old and die in Isabel like everyone else does." She directed her gaze back to the stars. "But I hope to see the ocean someday—especially before it becomes all polluted and ugly." She hazarded a glance at him from the corner of her eye to see if he had any kind of visible reaction to her observation. "You know what I mean? Sometimes man has a way of disturbing the ecological balance of nature, and I think that's just a shame. Don't you?"

"Yes."

"And isn't it just awful the way even the government is doing things that simply appall you?" she prompted.

She could tell she had his undivided attention now. "The government? What have they done?"

"Well, for instance. I think it's just terrible the way they're running around like a chicken with its head cut off looking for places to dump toxic waste . . ."

Again, she paused and allowed a moment for her words to sink in. Surely now he'd know she'd guessed his real purpose for being in Isabel and drop this innocent "I'm only a meat inspector" act. If he only would, then she'd let her growing feelings for him run free.

"Well, I know it isn't a pleasant thought, but I suppose they have to do something with it," he reasoned.

"They don't have to dump it on Isabel!" Her voice rose sharply.

He looked at her blankly. "No—I didn't mean they had to dump it on Isabel."

"You mean you'd find that objectionable?" She was searching for any small clue to show he wouldn't be a party to such a catastrophe.

He stood up and stretched. "Thank goodness I don't have to make that kind of decision." He extended his hand and pulled her to her feet. "Hey, it's getting late. I could walk you to the meeting if you'd like."

She suddenly felt disappointed that he'd be so blasé about a matter that held such importance to her.

She quickly brushed off the backsides of her jeans and tried to avoid his eyes. "Sure, you can if you want to."

"Are your parents going?"

"No, Dad has another meeting tonight."

They walked in silence for a good five minutes before Kenlyn's temper finally began to recede. She reminded herself over and over that she really didn't have any incriminating evidence against him, so why should she be so upset by such a simple remark? By the time they turned the corner leading to the pharmacy, she felt much better.

"Why don't you stay for the meeting?" she invited. "It shouldn't take very long and then I might buy you a chocolate soda afterward."

"A chocolate soda, huh?" He hadn't had one of those in years. "Well, why not." He put his arm around her waist and gave her a brief kiss. It was the second time he had done that, and she found herself longing for him to really kiss her.

"Great. I'll have one too."

"Is the owner of the diner going to be there?"

"Leroy? Yes, I'm afraid so . . . I mean, yes, Leroy wouldn't miss a meeting for love nor money."

"Why do I have the feeling he doesn't care for me?"

"Gee—I don't know," she hedged, suddenly feeling uncomfortable with the conversation.

"Maybe it's my imagination, but I could swear he watches me like a hawk."

"Oh, there's a bunch of nosies living in this town. Don't pay attention to any of them."

Perkins' Pharmacy was full when Kenlyn and Travis joined the meeting. All eyes focused in their direction as they walked in and took the last two empty seats.

Kenlyn noticed tongues begin to wag the moment she sat down, but she stared back at the troublemakers with a show of defiance.

Henry Perkins stood up. "Okay, folks. Looks like we're all here now, so we can get started." He turned to Kenlyn. "You want to take over?"

Kenlyn stood and smiled sweetly at the audience. "Good evening."

There was a low rumbling of returned hellos.

"First, I'd like to introduce my guest. I'm sure you have seen him around the past few days, but you've never been formally introduced." She glanced at Travis and smiled. "Travis Richmond, would you please stand?"

Travis slid out of his seat, embarrassed she'd go to such lengths to introduce him. A simple "this is Travis Richmond" would have done. He smiled lamely at the sea of unfriendly faces. "Hello."

The majority smiled back, but there were a few stony faces that puckered a what-is-she-up-to look.

"I invited Trav . . . Mr. Richmond, to sit in on our meeting tonight." Kenlyn paused to let the implication of her words sink in. "I thought it'd give each of you an opportunity to become better acquainted with our visitor."

The continued silence was so thick, you could have cut through it with a chain saw. Kenlyn's temper began to flare, realizing they weren't going to be charitable about this.

Leroy cleared his throat and stood up. "Hi-ya, Mr. Richmond. You feelin' any better?"

"Yes, thank you. I believe I'll survive now."

"You don't look too good yet. Better take it easy and not be in any rush to get back to Callyfornee."

Someone in the room chuckled until someone poked him in the rib and made him remember who Travis Richmond was.

The meeting got under way and, after thirty minutes or so, Travis leaned over Kenlyn's shoulder and offered to make a pot of coffee.

"Thanks. I think we could use it. You'll find a kitchenette right through that door."

The moment Travis disappeared through the doorway, Leroy was at her side. "Okay. What's going on?"

"What do you mean?"

103

"Why in the world did you bring *him* to the meeting?"

"He came as my guest."

"Your guest! Well, la-dee-da," he mimicked. "I thought you was supposed to be finding out why he was here, not cozyin' up to him!"

"I'm *not* cozying up to him," she denied heatedly, but the others had already begun to gather around her. "Travis simply offered to walk me over here tonight—"

"So it's Travis now," Sierra Laythrom accused.

"That's right. His name is Travis. And you should be ashamed of the way you treated him earlier. All of you should be!" she accused, determined to make them feel just as guilty as she'd been feeling.

"Ashamed!" Leroy demanded. "For what? Not trustin' a fed? Have you forgotten what that man's up to? Do you think he's here on some sort of a vacation, with all your 'visitor' talk!"

"Oh, for heaven's sake! I told you, the man is nothing more than a federal meat inspector. He's told me so himself at least a hundred times—and I believe him!"

"Well, if *he* told you that—I say we should believe him." Henry Perkins agreed with Kenlyn wholeheartedly—besides, the "Gunsmoke" reruns were on again tonight and he wanted to get the meeting over and go home.

"You hush up, Henry. What do you know 'bout government spies?" Leroy badgered.

Henry scratched his head worriedly. "Nothin', I

guess. I just thought if the man said he was a meat inspector, that's what he might be."

"There are no government spies in our midst," Kenlyn tried to patiently explain one more time. "Now, I think it's to all our best interest to stop this nonsense and get on with the meeting. Now, Marcella, about your booth—"

"Seems to me, Kenlyn, you've forgotten your assignment." Leroy glared.

"Assignment? You mean, my sentence!" she clarified curtly. "And I certainly have not. Not for one moment. I've done exactly what you forced me into doing. The only problem is, you don't want to accept my findings."

From the looks on their faces, Kenlyn realized part of them wanted to believe her and others didn't.

"I'm sure if you'll just take the time to visit with Travis after the meeting, most of your fears will be put aside—"

Again Leroy butted in. "If you ask me, it purely ole sounds to me like you just might have a thing for that federal man," he accused.

Again, all eyes turned on her, brimming with renewed suspicions.

"A what?" She demanded an explanation to his accusation.

"You know darn very well what I mean. Looks like you've up and fallen for that government man. That would explain the sudden change of interest."

"Who could blame her?" Sierra challenged from her perch on a bar stool. She continued to file a razor-sharp edge to an already dangerously pointed fingernail. "He's a hunk if I ever saw one."

Kenlyn whirled around, suddenly fed up with trying to make a bunch of narrow-minded people understand her point of view. She calmly went about gathering her purse and sweater as the room sprang alive with the renewed speculation of Kenlyn's suspected romantic involvement with the federal man.

"You have *all* gone off the deep end," she announced, then marched determinedly through the doorway leading to the kitchenette.

She found Travis still rummaging through the cabinets for coffee filters. He glanced up as she burst through the doorway. "Hi. I'll be through here in a sec—"

"Forget the coffee. The meeting's over." She wanted to get him out of there before he could discover the bin full of looneys on the other side of the door.

"So soon?" He had figured it would continue another hour or two.

"Oh, Travis!" To her mortification she dissolved in tears and went straight into the shelter of his arms.

At a complete loss about what was going on, he pulled her up tightly against his chest and tried to soothe her anguish. "Hey, listen . . . what's the matter?"

She was sobbing so hard she couldn't tell him— nor would she, even if she could. She was ashamed of her town, yet deep down she was torn between the conflict of the ever-nagging thought, What if they were right and he was here to do Isabel harm?

Never had she met a man who could turn her insides to mush when he looked at her or make her wish *she* could be the one to give him his dumb garlic pills every morning for the rest of her life!

"Kenlyn, honey . . . tell me what's wrong," Travis's voice had grown husky as he pleaded for a reason for her distress.

He was becoming intoxicated with the feel of her in his arms. The familiar smell of her perfume assaulted his senses as he wrapped his fingers in her hair and tipped her tear-streaked face to meet his. He was ready to demand that she tell him why she was in such a state, but when the huge pools of violet met his troubled gaze, words were forgotten.

Before he realized it, he was kissing her, a hungry passionate kiss that made him shove all previous thoughts of prudence aside. This was madness, he told himself—he had only known her a few days— and yet the kiss deepened into a searing urgency that left them both with a tantalizing weakness invading their very souls.

"Oh, Kenlyn, I've been wanting to do that for a long time," he admitted when their lips finally parted.

"Oh, Travis. I've been wanting you to do that." She smiled at him tenderly and for a moment her troubles were forgotten as their mouths met again and again . . . and again.

Only the sound of Leroy's raised voice coming from the other room dampened her newfound happiness.

"Travis, I want to leave here." She whispered her

107

heartfelt request against the tantalizing sweetness of his lips.

"Of course. Anything you say."

The gentleness in his voice brought fresh tears to her eyes. He was so kind, so thoughtful . . . so good! He couldn't be there to do harm. . . .

He slipped his arm around her and she buried her face in the sleeve of his jacket, and they quietly slipped out the back door.

Leroy watched with a jaundiced eye as the couple left the pharmacy, then let the curtain on the front window drop back in place. He turned to the critics of Isabel, who were sitting as quiet as church mice.

"I knew it! What did I tell you? She's gone and fell for that fella and now we're in an even bigger pickle than we was to begin with." He began pacing the floor. "Well?" He turned an accusing eye back to the assembled group. "Don't just sit there. Someone come up with something before it's too late!"

"As much as I hate to admit it, maybe we made a mistake by sending Kenlyn to get the lowdown on this federal man," Elmo offered.

"A mistake. A *mistake!* Well, Lord almighty, Elmo. We don't need you to tell us that! Of course we made a mistake! I want to know what you think we should do about it!"

Sierra yawned and stood up. "I don't know what all the shouting's about. As I've pointed out before, Kenlyn Grant is not the only woman in Isabel who's capable of dragging information out of Travis Richmond."

The eyes of the accusers were immediately on her.

"I mean, why don't I see what I can do?" she offered simply.

"That's smart, Sierra, that's smart," Leroy admitted. "I don't know why I didn't think of it before."

"But if the G-man's fell for Kenlyn, how do you think you're gonna get him to look at you?" Marcella asked, feeling a certain loyalty to Kenlyn. After all, she saw the government man first.

Leroy shot Marcella a dirty look. "Because, Marcella"—he reverted to a tone he would use with an imbecile—"just because Kenlyn went and fell for him don't mean he returns the feelin's. Good grief, woman! He's a man of the world. Comes from Los Angeles and all. You think he'd honestly be interested in a small-town gal like Kenlyn?"

"She's real pretty, Leroy" Henry pointed out.

"Yeah, and she's nice, too," Otis was quick to add. "She's not pouty or spoiled like some of those big-city women are."

"Dad burn it! We ain't here to talk about Kenlyn Grant's love life," Leroy objected. "We're here to get this government business nipped in the bud. Now I say we let Sierra have a shot at this. What do you say?"

Well, there was little they could say. Leroy seemed to be running the show.

"All right, then. We agree. Sierra, you stay after the meetin' and I'll help you think of some way to get to the G-man without arousing Kenlyn's suspicions. If she finds out what we're up to, why she just might sell us down the river, and we can't afford to let that happen."

The small group nodded solemnly. That was for sure. That was for *darn* sure.

CHAPTER SEVEN

Travis, ole man, you're nothing but a fake.

Travis stuck his tongue out and leaned closer to the mirror, hoping to see some lingering signs of illness. Nope—it looked all right to him. His hand automatically went to his forehead and he struck out again. His temperature appeared to be perfectly normal.

A week. He had been in Isabel one full week, and he had played this simple case of flu to the hilt.

What was wrong with him? Why did he keep postponing the inevitable? He was going to have to leave for L.A. soon. He couldn't stall Dan much longer with the feeble excuse he still didn't feel like traveling. Although his boss had been very understanding about this unexpected illness, Travis knew he was beginning to suspect something strange was going on.

Travis shuffled over to the side of the bed and sat down. He covered his mouth and burped, the strong taste of garlic bombarding him again. He might feel like an Italian meatball, but he had to admit he was strong as a bull moose from all those vitamins Kenlyn had been forcing down him.

Kenlyn. He crossed his arms and lay back on the bed, visions of the violet-eyed beauty dancing through his head. Kenlyn Grant was what was the matter with him, he finally admitted. The truth was, he didn't want to leave her.

Well, at least he'd been able to come up with another feeble excuse to stick around for another day or two. He'd sent his car to the local garage to be serviced and made it clear he wasn't in any hurry to get it back. He hoped Elmo Wilson was as slow as he looked.

Rising from the bed slowly, he went into the bathroom to fetch his toothbrush and extinguish the repulsive taste in his mouth, his mind going back to the night before.

He and Kenlyn had sat out on the porch long after the rest of the household had retired. They had been talking, and then kissing, and then downright necking. It had been very late when they had finally come into the house.

Travis laced the bristles of his brush with a generous supply of toothpaste and diligently attacked his mouth.

He was falling in love with Kenlyn Grant, and he wasn't going to fight it.

Kenlyn placed the grand finale, a crystal bud vase containing a solitary red silk rose, on the breakfast tray she'd spent the last fifteen minutes preparing. She hoped the rose would brighten Travis's day as easily as he seemed to brighten all hers. Her mind happily relived the night before, when he had kissed her until she was breathless and she had wanted much more.

And he had been so understanding the night she'd left the pharmacy so upset. He hadn't pressed her to find out what had happened—just let her lean on his strength until she felt better.

Her smile grew dreamy as she poured the orange juice and lay his daily supply of vitamins on the tray. She was in love with Travis Richmond. It wasn't an easy confession, especially considering what the town was accusing him of, but now she really didn't care *why* he was here. It only mattered to her that he was. To her way of thinking it might be childish, rebellious, and inconsiderate, but it was honest.

Besides, she still thought he was innocent, and nothing would change her mind. Even if what Leroy was saying was true, she'd have to believe Travis had a reason for being in the line of work he'd chosen. If by some miracle he could one day return her love, then he could always quit his job and they could move somewhere far away, where no one would ever know. . . . Oh, it was foolish to think such thoughts, she cautioned.

Anyway, she and Travis had only known each other a week. But her Grandmother Grant had been a mail order bride, and she and grandpa's love had surely flourished for sixty years.

She was humming softly under her breath when the faint knock at the back door caught her attention. Glancing at the clock on the microwave, she frowned. Who in the world would be knocking on the door this early in the morning? She stepped to the window and carefully pulled back the print kitchen curtains.

She sighed as she found Sierra perched on the wooden porch. What was she doing up and stirring around so early in the morning? Better still—what was she stirring around here for?

It wasn't as though she didn't like Sierra Laythrom. Kenlyn found her to be pleasant enough. But they weren't exactly the closest of friends and definitely not close enough for her to be on Kenlyn's doorstep so early.

Kenlyn hesitated before answering Sierra's repeated knocking. Glancing at the western omelet she had artfully created, she sighed again. It would probably taste like rubber when it reached Travis.

Opening the door a crack, she peeped cautiously around its corner. Maybe Sierra would take the hint when she saw that Kenlyn was still in her robe.

"Sierra . . . hi. Is there anything wrong?"

"Oh, hi, Kenlyn." Sierra seemed surprised that it was Kenlyn who had opened the door. "I didn't think you'd be up, yet."

"I barely am. Mom had to work the church rummage sale this morning, so I'm fixing our houseguest's breakfast."

She eyed Kenlyn's rumpled appearance. "Oh . . . how nice. May I come in?"

"Uh . . . sure." Reluctantly Kenlyn stepped aside, allowing Sierra to enter the kitchen, carrying a bulging wicker basket clenched tightly in her hand.

"Umm . . . what *is* that heavenly smell!" Sierra sniffed the aromatic air appreciatively.

"Blueberry muffins."

"Blueberry muffins?" Sierra lifted her brows knowingly. "Why, Kenlyn, I had no idea you were so domesticated. Homemade blueberry muffins. I'm sure Mr. Richmond will be delighted."

"I hope so." She smiled back at her coolly. Sierra had attended the town meetings concerning Travis, and her remark made it clear she thought Kenlyn was being a traitor to the cause, too. "Well, what has you up and about so early this morning, Sierra?"

The click of Sierra's three-inch high heels echoed loudly in the kitchen as she strutted across the tile floor. She paused and ran her hand across the slim curve of her hip and smiled sweetly. "I'm here as an official representative of the Isabel Welcome Wagon," she announced.

"The Welcome Wagon? In Isabel?" There was no such thing!

"Yes, the Welcome Wagon. And I've come to officially welcome Mr. Richmond to our fair city."

For a moment Kenlyn could have sworn a guilty look flashed across Sierra's face.

And it had. It had been Leroy's idea to use the Welcome Wagon approach, Sierra thought miserably. I'd have preferred doing it my own way!

Kenlyn momentarily felt at a loss for words, while Sierra strolled to the table where the breakfast tray was sitting. She began to absently rearrange the silverware. "You don't mind if I deliver this to your guest, do you?"

"Well, yes, as a matter of fact I do!" Kenlyn stepped protectively in front of the tray.

Sierra quickly sidestepped her and hurried to the doorway. "Okay, then I'll just go with you, while you deliver it."

Before Kenlyn could protest, Sierra had left the room, trailing a heavy scent of Charlie perfume in her wake. Sucking in an indignant breath, she swiped up the tray and marched out of the kitchen, mumbling under her breath about the unmitigated gall of some people.

"Really, Sierra. I don't know if Mr. Richmond is even dressed yet," Kenlyn protested as she overtook the unwanted intruder on the stairway.

"If he isn't, I'll wait," Sierra said, brushing her off in a breezy tone.

There was nothing Kenlyn could do but trail helplessly behind the curvaceous blonde, who looked as though she'd been poured into the red knit dress she was wearing. She would have chosen red, Kenlyn thought resentfully, recalling how it was Sierra's most complimentary color—and she *knew* it.

Kenlyn glanced down at the terrycloth robe she was wearing and she felt her heart sink. She had meant to change into jeans and a blouse, but she had been so preoccupied with impressing Travis with her culinary arts, she had only brushed her teeth and haphazardly run a brush through her hair before she started breakfast. But she'd had no idea she was going to be competing with another woman, she fretted, still trying to figure out why Sierra was there.

Her gaze was drawn again to the way the red knit clung provocatively to Sierra's backside, and she had to stifle another groan. Travis had never even *seen*

116

her in a dress, but she silently swore to correct that as soon as possible.

By now they had reached the top landing, and Kenlyn hurriedly pushed around Sierra. *"If* you don't mind, I'd like to at least warn Travis that he's going to have company."

Sierra tried to force herself back in the lead, but after a few moments of silent struggle, she finally conceded defeat. Soothing her dress down over her narrow hips, she glared at Kenlyn. "Don't you think you should get dressed before you go in his room, dear?"

"No, dear. I'm perfectly acceptable the way I am."

Sierra's eyes flicked over her distastefully. "Acceptable as what?"

The door opened while they were still hatefully eyeing each other and Travis appeared.

"Good morning! I thought I heard—" His words were interrupted as Kenlyn shoved past him in a huff and tramped over in her furry scuffs to slam the tray down on the bedside table.

The dishes rattled and clanged precariously as she whirled around to confront him. "I brought your breakfast and this is Sierra Laythrom. She's from the . . . Welcome Wagon." Ah-ha-ha, she added silently.

Travis seemed clearly puzzled by the unexpected intrusion, but he nodded politely at the attractive blonde. "Hi."

"Hi." Sierra gave him a radiant smile. "My, you look chipper this morning! I hope this means you're well on the road to recovery."

"Yes, thank you." He smiled at Kenlyn. "With all the good care I've received, I gain strength every day."

"And no wonder!" Sierra hurried to the bedside table and lifted the lid off the western omelet and blueberry muffins proudly, as though she'd concocted the contents herself. "Just look what I've brought you to eat this morning!"

I've! I've brought you to eat? Kenlyn flashed her a hair-pulling look, but Sierra snubbed off her glare as she motioned for Travis to sit down.

"And I've also brought you a few other lovely goodies I know you're going to enjoy," she said, tantalizingly, handing him the bulging wicker basket. "It isn't much—some fruit, chocolates, and a copy of our local newspaper, but we thought you might enjoy it. Just our little way of saying . . . welcome!" she explained with a merry laugh.

Travis was suddenly being propelled across the room to be hurriedly seated in the chair next to the table. "Now do go ahead and eat before it gets cold," she urged. "I'll just sit here and we'll have a nice long chat while you enjoy your breakfast."

Travis glanced helplessly at Kenlyn, who was standing in the doorway with her arms crossed Indian fashion.

Dropping down on the edge of the bed, Sierra crossed a smooth, well-defined leg and the side slit of her knit dress gaped open to show a substantial glimpse of her thigh.

Kenlyn rolled her eyes upward and stifled another groan. What was she doing?

Travis's eyes widened appreciably until he noticed the glower on Kenlyn's face, then he obediently dropped his gaze back down to his plate.

"My . . . this looks good," he complimented feebly.

It was bad enough that Sierra had taken the credit for the breakfast she'd prepared, but giving him a girlie show while he ate was too much! Kenlyn finally stepped forward, smoothing her hand over her tousled hair in embarrassment.

"Travis, I hope you like the muffins. I made them myself . . ." She swallowed her unfinished words. It was obvious he wasn't listening. He was too busy looking at Sierra's expanse of dark hosiery covering her thigh.

But Travis wasn't as interested in Sierra as he was amused with the way the two women were obviously struggling for his undivided attention. He was more than a little puzzled about why Sierra Laythrom would think she warranted such attention—although she sure had a nice set of legs. . . .

"It's my Grandmother Grant's recipe and I'm the only other person she's ever given it to," Kenlyn announced lamely.

And about Kenlyn, Travis was thinking—well, he was pleased that she would have such an interest, but she had never acted this strangely before.

"I'm sorry, Kenlyn, did you say something?" He snapped out of his meanderings and smiled at her. Her question about the muffins hadn't totally escaped his ears, but Sierra was in the middle of telling him about her cashier duties at the local grocery store, and out of politeness he'd extended an ear to the mundane accounts of leaky brown bags and miscalculated subtotaled sales receipts.

By now Kenlyn's patience was at an end, not to mention her bruised pride and her soaring jealousy. He could act like he wasn't thoroughly enjoying the view Sierra was giving him, but Kenlyn knew better!

"Who, me? Well, I wouldn't want to disturb your visit. All I said was, if the two of you'd be so kind as to excuse me, I really must be going."

Sierra glanced up, surprised to see that she was still in the room. "Oh, of course we will, dear. I know you must be dying to get out of that hideous bathrobe," she excused pleasantly. Immediately turning her attention back to Travis, she returned to rambling about her long and tiring hours at Petersen's Grocery.

Travis shot Kenlyn a panicked look that plainly said, "Don't leave me alone with her," but Kenlyn callously ignored it. She was going to make him pay the price for all that gawking!

But the moment the heavy oak door closed behind her, her true colors of rage appeared as she stormed down the stairs, threatening destruction to anything that dared to cross her path.

An hour later, she was sitting at her desk at the *Gazette,* still nursing her bruised feelings. A Butterfinger and a can of root beer usually buffered whatever was ailing her, but today they just didn't seem to pack their usual punch.

These confusing feelings were getting the best of her. She couldn't understand what was happening.

Anyway, she might be in love with the stranger, but she had no exclusive strings on him. Sierra had just as much right to visit with Travis Richmond as she did.

Then why did it hurt so?

She sniffed, fighting back tears of growing frustration. It would be absolutely absurd to even hope he might return her feelings, she reminded herself. One day soon, he'd hop in his car and forget he'd even heard of Isabel, Arizona.

He'd be a rat of the highest caliber if he didn't at least feel a little guilty about those last few nights they had spent on her front porch! But most likely he wouldn't even remember who Kenlyn Grant was a year from now. She hurriedly fumbled in her desk for another Butterfinger.

Travis walked through the open door of the *Gazette* as she was rummaging through the bottom of her purse for enough loose change to buy another root beer. For a moment, he stood watching her, a smile tugging at the corners of his mouth.

"What vitamin do you take to counteract all that junk?"

Kenlyn sprang upright in her chair, embarrassed Travis had managed to sneak up on her, especially while she was indulging in one of her many weaknesses. She hurriedly stuffed the second half-eaten candy bar in her desk drawer.

"Oh, hi."

"Hi." Travis strolled over and propped himself on the side of the desk.

His presence shouldn't have startled her so, it was

121

the third day in a row that he'd stopped by the office to visit. For some reason, she hadn't expected him this morning. She'd assumed Sierra would take her time making him "welcome." The mere thought of Sierra spending time with Travis ruffled Kenlyn's already disturbed feathers.

She knew she had no right to be angry with him. And even if she had, the wonderful, warm way his chestnut eyes melted right through her, she couldn't have harbored her resentment for very long.

"Is that what you're having for breakfast?" Travis scolded. "A candy bar and a can of root beer?"

She shrugged. "It's a bad habit I've gotten into."

"And I'm the one burping garlic," he sighed.

"I burp it, too," she defended. "I'm just sloppy in my eating habits."

He chuckled and his eyes grew warm as he leaned over and tweaked her nose affectionately. "Hey, why did you run out on me this morning?"

"You looked as if you were enjoying yourself," she accused.

He leaned closer and whispered in a teasing tone, "Did you see her *legs?*"

"And her thighs and her tonsils."

He flashed a mischievous grin. "Oh, *meowwww, meowwwwww.*"

"I didn't say they weren't nice thighs and tonsils," she pointed out, and then broke down and laughed with him.

They were so engrossed in their laughter, they were surprised to glance up a few moments later and find Leroy Blankenship and her father entering the room. Kenlyn hadn't realized Leroy was on the premises—he usually went out of his way to make his presence known when he visited the *Gazette.* Obviously, he and her father were discussing business, so she went on explaining to Travis that this morning was the first she knew about Isabel's Welcome Wagon.

It didn't take Leroy long to spot Travis sitting on Kenlyn's desk. He began straining his neck, trying to catch a stray word of their conversation.

Kenlyn's attention was drawn to his annoying actions and she felt her temper surfacing. He was beginning to remind her of a bird dog—always on point! She was grateful Travis had his back to Leroy. It was almost pathetic to see the way the little snoop was nearly breaking his neck to find out what she and Travis were discussing.

Kenneth noticed what was happening, and he smiled and shook his head apologetically at his daughter as he tried to hold Leroy's wavering attention.

"Well, I think it's my duty to try to sooth your ruffled feathers over dinner this evening," Travis was saying, totally unaware of the silent war raging around him.

"Dinner?" She perked up at the unexpected invitation.

He nodded. "My place or yours?"

She laughed when she thought of how his room was probably no more than eight feet directly above her own. "What do you say we simplify the situation and meet out on the front porch? Then we can decide if we have Chinese, Mexican"—she struck a dignified poise—"French, or American," she finished, as though there would really be a choice.

Leroy's was the only eating establishment in town and they both knew it.

"Fine with me," he agreed, admiring how pretty her hair looked this morning. He'd love to run his hands through the dark mass and . . . to break the hypnotic spell she had unknowingly cast on him, he quickly conceded to her suggestion. "I'll meet you on the porch. How's seven strike you?"

"Perfect." She blew him a hurried kiss behind Leroy's back.

A few moments later Travis left the office, but not before pausing for a few moments to say hello to Kenneth and Leroy.

Kenlyn cringed when she heard Leroy tell him that he still "looked a mite peaked," and not to be in any hurry to get back to L.A.

Through years of training, Leroy had managed to overhear a muffled tidbit or two of Travis and Kenlyn's conversation. When Travis was safely out the door, his little feet quickly carried him to Kenlyn's desk.

"I heared that Richmond fella say somethin' about seven o'clock." His beady eyes sparkled with renewed hope. "What's up? You decide to pump him again?"

"Nothing's up, Leroy," Kenlyn said dryly, thinking her dander might get that way real fast if Leroy started in on her again. "Mr. Richmond invited me to have dinner with him, that's all."

124

"Dinner!" He expelled a *whoosh* of disgust. "Well, ain't that just dandy!" He turned to Kenneth, pleading. "Did you hear that, Kenneth? Your daughter's eatin' supper with that G-man tonight!"

Kenneth meandered to his desk and sat down. "Leroy, you know you might be getting the town upset over nothing," he pointed out, using his most assuring tone of voice. "Mr. Richmond appears to be on the up and up . . ." He faltered momentarily as he saw the fire in Leroy's eyes begin to simmer. "Now, I've observed Mr. Richmond throughout the week and I haven't seen him do anything sneaky," he defended.

"Well, I never thought I'd see the day that you'd be suckered in by the government!" Leroy jammed his sailor's hat down on his head disgustedly. "If you'll excuse me, I've got things to attend to."

The front door slammed shut loudly as Kenlyn glanced at her father and smiled with gratitude. "Thanks, Pop."

"Don't thank me," Kenneth excused absently as he adjusted his glasses on the bridge of his nose, then picked up a piece of copy and began to proofread it. "Just don't be bringing me home any grandbabies who glow in the dark."

Travis was waiting on the porch that evening by six thirty. He spent the excess time nervously adjusting his tie, smoothing his trousers and wishing he'd suggested she meet him a half an hour earlier.

He couldn't wait to be with her. He'd thought of nothing else all day long and he wondered again if he was rushing things. A week was a pitifully short time to fall in love with a woman, and yet wasn't Kenlyn Grant the woman he'd searched for all his adult life? He supposed when he looked at it in that context, a week wasn't that unreasonable.

All day he'd found himself mentally comparing Kenlyn to Melody, and for the first time he felt confident he'd done the right thing by breaking the engagement.

Kenlyn was honest and forthright, and she'd never try to manipulate him the way Melody had. She was the woman he wanted to spend the rest of the days of his life with.

He chuckled when he thought about what his friends and family were going to say when he came home engaged . . . he caught himself before he went on. He still had to ask Kenlyn to marry him, and he wasn't sure she'd consent to his proposal. Doubts began to build in his mind again. A week was pushing it. . . .

"Am I late?" a familiar voice asked, breaking in on his troubled thoughts.

Turning around, he was unprepared for the "new" Kenlyn. He felt his heart skip a beat as she smiled and walked to him. The mesmerizing smell of her perfume drifted lightly through the air and he felt his mouth go dry.

"Do you like it?" She swirled around the porch, displaying the burgundy skirt and matching peasant blouse that dipped tantalizingly low at the neckline. Her hair was pulled back with a ribbon.

It was all he could do to keep from taking her in his arms and confessing his earlier thoughts.

But he didn't want to scare her. Because of the circumstances of their swift relationship, when he told her he loved her, he wanted the timing to be perfect.

"Yes, it's beautiful . . . you're beautiful," he told her in a voice that had suddenly grown husky with desire.

She felt herself releasing the sigh of relief she'd been holding. She'd retrieved the dress from the far corner of her closet where she'd tucked it away, having bought the ensemble for Otis and Marcella's wedding. True, it wasn't quite as sexy as the red knit Sierra had been wearing this morning, but with the aid of a few nips and tucks around the neckline, she'd tried to create a more alluring effect.

And from the look on Travis's face, she'd been successful.

"It's a very pretty dress," he complimented again, trying to regain control of his aroused senses. "You look beautiful."

"Thanks. You said that." They smiled shyly at each other.

"Remind me to say it a hundred times more before the night's over."

Reaching out, he took her hand and they stepped off the porch. The moon was just rising, and the evening promised to be a special one. As they strolled down the sidewalk, he put his arm around her waist, and she lay her head on his shoulder.

It wasn't difficult to decide where to have dinner; Leroy's was the only show in town.

The meal was pleasant despite the stares that accompanied every bite they put in their mouths. Still, nothing could dampen the simple joy of being with one another.

When Travis went to take care of the check, Leroy flashed Kenlyn a petulant look as he rang up the sale at the register.

When they left the diner to walk down the deserted streets of Isabel, the moon had begun to succumb to an occasional cloud, reflecting soft shadows around the contented couple. The air had developed a slight chill, so he offered her his jacket. She declined, though the thought of being wrapped in a jacket with the smell of his woodsy cologne still lingering in its material was tempting.

"Am I getting paranoid, or is it true the people of Isabel think I'm some sort of a freak?" Travis asked as Kenlyn again settled against the warm contours of his body.

"No, they don't think you're a freak. They just don't take to outsiders that easily."

She wrapped her arms around his waist and squeezed him tightly. She knew how puzzled he was by all the stares and hushed whispers he'd been receiving, and she longed to confess how Leroy had the town all stirred up with his wild accusations about Travis. But if she did, then she'd have to confess what role she'd played in this bizarre incident, and she positively didn't want to do that. At least, not yet. She still wasn't sure she believed his meat-inspector story without reservation, but she knew deep within her heart he would never intentionally hurt anyone. \

"Well, I'll have to be leaving soon," he conceded, and he felt her grow tense at his words.

"I don't want you to leave," she confessed in a small voice.

It was he who squeezed her affectionately this time. "I know, and I don't want to, but I think my boss is beginning to wonder just how long a simple case of flu can keep me here."

"Do you like your job, Travis?" She hated herself for prying again, but it was important to her.

"Yes, why?"

"Oh, I was just wondering. You've never thought of doing something different?"

He was silent a moment, as though he were carefully weighing his answer. "No . . . not until I met you."

If Kenlyn decided she'd be unhappy living in L.A., then he supposed he'd be willing to consider another line of work, but he'd sure hate to.

Her steps faltered and she turned her face to meet his in the filtering moonlight. "You mean . . . I would make a difference?"

He smiled down on her, love radiating in his eyes. "Yes, I think you would. If you haven't noticed, I'm in love with you, lady."

There was no candlelight and roses, but he couldn't hold his feelings in any longer.

Kenlyn thought her heart would burst from happiness. "Oh, Travis . . . I love you, too." Her arms went around his neck and they kissed long and hungrily.

The ever-present eyes of Isabel were upon them as Kenlyn suddenly remembered where they were and set their feet in motion again.

"Let's go somewhere where we can be alone," he murmured. There were so many things he wanted to say to her.

"I was thinking the same thing."

"Oh, wait . . . while we're this close to the garage, I guess I should stop by my car for a minute."

"Elmo closed hours ago," she reminded.

"Damn."

"Is it that important?"

"In a way, it is. I have a report that has to be on my boss's desk by Friday morning and I can't complete it until I consult a few notes I left in my briefcase."

For one unexplainable moment she felt a chill come over her. What type of a report was he going to make?

No—I trust him. Implicitly. Whatever the report is, it will not concern Isabel. She'd stake her life on it.

"Maybe if Elmo hasn't serviced the car yet, it'll still be sitting out in front of the garage," she suggested.

"Let's hope that's the case."

As they approached the garage, they could see the white sedan parked beneath the floodlight, and Travis breathed a sigh of relief.

"Good. I'll only be a minute," he promised as he leaned over and snatched a hurried kiss from her.

Kenlyn watched as he walked to the trunk of his car and quickly inserted the key. Suddenly, he paused, a frown forming on his handsome features as he bent forward and touched the area around the keyhole.

"What's wrong?"

"Oh . . . nothing. I found a few scratches around the keyhole I didn't realize were there," he said absently, thinking now he'd have to fill out another long, lengthy report.

But Kenlyn heard him swear irritably under his breath again as he flipped the trunk lid open and viewed the stray pages of his last month's report discarded on the floor of the trunk.

Startled by the sound of his angry voice, Kenlyn moved briskly to the car. "Travis . . . what's wrong?"

"It looks like someone's been rummaging through my briefcase," he said curtly, trying to rearrange the papers back in proper order. "Now who in the devil would do that?"

"Are . . . are you sure?"

"Yes I'm sure!" His voice echoed loudly from inside the trunk. "I'd like to know what's going on around here!"

Wanting to comfort him, she reached out and gently touched his arm as she moved to join him in his effort to restore order. "I'm sorry," she conveyed apologetically.

She felt rotten. This had to be the result of Leroy and Elmo playing Dick Tracy again.

131

"Hey!" Travis paused and immediately took her back in his arms. "It's not your fault. Vandalism can happen in any town," he soothed. He tipped her face to meet his, then touched his mouth tenderly to hers. "Give me a few minutes, then we'll find that time alone."

But it was her fault, she thought miserably, as she watched him turn back to the scattered papers. And was he going to be so consoling when he found out she *knew* who had been pilfering through the trunk of his car . . . and why? She seriously doubted it.

The incident still worried her as they walked through the deserted park a little while later. They sat down on one of the benches to rest, and Travis's arm automatically went around her.

"Travis . . . I really am sorry about your car," she apologized again.

"I don't know why you're still worrying about it," he soothed, nuzzling the lobe of her ear. "It wasn't your fault."

"But . . ." Her words were forgotten as he nudged her mouth open with his, sending shafts of sweet desire darting through her. For a moment the world was lost as she became immersed in his touch.

Being in his arms was a feeling she found hard to explain. It was like waking up on Christmas morning and finding everything you'd ever wanted wrapped in one big package—with your name on it. It was the exhilaration of the first snowfall of the season, the joy of a baby's laugh, the warmth of your mother's smile when it seemed the whole world was against you. It was a feeling she didn't want to lose.

"Travis—I think you should know something," she began when his mouth finally released hers, only to trail down her neck and send goose bumps racing up her spine.

"I do know something. I'm crazy about you, Kenlyn Grant."

"No, that's not what I mean," she protested, wishing her mind would think more clearly. She had to confess what she had been doing, but he was making it impossible to think clearly.

"You're not crazy about me?" He nipped at her ear and his hand slipped inside her jacket, coming to rest lightly on her waist. The blouse she was wearing was silk, and the heat of his hand made her go weak with longing.

"Travis . . ." Her voice held a distinctive warning as his hand began to explore.

"Yes?" He was playing a bewitching game, and she was caught in his spell.

She reached out her hand to run her fingers down his cheek. "I think we should talk," she pleaded softly.

"About what?"

"About your being here . . . about me . . . about what I'm doing . . ." Their mouths came together again, and she groaned and shifted closer in his arms.

But what he was doing was reason enough to make her forget her good intentions—or at least it seemed that way to her.

"Don't you think?" she finally managed to ask feebly.

"Absolutely."

But when he finally kissed her good night at her doorway an hour later, they had discussed nothing.

CHAPTER EIGHT

"I'm in love with him, Grandpa."

"I figured as much."

"Am I being totally foolish?"

"Everyone's got a little fools' blood in 'em, youngun."

"It was this way with you and Grandma, wasn't it?"

"You mean, did we fall in love that fast?"

"Yes."

"Yes, child. Exactly the same way."

"I told Travis about you and Grandma last night. He thought it was wonderful the way you ordered her from a catalog and then spent sixty years loving each other. Sixty years—that's a long time, you know."

"It wasn't nearly long enough."

Another two days passed, and still the government man lingered.

Kenlyn walked around with her head in the clouds, thinking of little but Travis Richmond. The hours they spent together were precious, but she knew it was long past time to be honest with him. More than once he'd made reference to the fact that she was more than a passing fancy, and she knew she had fallen in love with him.

She sensed he intended to ask her to marry him before he returned to L.A., but each time he'd broached the subject she had quickly changed it. Not that she didn't plan on accepting his proposal—she just wanted everything to be right, and it couldn't be until she confessed what she had been doing.

Most likely he'd get a big laugh out of all the misconceptions that had been going around about him, she'd think sometimes. Of course he would! He had a great sense of humor, and he'd probably be amused by her amateurish tries to play sleuth. Or else he'd tell her he wasn't ready to marry someone who was that big of a bubblehead and walk out the front door and she'd never see him again, she'd anguish at other times. Either way, she had to tell him.

"Pop, radiation doesn't have to be all that bad, does it? I mean, look at the way it's advanced medical technology. And *if* he's here to find a new dump site for toxic waste, don't you think the government is smart enough to use a safe and effective method to dispose of it?"

"I imagine."

"I mean, it has to be dumped somewhere. Why not Arizona? I'm sure *no* state's going to issue an engraved invitation to bring the stuff in . . . so maybe if the worse happens, then the whole world will look on Isabel, Arizona, as being darn patriotic—don't you think?"

"I suppose so."

"Why, he could end up making us all heroes . . . and . . . and the town would be eternally grateful to him—don't you think?"

"I thought you believed he was a meat inspector."

"He is, for heaven's sake!"

Friday morning, Travis was surprised to find Sierra standing outside his door when he answered the soft knock. He didn't know why he should be surprised. She had been underfoot for the past few days like a tenacious bulldog, asking some of the craziest questions about his job. There was something about being a federal meat inspector that unduly fascinated the citizens of Isabel.

Sierra wasted no time in her current mission, for fear that Kenlyn would catch her there again.

"Hello, again!" She smiled sweetly. "Oneida said you were up."

"Hi, what brings you around so early?"

"I thought I'd stop by and invite you to join our festivities at the Winter Carnival."

"Thanks. I'd planned on coming."

The Carnival was the following night—he knew that by heart. He had walked Kenlyn to more meetings than he could count on one hand since he had been here. After talking to Dan again yesterday, he also knew he couldn't delay his return to L.A. longer than Sunday, so he planned to ask Kenlyn to marry him sometime tomorrow night.

137

Naturally, she had to be at the Carnival, but afterwards. . . .

"Would you like to go with me?" Sierra invited.

"Well . . . thanks, but I'd planned on taking Kenlyn," Travis admitted.

"Oh . . . poop!" Sierra's lower lip jutted out. "I was hoping you'd go with me."

Travis grinned. "Now you'd never make me believe you'd have a hard time getting a date for Saturday night."

"Well, no . . . but I wanted to go with you."

"Sorry, maybe next time," he excused as the phone beside his bed began to ring.

"Excuse me?"

"Sure. I'll wait."

While he went to answer the phone, Sierra slipped into the room and promptly made herself comfortable in an overstuffed chair sitting in the corner. She cocked an ear, preparing herself for any bits of stray information the phone call might provide. So far, she had been a complete washout as far as getting any information out of him. There was another town meeting tonight and she dreaded the thought of facing Leroy empty-handed again.

Dan's voice was a mildly unpleasant reminder that Travis had a life waiting for him on the other side of the Arizona state line. "Yeah, I should be leaving Sunday."

"Well, it's about time. I was ready to come down and bring you home myself," Dan joked. "What in the world have you found so interesting down there in . . . what was the name of that town . . . Jeze-bel, Arizona?"

"Isabel."

Sierra's ears immediately perked up. Probably con-firming his location again, she surmised shrewdly.

"Oh, yeah . . . Isabel. Well, Annie says it's prob-ably one of those wild little out-of-the-way places you hate to leave."

"Negative," Travis grinned, thinking how boring Isabel would be if Kenlyn hadn't been around.

"What! You're going to try to tell me you've hung around a town for the better part of a week and a half that's no bigger than a dry spot in the middle of the road and has nothing but a greasy café and a corn feed silo?" Dan reared back in his chair and roared, thinking how unlike Travis Richmond that would be.

"Oh, let's do it up right," Travis bantered. "Add at least a couple more silos."

Sierra's mouth went slack.

Travis glanced over and noticed the funny look on her face and immediately regretted poking fun at her town. After all, when he married Kenlyn, he'd have close ties in Isabel himself.

"Listen, Dan—could I give you a call back this afternoon?"

"Sure, no sweat. It's sure good to hear you sound-ing like your old self again."

"Thanks. Talk to you later."

Sierra squirmed in her chair uneasily. "You . . . uh . . . didn't have to hang up on my account."

"Oh, it wasn't that important."

"Well, listen, I have to be running along." She

sprang out of her chair and hurried to the door. "I just wanted to invite you to the Carnival."

"Yeah . . . thanks. I'll probably see you there—"

Sierra never heard the rest of his sentence, because she had already slammed out of his bedroom in a mad rush.

Perkins Pharmacy was hot and crowded when Kenneth, Oneida, and Kenlyn arrived that evening. It had been against Kenlyn's wishes to attend the meeting, but Kenneth had insisted she be present as usual. She'd cornered Travis and told him she had another brief meeting to attend. He'd innocently mistaken the meeting to be yet another one about the Winter Carnival, and she hadn't bothered to correct him. He'd been visibly disappointed they couldn't have the entire evening together, but she'd given him a lingering kiss and promised to be gone no longer than an hour. Wild horses couldn't have made her break that promise.

Kenneth called the meeting to order, and Leroy immediately took command.

"Well, now you know me and Elmo didn't turn up anything real incriminatin' when we searched the fed's car—"

"Searching the 'fed's' car is a federal offense," Kenlyn was quick on her feet to point out, still peeved they had gone through Travis's car like a bunch of pack rats.

"Well, I know, I know, but sometimes you gotta bend the rules a little," Leroy excused.

"Tell us what you found in the 'fed's' car," Kenlyn baited.

She knew they had found nothing out of the ordinary, and she wanted Leroy to publicly admit it.

"Well, nothin' really—just some papers indicatin' he was doin' some meat inspectin' over around Phoenix. But that was just to throw us off track. Of course they'd give him the proper papers so's he could back up his willy-nilly story."

"Of course," Kenlyn groused under her breath as Oneida patted her knee sympathetically.

Fully expecting him to finger her for a full report, Kenlyn braced herself to give him her lack of news, when Leroy suddenly turned to address Sierra Laythrom.

"All right, now, ladies and gents. I'll admit we ain't done too good so far on gettin' anything real solid on this G-man, but I think, due to a stroke of luck, we just might have stumbled over the first real bit of evidence we can really sink our teeth into. I think our own"—he shot Kenlyn a snooty look— "Sierra Laythrom has something you're all gonna find real interesting. Sierra, dear, you tell 'em what *you* heard." Leroy wiped the gathering perspiration off his face and sat back down.

Kenlyn glanced at her father and Kenneth raised his shoulders as though to say, "I have no idea what he's up to this time."

Sierra stood up slowly, her eyes darting to Kenlyn uneasily. She cleared her throat a couple of times, then began. "Well, as you know, I was supposed to . . . uh . . ." She glanced sheepishly at Kenlyn

141

again, then back down at her hands. ". . . uh, see what I could find out about Mr. Richmond—"

"What!" Kenlyn slapped her hand on the table and shot up out of her chair. "I thought that was *my* job!"

Sierra stiffened her back defensively as Kenneth ordered the crowd back to order.

"As I said," Sierra continued in a firmer voice, "since Kenlyn could not accomplish anything, I was appointed by all of you to see what I could find out about the government man."

Oneida tugged on her daughter's shirttail and urged her to sit back down.

"But she said . . . she's been *spying* on Travis, Mom!"

"Yes, dear. Now sit down and don't act ugly."

The following five minutes were devoted to Sierra's detailed account of her attempts to gain information from Travis Richmond.

With each word, Kenlyn submerged into a slow, jealous burn.

"And after giving this matter considerable thought, I'd like to assure the counsel that I honestly don't think that Travis Richmond is in Isabel to scout out a toxic dump," Sierra concluded.

The crowd spontaneously let out a sigh of relief and burst into a round of applause, and it was several boisterous minutes before calm could be restored.

Kenlyn was still seething at the thought of Sierra dominating Travis's time, but at least the truth was out now, and she was more than a little relieved to have this whole silly affair over.

"Please . . . please! If I may continue to have your attention, please!" Sierra sought to gain the floor again. "I do feel, however, it is my civic duty to report to you a conversation I overheard this afternoon while I was in Mr. Richmond's room."

"You were in Travis's room this afternoon!" With lightning speed Kenlyn was on her feet again, and it took both Oneida and Kenneth to prevent her from going nose to nose with Sierra.

Sierra, feeling considerably more courageous with the support of the crowd, turned her nose up haughtily. "Yes, I was, and I overheard Mr. Richmond telling someone that they should 'do it up right' and for them to order at least a couple more 'silos' for Isabel!"

Kenneth Grant's brows shot up in surprise. "Are you implying they were talking about missile silos?"

"Well . . . I . . . I suppose that's what they meant. He clearly said silos. I was sitting not ten feet away from him when he said it."

The immediate ohs and ahs filled the room ominously. Not a person there wasn't aware of the horrifying implications of such an intrusion.

"Well, sheet!" Leroy bound to his feet as Kenneth grabbed the gavel and banged it down hard on the tabletop.

"Now, Leroy! We have women present and you're gonna have to watch your mouth!" he demanded.

"Well, I'm sorry, your mayorship, but do you have any idea what that lets us in for?" Leroy had grown quite wild-eyed by now. "Why any town housing such missile sites is gonna be the first on Russia's

143

bombing list!" he was quick to point out, the familiar beads of sweat popping out everywhere on his forehead.

"Now listen, folks." Claude Grant tried to speak above the raised voices. "You have to bear in mind Sierra said she overheard Mr. Richmond's conversation—that don't necessarily mean he was talking about missile sites. Why, he could a been talking about corn silos for all we know!"

"Corn silos!" Leroy slapped his forehead in complete exasperation. "Get real, Claude!"

With Leroy's all too clear visualization of being bombed clean off the face of the earth, the crowd soon swelled to an angry mob. Kenlyn couldn't believe what she was hearing! She grabbed the gavel from her father's hand and started pounding on the table for order, but the citizens of Isabel had gone berserk.

Marcella was openly weeping and Otis was beside himself trying to lend comfort. Henry Perkins was trying to remind everyone there was an old bomb shelter in the basement of the pharmacy and they'd better have a meetin' first thing tomorrow morning and get the blasted thing cleaned out.

"This is crazy!" Kenlyn shouted above the din. *"Travis Richmond is a meat inspector!"*

"I don't think they're listening, dear." Kenneth took the gavel out of her hand as she burst into tears.

Claude Grant sat back and watched the zoo going on around him, shaking his head in disbelief.

Scooping up her purse, Kenlyn ran out of the frenzied meeting, scalding tears running down her face.

She had to get to the only sanity she had left in her life—Travis.

When she burst through the kitchen doorway ten minutes later, she found him standing at the counter, dipping up a bowl of ice cream.

"Oh . . . hi! I didn't expect you back this early—"

His voice faltered as he noticed Kenlyn's tear-stained face. She was out of breath from running all the way home, and her mascara was running down her cheeks in black trails.

"Kenlyn—what's wrong this time?" He dropped the ice cream scoop and stepped to gently cup her chin in his hand, tilting her face to meet his.

"I *hate* this stupid town!" she blurted, then burst into another fresh round of tears.

"What?"

Kenlyn fought to avoid his compassionate eyes. "Oh, Travis! I don't know what to do!"

"Did someone hurt you?" he demanded, his voice suddenly taking on an edge as the thought of someone trying to do her harm made his temper flare.

"No . . . it's nothing like that," she insisted, adding with a sob, "would you . . . please come with me?"

"Sure . . . where do you want to go?"

Handing him the keys to the Volkswagen, she could think of only one place where she would be assured the privacy she needed to sort this thing through. "I want to go to Grandpa's house."

"But he lives over the garage—"

145

"No, not that house. I want to go to the house he shared with Grandma."

"You've got it. Just point the way."

Few words were exchanged as Travis and Kenlyn drove along the winding gravel back roads that led to her grandfather's deserted ranch. Except for a "Turn right here" and "take a left there," Kenlyn's thoughts were consumed with retracing the course of events that comprised the last week and a half.

She was still far from being over her anger to her fellow council members—and Sierra, specifically—but even as her blood continued to boil, she knew that her neighbors and friends were good, hardworking, honest people. They just got carried away sometimes.

Deep down, she could understand their reason for panic. In their eyes Travis Richmond was a threat to the security of a safe little world they'd known all their lives. They were frightened, reacting in the only way they knew how.

If only she'd been able to convince them that their fears and suspicions were unfounded and totally absurd, she sighed to herself. If they only knew the Travis Richmond she knew, they'd quickly realize they had absolutely nothing to fear from this kind and gentle man.

Travis respected Kenlyn's need for solitude and allowed her the twenty minutes the ride supplied to sort through whatever was troubling her. He hated seeing her so upset, but obviously something had taken place at the meeting that she didn't want to discuss. If the Winter Carnival was going to cause so much trouble, he wished she'd resign from the committee and let someone else have the headaches.

Kenlyn broke the heavy silence they had succumbed to, softly pointing out, "There's a lane to your right, just up the road."

"Here?" he asked.

"Yes. This is it."

As Travis turned onto the dirt lane, the headlights of the car reflected ghostly images on the silhouette of the abandoned ranch. The house was surrounded by a fading white picket fence. A barn out back looked weathered and in need of repair. Pieces of its tin sheet roof were curled upward, a symbolic surrender to the passing of time and its elements. A towering windmill stood idle in the calm night air.

Travis brought the Volkswagen to a gentle halt. Walking around the car to open Kenlyn's door, he could not help notice the bright mass of stars that seemed to hang heavily above their heads.

Standing by the opened car door, he waited while she slowly emerged. "I can see why you wanted to come here," he offered, as he continued to gaze at the innumerable stars that seemed to pulsate in the darkened sky.

Kenlyn's watery gaze joined his. "I used to sit out here for hours, trying to see if I could count them all." She sighed, a small hopeless sound. She blew her nose for the tenth time since they had begun the trip. "I never did."

He grinned and leaned to touch his mouth to hers tenderly. "Well, don't give up, sweetheart."

"Would you like to see the house?"

"Sure. Do you have a key?"

"Yes." She leaned over and reached for the keys still in the ignition. Retrieving a flashlight from under the front seat, she flipped its beam on.

Travis shook his head. "You really come prepared, don't you?"

With a soft laugh, Kenlyn dropped her head guiltily. "Oh, you're probably going to be shocked at how prepared I am."

The boards creaked as they stepped on the huge front porch. Kenlyn jiggled the house key in the lock and pushed the large wooden door open. Hardwood floors echoed the sound of their footsteps as Travis trailed behind her through the darkened rooms. She went straight to the writing desk by the paned window, picked up a box of matches and ignited the glow of a flickering flame to the oil lamp.

"So . . . what do you think?"

A rock fireplace dominated one wall of the cozy room. Except for the sheets that covered the furniture, it looked as though the occupants had simply gone away on vacation. Pictures were still hanging on the walls, freshly laundered curtains draped the big window—nothing looked out of place.

"It's nice," he complimented, noticing there wasn't so much as a speck of dust on the walnut writing table.

"I try to get out here at least once a week. No sense in letting the place go to pot," she reasoned as she walked to the half-filled wood box.

"I'll do that." Travis began gathering a handful of kindling and several small logs to start a fire.

Within minutes a soft glow bathed the room from the welcome warmth of the fireplace.

Kenlyn sat on the oval rug in front of the fire. With her arms wrapped around her drawn legs, she patted a silent invitation for him to join her as she stared thoughtfully into the dancing flames.

Travis watched as the subtle light from the fire played softly across the contours of her face, its subtle glow reflecting a magical sparkle in those mysterious violet-blue eyes.

As he continued to watch Kenlyn deep in thought, Travis realized the room was becoming increasingly warm. And he knew that the fireplace alone wasn't responsible. It must be all that damn zinc she's been giving me, he thought with amusement. In the pamphlet she'd given him to read about vitamins, it stated zinc was important to male hormone production.

"You want to talk about why you're upset?" he offered again, hoping to cool the flame her beauty had so innocently ignited.

"I do . . . but not yet." She glanced up and smiled at him. "I will before the night's over, I promise."

"You don't have to, you know. I'm here whatever."

"I know."

For a brief moment, brown eyes searched violet-blue ones, understanding shining deep within them.

"Do you know why I brought you here?" she asked softly.

He shook his head negatively.

149

"I want you to make love to me."

He felt his stomach jump. "What?"

"You heard me."

"No, I don't think I did."

"I want you to make love to me."

"Oh, hell, Kenlyn." He ran his hand through his hair. "What sort of mood are you in tonight, anyway?"

She scooted closer. "A romantic one."

He moved away. "This is your grandparents' house," he warned.

She moved closer yet. "I know. It holds special meaning to me. That's why I brought you here. I think they'd approve."

He looked at her wryly. "Are we talking about the same white-haired gent who sits out on your front porch and preaches to me about the evils of today's world?"

"Evils, yes. True love, no. He understands love. Ask him how he felt about Grandma." Kenlyn leaned over and gently ran the tip of her tongue across his bottom lip. "Better yet, ask him how I feel about you."

Travis groaned as she stole a long, suggestive kiss. When their lips parted, he whispered huskily. "What would he tell me?"

"He'd tell you I loved you."

They kissed again and Travis felt the zinc kick in overtime.

"Maybe you should ask how I feel about you," he murmured as his mouth explored the tender outline of her lips and tasted the alluring curve of her neck.

The subtle perfumed fragrance of her hair drove away any last trace of control from his aching body as he buried his face in its long layers and whispered her name. "No, you don't have to ask me, I'm telling you. I love you, Kenlyn. I know we haven't known each other very long, but in a way I've known you all my life."

She was in his arms fully now and their kisses took on an unexpected urgency.

"I don't care how long we've known each other," she whispered between snatches of heated kisses. "I love you, Travis, and I want to be completely yours."

"Oh, Kenlyn," he groaned. "You're making it very hard to say no."

"Then don't say it."

Travis tenderly lowered her onto the soft pile of the oval rug as his mouth claimed hers again. Raising his head a few moments later, he gazed into violet pools that were overflowing with love. "There are so many things I wanted to say to you before we reached this point."

"I know . . . there are so many things I should tell you."

"I suppose neither one of us has anything to say that's so important that it can't wait until a better time, do we?" he coaxed.

She grinned up at him. "No."

He captured her mouth masterfully again and she forgot what she'd have said anyway.

"Oh . . . uh . . . maybe we should discuss one thing. . . ." He searched for a tactful word to express his concern for precaution.

"Oh . . . you mean . . . oh that. Well"—she raised her eyes to him guiltily—"I drove to Millville a couple of days ago to do a bit of shopping . . ." When she saw the shocked look on his face, she grinned again and shrugged. "Well, I *said* you were going to be shocked to see how prepared I really was. . . ."

He shook his head solemnly. "You mean you planned this?"

She nodded. "For at least three days."

"Well, I'll be damned." They both laughed.

"Then you don't think badly of me?" she asked.

"No, I don't think badly of you." His finger gently caressed the outline of her face. "But what would you have done if I had said no?"

"Cried a lot."

With outstretched hands, she urged his mouth back to hers in order to smother his disgusting, low male chuckle.

He wasted no time in obliging her request, covering her feminine form with his masculine physique, as his mouth again sought the moist magic of hers.

She clung to his firm body and knew the joy of loving someone so completely that it almost hurt. Her fingers explored the thick mass of his dark hair, gently tracing tantalizing trails down the back of his neck, as she whispered his name and told him over and over of her love, glorying in the realization he returned that love with no reservations.

Slowly he lifted his weight and began to unbutton his shirt, allowing it to fall to the floor.

"You're sure?"

"I'm sure."

"I love you."

"I love *you.*"

In moments the last traces of his clothing, as well as hers, joined his discarded shirt, and they melted back in each other's arms.

And as the embers of the smoldering fireplace reflected dancing images on the wall, Grant proceeded to take Richmond, and this time there was absolutely no opposition.

Only history was altered somewhat, and Grant found Richmond taking her with a beauty and a reverence that left her breathless. She had never heard her name whispered so sweetly, so possessively, so longingly. She had never felt so loved.

When the fires of passion had reached their glorious peak, and they lay limp and spent in each other's arms, he still gazed at her with eyes filled with so much love it brought tears to her own.

"I hope you never tire of hearing me say it, but I love you," he whispered.

"I can promise, I'll never tire of that."

They lay entwined in each other's arms, basking in the warm afterglow of their lovemaking long after the old clock on the mantel had struck two. Kenlyn knew nothing had changed, and yet nothing would ever be the same again.

Tomorrow she had to tell him.

CHAPTER NINE

"A letter for you, sweetheart." Kenneth stopped in front of Kenlyn's desk Friday morning to deposit the morning mail.

"Thanks, Pop." Her eyes hurriedly scanned the postmark, then, assured it was what she had been waiting for eagerly, ripped into the envelope. A few moments later she let out a squeal of delight as she threw the enclosed paper in the air and rushed to throw her arms around her father's neck. "Better get your suit cleaned, Pop. I think there's going to be a wedding!"

"A wedding!"

"You bet. Mine!"

"Yours!"

"And your grandchildren will be pink, not green!" she squealed again, then whirled around and bolted out the front door before Kenneth could find out what in the world had come over her.

Stooping to pick up the discarded letter, he began to smile as he read the letterhead; U.S. Department of Agriculture, Food Safety and Quality Service Compliance Program, Los Angeles, California.

Dear Ms. Grant:

Regarding your recent letter about Travis Rich-mond. We want to thank you for taking the time to let us know you have found Mr. Richmond to be superior in conduct and his attitude and mannerisms of professionalism of the highest caliber.

Mr. Richmond has been associated with our department as a Federal Meat Inspector for the past five years and is highly respected among both his superiors and co-workers.

If we may be of any further assistance to you, please do not hesitate to let us know.

Cordially,
Dan Williams
Circuit Supervisor

Kenneth smiled happily as he carefully refolded the letter and replaced it back in the envelope, wondering if he should have the brown or the black suit cleaned.

Kenlyn was among the first to arrive at what was once the old train depot that evening. When the railroad had pulled out of Isabel two years ago, the vacated building at the edge of town had become the site for their annual Winter Carnival.

She'd searched for Travis all day, but he'd simply disappeared. She couldn't wait to tell him what had been going on, confess what her part had been in the deception—and apologize.

The idea to write Mr. Williams had occurred to her one day while she'd been cleaning the guest room. She'd found his address among the papers Travis had strewn around the room. By that time, she had already come to the firm conclusion that Travis was exactly who he said he was, but she reasoned that if she had the information in black and white, she could present it to the council and then the wild speculations about his purpose in Isabel could finally be laid to rest.

The depot was beginning to fill with early arrivals as she hurried about checking on various last-minute details, her mind still centered on how she was going to explain to Travis what her part had been in the town's deception. They'd spent the past few days drinking in as much of one another as possible, but she still hadn't found the right time to tell him.

But tonight she would.

He'd undoubtedly take the news in his usual good-natured stride and then the whole shadowed past would blissfully be put behind them. She loved him. Oh, how she loved him! And he loved her. She had no doubts about that. And now that this whole silly misunderstanding was over, she could accept the marriage proposal she knew would come.

Powerless to keep the good news to herself, she cornered Marcella and Otis and informed them of the wonderful news about Travis's innocence. Marcella in turn told Marge Hopkins, and Marge told Betty Gordon and Betty told Helen Lowrey, and Helen told Shirley Netson, and Shirley told her best friend, Jean Littleton, and before Kenlyn knew it the whole room was abuzz with the latest gossip.

She went in search of Leroy, itching to tell *him* the

news when she was sidetracked by Olive Smalley, who was searching frantically for an extension cord.

As Kenlyn went in search of the needed item, she passed the booth where her mother and several other women were busy arranging their displays for the cakewalk. A long table was being covered with a red table cloth and topped with pineapple upside-down cake, Bavarian cream, chocolate chip cookies, and a host of other equally delicious-looking sweet treats. Kenlyn had thought it best to play it safe and skip the bake contest this year, opting instead to devote her time to the kissing booth.

The local musicians were bringing in their limited assortment of instruments when she finally located the cord. An overall-clad Elmo Wilson sat down on a bale of hay and began to rosin up the bow of his fiddle, while Burl Hopkins strummed on the strings of his banjo with an off-key rendition of "Cotton Eyed Joe."

Kenlyn sighed with pure contentment. The atmosphere was set for a gala time, and she thought her heart would burst from sheer happiness. Travis Richmond was going to be hers, and she could hardly wait.

The festivities were just getting started when the handsome government man finally arrived. Lingering in the doorway, his eyes immediately sought to find Kenlyn. She spotted him, too, feeling her heart skip at least a dozen beats from the mere sight of him. She waved to him from the kissing booth and he grinned, then walked to hurriedly take his place in the back of her line.

Kenlyn peered eagerly around the sea of faces and smiled and waved at him again, and he smiled and waved back.

A few moments later, he quietly nudged the teenager in front of him. The starry-eyed youth momentarily averted his attention from Kenlyn to see what the stranger wanted.

"Listen, buddy," Travis reached into his pocket to secure a folded bill. "I'll give you five dollars if you'll trade places with me."

"Huh?" The adolescent's puzzled filled eyes clearly reflected he thought the stranger must have more money than he had brains.

"Five dollars for your place in line." Travis reiterated with a smile.

The youth hesitated for a moment and scratched his head. "I don't know. Why you wanna give me five dollars when you'll get to kiss her in a few minutes anyway?"

Travis leaned closer and teased in a confidential voice. "How old are you?"

"Thirteen."

"That's what I thought. Well, if you trade places with me, the extra five dollars will buy one of those good-looking cakes I saw a few minutes ago."

"Yeah? Well . . . okay." The teenager still sounded leery about the swap as he stepped behind Travis.

Travis was now within five kisses of reaching Kenlyn and his impatience grew. His hand automatically went into the pocket of his jacket and closed around the small jewelry box, which contained the engagement ring he had driven all the way to Millville to buy that afternoon.

If he could manage to get a few minutes alone with her, he planned to propose. He knew he should wait until the Carnival was over, but he couldn't. He had waited long enough.

Travis advanced to the fourth in line and discovered he was jealous of the ninety-year-old man Kenlyn had just pecked on the cheek.

And then he was third.

Their eyes sought each other again, and Kenlyn found it extremely hard to concentrate as she dutifully kissed another customer in return for his two-dollar donation. She smiled and hurriedly dispensed with the next two customers, and then Travis was standing before her.

Her gaze grew tender. "Hello, stranger. I've been looking everywhere for you."

"That's good. Did you miss me?"

"You bet. Where were you?"

"I went shopping."

"In Isabel?" She laughed. "For what?"

"For a present for my girl."

"Hey, mister. You wanna hurry a little bit?" The teenager was growing tired of all the superfluous chitchat.

Kenlyn blushed as Travis sheepishly rummaged through his wallet and pulled out a ten-dollar bill. "I'll take ten dollars' worth."

The teenager let out an exasperated groan.

Kenlyn smiled as she looked longingly into Travis's warm chestnut eyes. "Only ten dollars?"

"To start with."

Nine kisses later, the teenager was grumbling something about how he was *never* going to get his turn and decided to try his luck on a cute little red-headed schoolmate who was standing alone at the color-analysis booth. Neither Travis nor Kenlyn seemed to notice his departure.

Gazing at Travis lovingly, Kenlyn scolded, "You're driving away all my business."

"I know. Can you leave for a few minutes?"

"Oh, I'm sorry, darling, but I'm stuck here for the next hour."

He wasn't sure he could contain himself another hour. "Couldn't you get someone to take over for you just a few minutes? We need to talk."

Kenlyn glanced around the crowded room for any likely replacement, but found none. Everyone was busy with their own booths. "I'm sorry . . . I only have to work another hour," she consoled.

He sighed, reaching in his billfold for another ten-dollar bill. "Then give me another ten dollars' worth."

"Travis, you're spending an awful lot of money. You'll be broke before the night's over," she laughed.

"I still have my American Express Card," he assured, then growled playfully and pulled her close for another long kiss.

At the sound of a drumroll, Kenneth Grant stepped up a platform and tried to get the noisy crowd's attention.

"All right, ladies and gentlemen. If I may have

your attention, it's time to start the annual 'Isabel's Most Beautiful Legs Contest.' "

The crowd broke into thunderous applause and all eyes centered on the mayor.

"Surely, you're going to be in the contest," Travis whispered, recalling all too well how beautiful her legs were. "You'd win hands down."

"Oh, I think I'll pass," she said modestly.

The contestants began filing out on stage and from the audience came catcalls and shrill whistles.

"Hubba, Hubba, Hubba!" someone shouted.

Old Henry Perkins right down stole second place. Coming in a close third, was Jim Blanchard. But, it was Leroy Blankenship—who'd even shaved his legs and wore panty hose for the occasion—who captured first place, hands down.

The audience roared when Leroy did an accompanying pirouette as he strolled to accept his first-place prize of pickled peaches—the only jar the committee had been successful in wringing out of Maude Willows. Kenneth removed Leroy's sailor hat and placed a construction paper crown on his head, then playfully gave him a congratulatory kiss on his weathered cheek that made them both blush beet red.

After the legs contest, the cakes and pies were judged, and to no one's surprise, Marcella Clever's Mississippi mud cake received the most raves. At a penny a vote, her cake was bought for the unbelievable and record-breaking price of $24.97!

Travis was digging in his pocket for another ten-dollar bill, when Kenlyn laughed and lifted a reluctant hand in protest. "Lighten up, Hot Lips! I think you'd better move on before someone throws you out!"

The line at the kissing booth was beginning to build again, until it was blocking the flow of traffic.

Travis flashed the line of hopefuls a sheepish grin, realizing he had dominated her time long enough.

"Oh, all right. I'll go to the end of the line," he conceded halfheartedly.

The customers behind him applauded loudly.

"Why don't you go get me something cold to drink," Kenlyn bargained, trying to soften the blow to his ego.

He turned and called to the youth who had stepped in line again. "Hey, kid. I'll give you a dollar if you'll go get her something to—"

"Travis! No, you go get it," Kenlyn insisted.

He shrugged and stepped aside, so the other Carnival participants could patronize the booth.

"Root beer?"

"Naturally." She winked and blew him a free kiss.

"I'll be right back," he promised.

In a flash he returned with two soft drinks. In the short time it had taken him to go to the refreshment stand, the line had grown to a ten-head count, ranging in ages from ten to what appeared to be a kindly gentleman of eighty-some-odd years. He walked to the front of the booth and placed their drinks on the plywood counter.

"Hey! No cuttin' in line, mister!" A boy of about ten protested from his place as first in line.

Kenlyn was unsuccessful in stifling a giggle at the irritated complaint coming from a boy who could barely see over the counter. Travis made an attempt at a serious apology, quickly explaining he was only there to deliver the soft drink. But Kenlyn noticed the young customer kept a watchful eye on Travis until he was safely positioned at the back of the line again.

Sierra Laythrom, having witnessed the incident, took the opportunity to attract his attention. She had to admit she had been relieved when she had heard the news about the letter confirming his innocence, and she couldn't wait to tell him so.

"Hi, there!"

"Well, hello," he returned, still watching Kenlyn as she went about placing kisses on the cheeks of young boys and the foreheads of the old-timers.

"I've been looking for you. Have you got a minute?" She had to raise her voice as the band began to play again.

Travis reassessed the long line and decided he did. He was at least twenty minutes away from the front.

As though she read his thoughts, Sierra smiled about the long line. "Looks like you're in for quite a wait."

"Yes . . . I guess it looks that way."

"Don't know about you, but it sure is getting stuffy in here to me." She started to fan herself with an opened hand. "Would you like to join me for a breath of fresh air?"

"Sure, why not."

They quickly worked their way through the crowd and stepped out of the crowded room. Leading him to the old waiting bench the railroad had left behind,

Sierra motioned for him to sit down. They made themselves comfortable.

Gala colored patio lights were strung decoratively along the concrete platform. The cool night air amplified the sparkle of a million stars brilliantly lighting up the cloudless sky.

Momentarily Travis forgot he was with Sierra, as he leaned back and blissfully recalled the intimacy he had shared with Kenlyn at her grandfather's ranch a few nights before and the nights since.

With this beautiful sky as a backdrop, he could hardly wait until he had her alone tonight. He planned to make love to her again . . . and again . . . and again. . . .

"Sure is a nice evening." Sierra sighed.

"It sure is." Travis agreed.

"I heard you're leaving tomorrow."

"That's right . . . for a while at least."

Kenlyn would probably want to marry in Isabel, he thought absently. But he'd have to return to L.A. for a few days and arrange for a leave of absence.

"Gosh, I wished I'd gotten to know you better," Sierra confessed, then turned to smile at him in the moonlight. "Wouldn't have done me any good though, would it?"

Travis knew what she was implying. "If you're accusing me of only having eyes for Kenlyn, then I'm afraid I have to plead guilty."

"Yeah, that's what I meant," she confessed. She turned her face to the heavens and closed her eyes. "Well, I suppose I should be a good sport and tell you I'm glad it's worked out the way it has."

"Thanks. I appreciate that."

"I mean, when I heard about the letter I guess I just knew deep down you weren't trying to do anything bad to Isabel. You just weren't the type," she conceded.

"Thanks." He leaned back and let the cool air drift over him.

Sierra sighed longingly. "Looking back on it, it's really funny. Kenlyn was supposed to spy on you and then I was supposed to spy on you and neither one of us could come up with a darn thing because you really were a meat inspector. Isn't that a hoot?"

"Yeah—a real hoot." He crossed his arms behind his head and wondered if the line at the kissing booth had receded any.

"Well, I can tell you I sure had the town in an uproar when I reported that I thought you were going to put a new missile site in Isabel," she chuckled. "You should have seen their faces that night. White as sheets. Every last one of them."

Travis laughed. "Oh?" He was only halfway listening to Sierra's ramblings, but "missile site" suddenly caught his attention.

"Yes, but they were all just as pale-faced the night Kenlyn told them she thought you were here to conduct a marijuana raid." Sierra broke into a fit of laughter as Travis slowly sat up.

"A what?"

"A marijuana raid!" she roared.

Travis eyed her warily. "A marijuana raid?" He didn't have the slightest idea what she was talking about.

"I'm telling you I thought Leroy was going to get thrown out of the town meeting that night the way he was cussin' and ranting around . . . saying we were gonna to have to stop you before it was too late. He said the government was gonna come in and take over Isabel and we had to find out what you was up to so we could stop it. Kenlyn was supposed to use her feminine wiles to get you to confess what you was up to . . . and then she got mad at Leroy and said, No! you *was* a meat inspector, but he didn't believe her and neither did most of the town, and then she wrote that letter to your boss and he confirmed you were a meat inspector and, oh . . . brother! Can you imagine getting all worked up like that over a simple meat inspector?" She roared again, caught up in the absurdity of the story.

But Travis's curt voice brought her hilarity to a screeching halt. "Sierra! What in the hell are you talking about?"

She stared back at him vacantly. "Why . . . the letter verifying your innocence, of course."

"What letter!"

She began to squirm in her seat uneasily. Surely, Kenlyn had told him about the letter by now—hadn't she? "Travis . . . uh . . . have you spoken with Kenlyn today?"

"No. I've been in Millville shopping." His face had lost its usual pleasant look, replaced by one that wasn't so pleasant.

"Oh, dear."

Travis rose to his feet slowly. "What's going on, Sierra?"

166

She glanced up to confront his intimidating size and she swallowed hard. She had undoubtedly put her foot in it this time.

"Oh, dear, Travis, what have I done?"

"Just tell me what's going on, Sierra," he said in a voice that had suddenly grown grave.

The story came out slow and halting at first, but she gained momentum as she went along.

Travis listened as he periodically rubbed a hand across the growing anger etched into his puzzled brow.

When the last acidifying detail had been revealed, Sierra took a deep breath and waited for his reaction. It wasn't long coming.

He looked stunned and bewildered, and hurt. Hoping to steady his shaken spirits, she quickly acknowledged and apologized for her own part in the plan.

"I really am sorry," she pleaded. "If it's any consolation . . . I believed your story about being a meat inspector—and I think Kenlyn did too."

But from the look on his face, Travis was not comforted by her admission. "Let me be sure I understand you, Sierra. Kenlyn has been playing up to me to gain information about some sort of secret mission I'm supposed to be on for the government?" His eyes sought hers solemnly.

Sierra nodded.

"And these meetings the town's been having since I arrived have been about *my* intentions here in Isabel, and Kenlyn's been giving the town a report at each meeting?"

"Well, not really. She never had anything to report," Sierra defended.

"But that was her duty?"

Sierra nodded lamely again.

"And she's received some sort of letter verifying that I am who I have contended I am?"

She nodded again.

"Well, I'll be damned." The sense of betrayal he felt was incredible.

Kenlyn Grant was no different from Melody Winslow—except Melody would never have used her body to do her manipulating. At least, not with a complete stranger.

"We thought it was terribly suspicious for a government man to come to our town," Sierra defended. "That doesn't happen often—actually, you're the first—and Leroy is always looking for trouble, so we thought—oh, Travis, I'm so sorry . . ." Her apology dissolved in tears as she turned and quickly fled into the safety of the depot.

After she left, Travis heatedly paced the platform, trying to control his growing anger. For a moment, he was tempted to storm in there and confront Kenlyn with the knowledge of what Sierra had just told him and ask her just what in the hell she thought she'd been doing!

Then despair took over and he thought, What's the use? Apparently, she'd played him for a fool, and won. But this is where his stupidity ended. Glancing through the plate-glass window, the sight of Kenlyn laughing with a little boy tugged at the strings of his heart.

No, he wouldn't confront her. He wasn't up to that yet.

He'd foolishly permitted himself to get so close to her that he knew, as weak as he was at the moment, he'd swallow whatever excuse she had to offer—hook, line, and sinker.

And no woman was going to make a fool of him, he promised himself as he walked away.

CHAPTER TEN

From the busy confines of the kissing booth, Kenlyn tried to keep an eye on Travis, but she'd found herself so involved with her assignment, she hadn't noticed when he had slipped away from his place in line.

Around midnight, the townspeople started slowly drifting out of the old depot, heading for home. The Winter Carnival had been a tremendous success, keeping with the tradition of past festivals. There had been good times and laughter shared among friends and neighbors, and although there were a few aching feet in the crowd, the ladies all agreed they couldn't wait to get started on plans for the following year.

When the last of Kenlyn's customers had melted away, she heaved a relieved sigh, ran the tube of ChapStick over her lips again and shut the door to the booth.

Still, there was no trace of Travis. When she had taken her break earlier, she couldn't find him. The crowd had been so thick and she had been cornered by several people just wanting to talk. By the time she had been able to get away, her break had been over.

Spotting Sierra in the midst of the dwindling crowd, Kenlyn thought maybe she might know where he had gone.

"Sierra?"

Sierra turned at the sound of her name and froze when she saw that it was Kenlyn calling her. She had dreaded this moment for the last hour.

"Hi! Have you seen Travis?"

"Umm . . . yes . . . I saw him earlier." Sierra hurriedly dabbed at her tear-reddened eyes.

"Where?" Kenlyn called, glancing around the near-emptied room.

"Ah . . ." Sierra stalled, realizing again what a mess she'd made by inadvertently spilling the beans to Travis. It had been so obvious that he had fallen deeply in love with Kenlyn. She felt like crawling in a hole as she saw the same happy sparkle reflected in Kenlyn's eyes as she continued to search the room for him.

Kenlyn finished closing her booth and walked across the room to where Sierra was busy packing away crepe-paper streamers.

"Hey, I asked if you'd seen Travis," Kenlyn reminded, thinking maybe Sierra had forgotten the inquiry.

With a sudden outburst, Sierra suddenly buried her tearful face in her hands and said through muffled sobs, "Oh, Kenlyn! I'm so sorry!"

Kenlyn immediately placed a soothing arm around Sierra's quivering shoulder.

"For heaven's sake, Sierra. What in the world is wrong?"

The sound of Kenlyn's sympathetic response was all it took to send Sierra into a nonstop, guilt-ridden confession. "Kenlyn, I didn't mean to tell him. . . . It all just came pouring out. I thought he knew or I'd have never said a word, and now I'm afraid he's mad at you and . . . oh . . . I'm *so* miserable!" she sobbed.

Feeling her heart momentarily stop, Kenlyn's hand dropped from Sierra's shoulder to cover her mouth in horror.

"Sierra—you told him . . . What did you tell him?" she asked, holding her breath and bracing herself for the bombshell.

"Everything . . ." Sierra confessed in a small voice.

"Everything?" Kenlyn repeated weakly.

Sierra nodded.

"He knows everything—even including the part about me supposed to be spying on him?"

She nodded again.

"Oh, *no!* For heaven's sake—*why,* Sierra?"

"I told you . . ." Lifting her tearstained face to meet Kenlyn's, who by now had signs of her own tears developing, she said, "I'm sorry! I'm really so sorry! I didn't realize he didn't know yet about what the town had been doing. Why, *everyone* knows about the letter you received this afternoon, so I just naturally thought that by now Travis knew."

Recognizing the sincerity in Sierra's voice, Kenlyn couldn't stay angry with her. She had no right to. Because in some respects she was at fault as much as Sierra. She should have tried harder to find Travis this afternoon, but with the Carnival and all the last-minute details, she'd been so busy. . . .

"Sierra, it's all right," Kenlyn soothed. "Now think—what did Travis say when you told him?"

"Plenty. He was *real* mad!" Sierra sniffed, wiping a stray tear with the back of her trembling hand.

Tears welled up in Kenlyn's eyes again. "He was?"

"He certainly was."

"Where is he now?"

"I don't know. I've tried to find him all evening, but he's disappeared."

Disappeared. Well, that's just dandy! Kenlyn thought. He must have gone racing off into the night half-cocked without giving her a chance to explain her side of the story! For all he knew, Sierra could have been slanting the story to make her look less guilty. But did he come and ask her for the facts? No, he sure didn't! Apparently, he had left without saying a word to anyone. If anyone had a reason to be mad, it was her, she decided.

She turned and made a dash for the doorway, determined to give Travis Richmond a piece of her mind before she sat him down and tried to straighten out this whole mess. His white sedan was nowhere to be seen in the deserted parking lot.

The loose gravel spun beneath the tires of the Volkswagen as she made a hasty exit from the depot's driveway. She kept assuring herself she'd find his car parked in front of her house. But it wasn't. As she turned the corner, her heart sank as she saw the empty spot where he usually parked.

Racing up the stairway to the bedrooms, she stood

173

outside his door long enough to catch her erratic breath and slow her racing pulse. She knocked softly, hoping against all the odds that he would be waiting for her on the other side of the heavy wood.

At the moment, she didn't even care if he was furious with her. All she wanted was a chance to undo the damage that had been done. She desperately needed him to be there.

She knocked again, louder this time, and called his name. Still no answer, so she flung the door open. The undisturbed bed, and the absence of the leather briefcase he usually kept sitting beside the nightstand sent a sick feeling surging in the pit of her stomach. A thorough search of the closet that was now emptied of any of his belongings confirmed her dreaded suspicions.

Travis Richmond was gone.

Flinging herself across the big featherbed, she succumbed to the hot swell of the tears that had threatened to spill the moment she'd entered his abandoned room.

She sobbed bitterly as she thought of the precious hours of intimacy they had shared—wonderful, joyful hours of intimacy. She had been so sure he loved her.

But tonight he hadn't cared enough to even let her explain.

The following day dragged by as painfully slow as the eternal night she'd spent tossing and turning. Futilely trying to drown her sorrow in the submersion of her work, Kenlyn's wavering attention was distracted with the sound of each car that periodically passed the plate-glass window by her desk.

Having Leroy call to inform her of the town council meeting for later in the evening didn't lift her spirits any.

"Why?" she asked, trying hard to keep the sarcasm she was feeling from spilling over in her voice. "Everyone knows Travis left Isabel last night."

"Yeah, I heard." Leroy admitted. "I heard about the letter too. That's why I called the meeting. We need to get together—sort of fill the town in on what's happened."

"I thought everyone already knew."

"I think most of them do, but we'd better make sure. You'll be there, won't you?"

"Yes, I'll be there."

She wouldn't miss this meeting for the world.

It didn't take long for the citizens of Isabel to realize that the main purpose of the hastily called meeting was to admit there had been a mistake and formally close the case of the mysterious government man. Kenlyn's aching heart took little comfort in the admission.

Leroy summed it all up with a heavy sigh. "One thing for sure, we gave it a mean tussle. We done our best to try to put a stop to the government's meddling. Yep, we sure gave it a helluva fight—excuse me, ladies. And who knows, we could have been onto something big. But we weren't, so I guess we can sleep better nights knowing they ain't gonna bring any missile silos or toxic dumps in on us—least ways,

175

not that we know of. Turns out this Richmond fella's on the up and up," he admitted humbly, casting a sheepish grin in Kenlyn's direction.

From the muffled conversations floating throughout the room, apparently, for the first time, most of the council members were more than ready to admit that maybe their imaginations had gotten the best of them.

Jim Blanchard stood up. "Well, personally, I think the town owes Mr. Richmond an apology," he announced with a hint of irritation. "Seems to me he was a right-down likeable fella and we didn't treat him very nice." He glanced at Leroy who sat red-faced, nodding his balding head in agreement for a change.

"Yes, I think he *was* nice," Marcella added. "Why, he helped me change a flat tire on my car the other day when it was raining cats and dogs. I thought that was real nice of him."

Other members in the room suddenly recalled how pleasant Travis Richmond had been in the short time he had been with them.

"I thought he was a fine man, and I think we as a town should be ashamed of ourselves for the way we treated him," said Oneida, who laid aside her knitting and pressed her handkerchief against her moist eyes. "I'm going to miss him. He always seemed to enjoy the way I fried liver."

Travis irritably swore under his breath and pounded his fist on the steering wheel in frustration as he turned off the main highway for the third time.

176

He'd spent the better part of the night and all day driving in ambivalent circles. Once he'd even made it as far as the California state line before locking up the brakes and spinning the white sedan back in the direction of Isabel.

The pain of her deception was still so sharp it sliced into him like a razor. Kenlyn had tried to play the same manipulative tricks that Melody had been guilty of, he argued with himself. She was no different—conniving, cunning, deceitful, and dishonest.

Why hadn't she come to him and confronted him with the town's suspicions instead of running around trying to play detective behind his back? All this misunderstanding could have been cleared up in a moment if she had only loved him enough to be honest with him.

But did she love him as she had professed? And if she did, did it really matter to him any longer? Was her affection showered on him only to gain information? That thought hurt more than all the others combined. He thought they had had something real. Was he mistaken? That question had tormented him all night and he seemed powerless to find an answer.

Had she deliberately led him down the garden path to trick him, or had *he* been unfair by not confronting her with the accusations? Would her explanation be entirely different from Sierra's?

With the town of Isabel visible on the horizon again, he braked the car to a sudden stop, debating on turning the vehicle around and heading back to California.

Hell, yes! I'm going to confront her, he decided,

suddenly realizing that if she *were* guilty of deceiving him, he was at least going to give her a hefty piece of his mind. Oh, yes, Ms. Grant. He was going to straighten out the sordid details of this misunderstanding—then ask her to marry him. . . .

He loved her. Who was he kidding? And he loved her enough to fight for a relationship that would include honesty and trust. It might take time, but he was willing to exert the effort.

Driving down the town's main street, he spotted Kenlyn's Volkswagen parked in front of Perkins' Pharmacy. He recognized the familiar gathering spot for the town council. Guess they're all in there comparing notes, he simmered, wondering what Kenlyn had to say now.

Travis parked and quickly walked into the pharmacy to stand unnoticed in the open doorway. All eyes were glued to Kenlyn, who was ready to speak. Perfect! At least he'd get to hear firsthand her side of the story.

Kenlyn rose to her feet and in a soft voice began. "I just wanted to say how very deeply I regret having been a part of a scheme that has hurt Travis Richmond. We were wrong. As a town, we've always walked with the wind, and I think the time has come for us to stop and examine our lives.

"Are our lives so boring, so monotonous that we have to continually go looking for trouble to give us some sort of unified purpose? Well, I hope not. I think we're all pretty decent people who just let ourselves get caught up in wild fantasies occasionally.

And I think it's going to have to stop before anyone else gets hurt.

"From now on, if we want something exciting to talk about, let's get together on Monday nights and visit our families in the nursing home. Or let's get together and plant those new trees on main street like we've talked about for years. Or better yet, let's get in our cars and drive to Millville and visit the soup kitchens and talk to the street people. It'd do us good to see how richly we've been blessed. I think we forget that sometimes. Maybe then we wouldn't have to always look for trouble. I think we've exchanged the warmth and the caring this town was built on for doubt and skepticism."

She paused to blow her nose, then continued in a trembling voice. "We were wrong about Travis Richmond. We found him guilty when he had committed no crime. He's an honest and gentle man. And as this letter from his superior, Dan Williams of the United States Agricultural Department, will explain, he's, as he said he was, a federal meat inspector." She lifted her eyes again to face the citizens of Isabel. "And I'm in love with him—and not at all ashamed of it."

The room had succumbed to a deadly silence as Kenlyn hurriedly gathered her purse and prepared to leave.

Sierra was fumbling in her coat for a tissue when she glanced up and spotted Travis standing in the doorway. She was ready to speak when he quickly silenced her with an index finger held to his lips.

She acknowledged the code with a joyous smile and flashed him a relieved wink of approval.

Kenlyn had turned to walk out of the room when she saw him. Her emotions took a roller-coaster ride at the sight of him. She had all sorts of mixed emotions. She loved him so badly it hurt, but she was furious with him at the same time for causing her so much anxiety and grief.

"How long have you been standing there?" she snapped.

He smiled at her guiltily. "Long enough."

Without a word, she swept past him and headed for her car. Travis wasn't surprised by her actions. He stood and watched helplessly as she walked out the door.

Leroy was on his feet in a flash. "Well, don't just stand there like a blame idiot! Go after her, boy!"

"Oh, brother—this will mean war," Travis predicted, realizing she was more than a little put out with him.

Leroy turned to Elmo, his eyes narrowing. "Did he say somethin' about Star Wars?"

Elmo shot him a dirty look. "Sit down, Leroy, and be quiet!"

Travis bolted out the front door as the room exploded in a loud round of cheers and applause.

"Atta boy, Travis! Go get her," Marcella yelled.

"Yeah, show her who's boss!" Howard Hopkins cried gleefully.

"Sit down, Howard," Marge ordered.

"Yes, dear."

Travis reached Kenlyn just as she was grinding the key in the unresponsive Volkswagen ignition.

Of all the times for you to get stubborn on me, she

180

was fuming, tears streaming down her cheeks. "Start, darn it!"

He leaned his head into the open car window. "Kenlyn, honey . . . wait. We have to talk."

"You sure didn't feel that way last night!"

"I know, and I'm sorry. That's why I'm here now. I want to talk."

Kenlyn was torn between protecting her already tattered pride and the electrifying shivers his pleading sent racing down her spine.

"Kenlyn . . . please. I love you."

She finally nodded a silent agreement, but not without making him suffer for a few agonizing moments. She moved over to make room for him. He quickly slid into the driver's seat, and with one easy turn of the key the motor purred into life like a contented kitten.

"Where are we going?" Kenlyn asked.

"Home."

It was Travis who did the honors of retrieving the flashlight and unlocking the bolted front door when they arrived at Claude Grant's ranch. Kenlyn started to enter the abandoned house, when he turned and lifted a protesting hand.

"Not just yet," he whispered, lifting a permissive but bewildered Kenlyn in his arms and carrying her across the weathered threshold.

She buried her face against the warmth of his neck and the tears came faster. The subtle smell of his after-shave lingered enticingly on his skin, awakening her ever-present need for him. His touch had left her weak with desire, and once inside the living room, he

181

gently lowered her to her feet and kissed her. Long and with such feeling she knew she could never remain angry with him.

Then they were kissing with an insatiable urgency. Lifting her back in his arms, he carried her to the sofa, where their clothes melted away like wet snow.

Though she had known him intimately, his body suddenly became mysterious and unknown territory, which she longed to discover anew. Her hands gently caressed the firm ridge of muscles along his rib cage as their lips touched softly, brushing over each other's in provocative short kisses.

"I'm so glad you came back," she whispered, the truth of her words clearly evident in the lavender pools of her eyes.

"You surely knew that I would."

"No, I could only pray that you would."

He chuckled and tried to capture her mouth again, but she pulled back warily. "You're laughing at me."

"No, I'm not. I'm laughing at how foolish we've both been. Let this be a lesson. From now on if there's anything bothering you, let me know. We can save ourselves a lot of trouble." Slowly, his mouth came back to meet hers, and she accepted the invitation, feeling the slow languorous heat he had been steadily building begin to seep deeper into her body.

She could hear the pleasure in his throat as he lowered himself over her, and then the world was nothing but each other while they made love with a passion that left them weak and spent but completely at peace.

Afterward, they dressed and Travis built a fire.

When the embers were softly aglow, he led her to the braided rug that Altera Grant had brought with her as a bride, and they sat down.

"Now, then. I'm sorry I lost my temper and left without confronting you," he apologized as he kissed the palm of her hand gently. "I know it was a childish thing to do, and in the future it won't happen again."

"I'm not saying that you didn't have every right to be angry, but I wish you had come to me, first."

"I should have. I'm sorry, but I was so angry to find out what had been going on. Why didn't you tell me what the town suspected?"

"I wanted to—many times. But then I would have had to confess that at first I suspected the same thing."

He shook his head, still finding the story about his being in Isabel to bring harm impossible to believe. "After what we shared together—didn't you feel you could confide in me?"

She lowered her eyes shamefully. "I would have felt foolish."

"Foolish?" Cupping her chin in his hand, he stared into the depths of the beautiful violet-blue eyes that from the very start had been successful in stealing his heart. "You should never feel foolish with me. That's what love's about—being able to make a fool of yourself to someone and they don't care."

His honest evaluation brought a soft laugh from her. "What did I ever do to deserve you, Travis Richmond?"

"I think the question is mutual," he assured, as his

lips met the moist softness of hers. Kenlyn responded with a shamefully amorous kiss, clinging tightly to him for fear he'd disappear again.

"Kenlyn, I have to know. Were you only trying to get information out of me? It doesn't really matter, but—"

Her hand covered his mouth and her eyes told him what a foolish thought that was. "I love you, Travis. And other than a few brief moments of lunacy, I've always believed in you."

"And if I *had* been here for any of the reason's the town suspected?"

"I would have still loved you. You just would have had to change jobs." She grinned.

Gently, he pulled her face toward him and they kissed.

"Hey—before we get carried away again, I have something that belongs to you."

"To me?"

"Yes. I was going to give it to you last night, but . . . uh . . . something came up."

"You mean, someone flew the coop."

He grinned. "Something like that." Reaching in his pocket, he withdrew the jewelry box and flipped it open.

"A ring?" she questioned softly.

"No, my heart . . . my life, my love."

She gazed at him lovingly as he slipped the diamond on her hand.

"Will you marry me?"

"Did you ever doubt it?"

Expelling a heavy breath, he looked immensely relieved. "I was afraid maybe I'd blown it."

The kiss she leaned to give him assured him he hadn't.

"When did you buy the ring?"

"Yesterday. I drove to Millville to buy it."

"That must have been why I couldn't find you."

"Were you looking for me?"

"Yes. I'd planned to show you the letter from Dan Williams and admit what had been going on." She sighed. "Oh, Travis, if I had only told you sooner, then you wouldn't have felt so bad toward me. I started to . . . so many, many times . . ."

"I think we're going to have to work harder at being honest with each other." He smiled at her tenderly. "That shouldn't be too hard, should it?"

"No, not at all."

He sighed and looked around the room contentedly. "I love this old house. How would you feel about buying it?"

Kenlyn seemed surprised. "Are we going to live in Isabel after we're married?"

"How do you feel about that?"

"It doesn't matter to me . . . but I'd like to see the ocean," she admitted. "With you. And it might be exciting to work on a large paper."

"Then we'll live in L.A. for a while. I like my job and the security it will give us. But I thought it would be nice to know we could move back here someday and live in this house."

Her eyes grew misty again. "Grandpa would love that."

"There's only one other thing . . ."

"Yes?"

"Do I have to keep pretending to like the liver your mother keeps poking down me?"

Kenlyn laughed out loud this time. "No, but you have to keep taking vitamins."

He frowned. "The garlic, too?"

"Of course. That's part of the reason you're up and about . . . and feeling so 'chipper.' "

"Believe me, 'chipper' isn't what I'm feeling right now," he confessed as he stole another hungry kiss.

"Oh? What are you feeling?"

"Umm . . ." He nuzzled his face into the silky floral scent of her long dark hair. "I'll let you guess."

"I think I already have," she sighed.

"And how are you feeling?"

"I feel very lucky." She kissed the tip of his nose. "You're not still angry or disappointed with me, are you?"

"About thinking I was here to bring Isabel harm? Naw." He chuckled. "What about you? Are you disappointed I'm just your average, run-of-the-mill meat inspector and not some mysterious CIA or FBI agent?"

"Naw!"

They kissed again to make it official.

"Oh, incidentally. I think I should mention your feeding me all that zinc tipped me off that you were after me."

Kenlyn felt her face grow a throbbing red. "After you! Well . . . the zinc . . . I didn't give it to you for *that* reason," she stammered.

186

"Oh, yeah? Then why, all of a sudden am I always . . . ?" He was embarrassed to finish his question, but she understood the painful problem he seemed to have been having since they met.

"Why are you amorous all the time? Oh, it's just because you're with me—or it better be," she warned.

He was still skeptical. "I read the pamphlet you left in my room and it distinctly stated zinc was for male hormone production—"

She stopped his words with another firm kiss. When their lips finally parted, she grinned at him mysteriously. "It isn't the zinc that's been making you so amorous, dear, it's all that E I've been cramming down you."

"E?" He looked at her warily. "What does that do?"

She began to pull him down on the braided rug, slowly beginning to unbutton his shirt. "Oh . . . it's too complicated to explain. Why don't I just show you?"

HOT
ON HIS TRAIL

For Fayrene Preston —
My bright and shining star in a
sometimes cloudy sky

CHAPTER ONE

"Drat!" CeAnn Masters sat straight up in bed and peered groggily at the clock on the bedside stand. "Five minutes before eight! I've overslept again!"

Pushing the blankets back, she jumped out of bed and rushed to the bathroom, showering and pulling on her clothes in record time.

While she quickly but meticulously applied her makeup, she found herself wishing once more she had a job that allowed her to be herself.

For the last two years she had sold cosmetics behind the counter of a large department store, and although she had always prided herself on being fashionable, she would probably never have worn anything, if left to herself, but a little lip gloss and a soft touch of blusher. Her skin had the delicate, clear beauty that would allow her that luxury, but the manager of the store thought it best that the employees visibly display the product they sold. So every morning CeAnn grudgingly went through the ritual she had come to resent.

Rushing to the kitchen, she hurriedly filled an assortment of mismatched bowls with dry dog food, then quickly rinsed and refilled the large water basin and opened a can of tuna for the cats.

Sprinkling a handful of birdseed in the canary's dish, she blew him a hasty kiss, then grabbed her purse and car keys. "Sorry to rush, Poops, but I'm late again!"

She got into her car a few minutes later, still grumbling under her breath about the fact that it was only Tuesday and yet it was the second day this week that her undependable alarm had failed to go off. Then she paused. Looking down, she groaned at the sight of a large run in her left stocking. She sighed and mentally added changing her hose to the ever-growing list of things to do when she got to work—if she ever did.

As she pumped the gas pedal, trying to bring her car to life, CeAnn desperately wished she could change her means of transportation too, but quickly discarded that tempting thought. It would be at least another year before she'd be financially able to trade in the old Chevrolet for a newer car.

With a racking cough and a backfire that rivaled a sonic boom, the motor finally roared to life, with a blue puff of smoke billowing out of the tailpipe. Putting the car into reverse, she backed out of the drive and sped down the road, hoping to make up for lost time. Glancing at her watch, she sighed. At the rate she was going, she would be about forty minutes late this morning. Not good—but better than the day before. She had been nearly an hour late then, and although her boss hadn't actually said anything, she had had a definite pinched look about her face when CeAnn rushed by with a hurried good morning.

No matter how badly the day had begun, it was impossible to ignore what a truly glorious day it was. The crisp autumn air was heady and invigorating as CeAnn sped along the country road. The sky was a brilliant shade of blue over the large midwestern town of Donovan, with only an occasional puffy cloud drifting across the horizon. The first hard frost had gripped the old maples and they were just beginning to don their glorious multicolored finery. In another few weeks the array of colors they proudly displayed would be breathtaking.

Her mind was completely absorbed in the lovely day as she pulled onto the interstate and gunned her way downtown. It took a minute for the faint wail of a siren to penetrate her senses.

"Oh, good grief, I hope he isn't after me!" she muttered, glancing down guiltily at her speedometer, then casting a wary eye in the rearview mirror. "I can't get another ticket!"

There was already one parking ticket in her glove compartment from the day before. She had been forced to park in a thirty-minute loading zone, reasoning that with any luck at all she could simply move the car during her lunch hour. Unfortunately, it hadn't worked out that way. She had been dismayed to find a ticket on the windshield.

The sound of the siren drew closer. She grimaced and took another hesitant glance in the mirror. There was no longer any doubt about it. The policeman was after her.

Flipping on her turn signal, CeAnn pulled out of the line of traffic and brought the car to an abrupt halt. I can't afford to waste any more time, she thought, so I might as well get this over with and be on my way.

A squeal of tires cut through the air as the man in the patrol car slammed on his brakes to avoid running into her car.

Turning around to give him a cool look, she wondered where he got the right to stop someone else for *any* reason!

The officer took his time getting out of his car. She decided to use the extra moments to check her makeup. Then she'd have one less thing to do when she got to the store.

Taking her compact out of her purse, she snapped it open and critically studied her features. The policeman sauntered up to her car and patiently waited for her to finish her preening.

Moments later she decided she was presentable and rolled down the window, forcing a pleasant smile. "Good morning, Officer. I hope this isn't going to take long, because I'm already late."

Calmly removing his hat and sunglasses, the policeman smiled politely. "Lady," he replied in a controlled tone, "are you aware of how close I came to hitting you a minute ago?"

"I certainly am. You should be more careful," she returned curtly. Normally, her answer would have been as meek as a church mouse's—that was her nature—but this particular morning was far from normal.

"Me?" His eyebrows shot up in disbelief.

"Well, I hope you're not trying to imply that I was the one at fault. You motioned for me to pull over, and I did," she pointed out briskly.

"But you pulled over and stopped all at the same time." He struggled to retain his composure and keep his tone moderate. He hadn't been able to believe his eyes when she'd slammed on her brakes so suddenly.

"I was under the impression that that's what you wanted me to do," she argued, failing to get his point.

Steve Hayden reached up and ran one hand through his hair, trying to control himself. I'm going to have to put in for a desk job, he thought wryly. The public was getting to him—fast. "Can I see your license, ma'am?"

"Of course." She reached over and picked up her purse. "I know I was going a little fast, but I overslept this morning, and since I've now been late for work twice this week, I really would appreciate it if you could hurry. . . ." CeAnn's voice trailed off as she realized that in her haste she had left her combination checkbook and billfold on the coffee table at home. She had been paying bills last night and had neglected to replace it in her purse, thinking she would do it this morning. "Oh, dear."

The officer restlessly shifted his weight while she shuffled through her purse. "Is there a problem?" he asked finally.

"No, not really," she hedged, then laughed. "You'll never believe this! I just realized I left my billfold at home—with my driver's license in it. I

195

left the house in such a rush this morning, I forgot to put it in my purse. Isn't that crazy?"

He smiled blandly. "Crazy."

"Well." She took a deep breath and put on her prettiest smile. "What happens now?"

If she'd been smart, she would've tried to flirt her way out of a ticket. But the one time she had deliberately tried to flirt with a man had turned into a disaster, so she quickly decided against that tactic. CeAnn Masters was not the flirting type, no matter how much it might've been to her advantage at this precise moment. But a few seconds later her eyes widened appreciably as, for the first time, she took serious note of the man standing before her.

For a moment she thought her eyes were playing tricks on her. He looked exactly like a guy she had fallen in love with in college. Although this man was taller and a bit older than Jess, the resemblance between the two men was striking.

She could feel her cheeks flood with color, but she was powerless to prevent her eyes from literally devouring the blondish brown hair and blue eyes she had seen so many times in her young daydreams.

Sensing he was being unduly scrutinized, Steve cast his eyes back down to the clipboard in his hand. "Ms.—" He paused, searching for a name.

"Masters," she supplied helpfully.

"Ms. Masters. You do have a valid license, don't you?"

"Oh, yes, I do," she assured him, her eyes refusing to stop their lusty wandering. "It's lying home on the coffee table. . . . Um, you'll have to forgive me, but you look exactly like a man I used to know," she said in the manner of an apology, her voice barely concealing her surprise.

He glanced at her briefly. "Oh?"

"Yes, Jess McIntosh. . . . You wouldn't happen to be related to him, would you? The resemblance is really uncanny." Her gaze trailed down to the third finger on his left hand, and for some strange reason she was delighted to see he wasn't wearing a wedding band.

"No, ma'am. I'm afraid I'm not." He again noted her wandering gaze and cleared his throat. "Excuse me for a moment. I'll have to check this information out with the computer." He moved away from the window and went back to his car. She sat watching him in her rearview mirror. It was absolutely uncanny. He looked exactly like Jess!

A few minutes later he returned, satisfied she did have a valid license. "I'm going to let you off with just a warning this time," he said in an authoritative voice, "but if I catch you without your license again, I'll have to give you a ticket. The same goes for speeding. You were doing fifty-three in a forty-mile zone."

"But I was late for work."

"I understand that, and as I said, I'm willing to let you off easy this time. Just watch it from now on."

There was something about the way she was looking at him that made him uneasy. She looked like the sort of woman who was looking for a good time, the type of woman who had always made him nervous. Steve Hayden liked good-looking women as much as the next man, but he always had trouble when it came to starting a relationship with one, and it was his own fault.

Steve Hayden was downright shy.

He had fought it all his adult life, but most of the time when it came to dealing with the opposite sex, he would just as soon not. He had female friends of course, but when it came to a more intimate relationship, or even asking a lady out, he avoided that type of situation as much as possible. His shyness always made him balk at pursuing a woman or making a pass, and for the last few years he had been content to let his personal life drift aimlessly.

Not that this woman doesn't have what it takes to turn a man's head, he thought fleetingly. She was certainly attractive enough. He discreetly looked at her lustrous coal-black shoulder-length hair, styled in carefree disarray. Yes, she had a look of worldliness and a beauty about her that made his heartbeat accelerate. No doubt she would know how to attract and keep a man's interest, he thought.

Noting his interest in her, CeAnn summoned up enough courage to give him a sassy smile.

Steve immediately stiffened with disapproval and let his eyes drop back to the pad he was holding. She was trying to come on to him and he didn't like that in a woman. A man would have had to be blind not to be aware of how her wide gray eyes had systematically stripped him at least twice in the last five minutes.

"You're not wearing your seat belt either," he added curtly. "From now on, wear your seat belt, carry your license, and watch the lead foot."

"Oh . . . yes, sir. I will." CeAnn was surprised at the way his voice had suddenly turned frosty. For a brief moment she could have sworn she had seen a faint glimmer of male interest in his appraisal of her. She couldn't help but feel let down at his obvious dismissal of her. But then she wasn't doing much to hold his interest either.

Of course, there was always the possibility that he *was* married and simply not wearing a ring. That could account for his aloofness.

With a curt dismissive nod the officer placed his hat back on his head and returned to his patrol car.

In her rearview mirror CeAnn watched his retreat with a sense of disappointment. Jess McIntosh. She just couldn't get over the resemblance. For a brief moment a feeling of nostalgia washed over her. There had been times over the years when she had questioned her refusal of Jess's offer of marriage. At the time she hadn't been ready for the responsibilities of home and a husband. She felt she had a lot of living to do before she could settle down, even though she had loved Jess. But he hadn't been willing to wait.

With a deep sigh she restarted the engine and absentmindedly put the car in gear, glancing back for one last look at the handsome officer getting into his car. There was no use crying over the past. Jess was married to someone else, and they were expecting their second child. Her foot found the accelerator, and for a moment she was disoriented as she felt the car lurch backward. Then CeAnn was horrified at what was happening. She slammed on the brakes, but not in time to prevent her car from colliding with the front bumper of the patrol car.

The sudden impact knocked the patrolman's hat off. He immediately looked up, his eyes narrowing angrily. Moments later he emerged again from his car, slamming the door with an impatient smack, fighting to calm himself as he walked over to confront her.

He might've looked like Jess, but she could sense their temperaments were very different. By now Jess would have been screaming to high heaven over her stupidity.

Lamely grinning up at him, she tried to explain the sudden turn of events. "I—I accidentally put the car in reverse."

Steve took a deep breath and let it out evenly, willing himself to be courteous at any cost. "Yes, I noticed that."

"I hope I didn't hurt you." She peered up at him hesitantly, hoping she would not find his teeth dropping out of his mouth one by one. The jolt had been unexpected, jarring, and she could tell he was struggling to remain calm. With a thankful sigh she noted that all his teeth seemed to be in place.

Getting out of the car then, she rushed over to examine his bumper, relieved to find there had been no damage to the patrol car.

"Doesn't look like mine's hurt," he admitted, "but I think your car sustained some damage." He knelt down to take a closer look at the rusted bumper. Letting out a low whistle, he glanced worriedly in her direction. "This thing's pretty mangled."

Leaning over his shoulder, she looked for new damage and found none. "No, I don't think there's anything new."

"You mean it looked this bad before the accident?" he exclaimed. The dented old bumper was an eyesore and he couldn't imagine anyone driving around with it in that condition.

Standing up, she smiled at him. "Oh, yes. I still haven't had it fixed from when I backed into a car at the grocery store a couple of months ago."

Casting one last assessing glance at the object in question, the patrolman stood up and brushed off his hands. "Well, if you're sure . . . but if it was my car, I'd want it fixed."

"Oh, don't worry about it. What's one more dent?"

"Look, I have to report this," he stated. "Even if you don't want to file an insurance claim, I'll have to let my superiors know about this."

"Well, you can if you want to, but I can assure you I won't make any trouble over it," she promised. "And I really do have to get to work." She lowered her eyes to read his nametag.

Steven Hayden. Steven. It fitted him perfectly. Filing his name away for future reference, CeAnn apologized for her carelessness once more as he walked her back to the driver's side of her car and helped her in.

"Oh, did you want my name and phone number?" she offered, hoping he would. Even if he didn't require it for the records, he could always use it for personal reasons.

"No, I can get any information I need from the computer," he returned politely.

She was sure her face fell with disappointment. "Oh . . . well, I guess I'd better be on my way."

"Buckle your seat belt," he said as she started the car. "And if you don't mind, I think I'll pull out ahead of you this time."

Once more she watched him make his way back to the patrol car and get in. Moments later he pulled out on the highway and cautiously passed her.

CeAnn in turn pulled out carefully into the line of traffic, then proceeded on to work, wishing for the hundredth time that she could be more aggressive when it came to men. It seemed to her that she was forever letting the perfect opportunity to meet an exciting new man pass her by. The incident that had just occurred was a perfect example.

That policeman had been the epitome of what she was looking for in a man, and what had she done? Stared at him like an idiot. Why hadn't she made witty, fascinating conversation and caught his eye instead of hitting his car and jarring his insides? Who knew, maybe one snappy rejoinder would have led to another and before they had parted he would have asked her for a date. If only she had been more aggressive.

CeAnn found herself laughing at the thought. Who was she kidding? Her? Aggressive? She wouldn't have dared look at him as long as she had if he hadn't reminded her of Jess. No, she just wasn't the kind to flirt with a man, no matter how much she wanted to. Besides, she had given the patrolman a perfect opportunity to further their brief acquaintance, and he hadn't even wanted her name!

By the time she had parked and hurriedly made her way into the department store, she was well over an hour late. It was another ten minutes before she had changed her stockings, clocked in, and walked the length of the building to her post at the cosmetics counter.

"Well, good afternoon," Jenny greeted her teasingly.

"Oh, gad, Jenny. Has Ms. Harrison been by yet?" CeAnn asked breathlessly. All she needed was for her supervisor to find out she was late again.

"Yes, but I covered for you. I told her you were back in the stockroom. What happened? Did you oversleep again?" Jenny studied her disorderly appearance sympathetically.

"Yes, that darn alarm didn't go off again. Thanks for covering, Jenny. I owe you one." CeAnn took her compact out of her purse and fumbled for a tube of lipstick. Although Jenny didn't mean to do it, CeAnn always felt intimidated by her. Jenny Cochran was not necessarily beautiful, but she was high fashion personified. Her clothes were always stylish, her makeup flawlessly applied, and although her flame-red hair was cut rather flamboyantly, she managed to put it all together and ended up looking just smashing.

"You'd better get that alarm replaced," her co-worker warned good-naturedly. "One of these days your luck's going to run out, and Amanda 'The Terror' Harrison is going to be here waiting for you when you finally do show up."

"I know she is. My luck's bound to run out if I keep this up. I plan to buy a new clock the minute I get off," CeAnn promised as she replaced the lipstick in her purse. "I really wouldn't have been all that late if I hadn't gotten stopped for speeding."

"Oh, no! You got another ticket?"

"No, I was lucky there. He just gave me a warning this time."

"How fast were you going?"

"It was no big deal, actually. I was going fifty-something in a forty-something zone. . . . But I forgot my billfold with my driver's license in it . . . and I wasn't wearing my seat belt." CeAnn tucked her purse under the counter and primly straightened her blue work smock.

"Good heavens. He must have been a saint to let you off." Jenny laughed as she opened a box of astringents, stamping the price on the bottom of each bottle. The melodious tinkle of the array of silver bracelets on her arms filled the air as her hands mechanically went about the chore.

CeAnn picked up another box, which contained moisturizers, and placed it on the counter. Then, leaning dreamily against the counter, she sighed.

"No, I don't think he's a saint, but you'd never believe who he looked like."

"Who?"

"Jess McIntosh."

Jenny looked blank for a moment. "Who?"

"Jess! You know, the guy I used to go with in college?"

"Oh, Jess." She paused in her work, her mind conjuring up the tall handsome man CeAnn had nearly married. "He actually looks like him?"

"The spitting image."

"Wow. What route did you take this morning? I think I'll speed by there on my way to work tomorrow morning," she bantered.

CeAnn picked up a knife and opened the box, realizing that Jenny probably wasn't kidding. She was the type who could do such a brazen thing without blinking an eye, if it meant meeting a good-looking man. CeAnn only wished she could be more like her, although the subject of men was beginning to get on her nerves lately. Although she hadn't been ready for marriage when Jess had proposed five years ago, she was now. The only problem was, she hadn't been able to find anyone she wanted to marry. Since she had always bordered on being shy, it was very difficult for her to date new men. It seemed the only ones she knew were out for one thing: a good time and nothing more. And since CeAnn wasn't inclined to become involved in shallow, meaningless relationships, that had narrowed down the field considerably. As each new day passed, she seemed to grow more convinced that she had missed her chance at happiness five years ago. But then, in all honesty, she knew she could never have been really happy with Jess. He was much too possessive. She sighed hopelessly. Maybe she should grow up and face reality for a change. Maybe she should just give up on her dream man and go for a little excitement in her life. Someone with a magnificent body and terrific good looks. . . . A vivid picture of Steven Hayden instantly came to mind.

Quickly deciding that it might not be such a bad idea, she debated whether to ask Jenny's advice on how to get the ball rolling. If anyone would know how, it would be Jenny. CeAnn took a deep breath and asked timidly, "Jenny, would you actually do such a thing? I mean . . . if you wanted to attract that certain policeman's attention, would you really go to such drastic measures to get him to notice you?"

"Sure," she said without a moment's hesitation.

"But that would be breaking the law. And wouldn't he know what you were doing?"

"So what if he did? The worst thing that could happen would be that he'd give you a ticket, and I think it would be well worth the money. The object is to get his attention, which it undoubtedly would." Jenny paused and turned to face her, remembering that CeAnn didn't ask her opinion concerning men very often. "We're not just making idle conversation, are we? You're really serious about getting to know this guy?"

CeAnn cast sheepish eyes back to her work. "I was just supposing," she hedged.

Jenny laughed and shook her head in disbelief.

Rarely did CeAnn ever express an interest in a man, and the thought that she had finally met someone who had caught her attention intrigued her.

"Well, first of all, I'd make certain he wasn't married," Jenny advised. "It saves a lot of trouble."

"He wasn't wearing a ring, although that doesn't necessarily mean he isn't married," CeAnn said.

"No, but it sounds encouraging. Do you know his name?"

"Steven Hayden," she replied softly.

"Hmm, Steven Hayden. Never met him."

"Good." CeAnn grinned and tossed the empty box to the floor. "I hope to keep it that way."

"My goodness! This sounds like it could get serious," Jenny chided. "And all this paragon did was to stop you and warn you about speeding? He must be dynamite."

"He is—or I think he probably could be." CeAnn's eyes clouded with apprehension. "Oh, Jenny, I don't know if it's because he reminds me so much of Jess or if there's really something special about him. But I really would like to meet him again."

"Then go for it!"

"But I don't know where to start. You know me! When it comes to men, I always feel like I'm jinxed!" Her cheeks grew red at the thought of what a fool she had made of herself earlier, when she'd hit his car. "And it would be very reckless of me to use speeding to gain his attention."

"Nonsense. All you have to do is be sure you're not endangering anyone by your tactics. If necessary, just speed up as you pass his patrol car, then let him take over from there."

"I don't know . . . I'm not very good at this sort of thing."

"You're as capable of snaring a man as the next woman," Jenny stated, caught up in her own plan. "If I were you, I'd certainly go after him."

"Well, 'snaring' wasn't exactly what I had in mind," CeAnn cautioned. "But I would like to pursue this a little further . . . I mean, who knows? He might be married, and then that would be that."

"Then again, he might be single," Jenny returned with an impish grin. She knew how hard it was for CeAnn to make the first move toward a man and it amused her. If only her friend knew how easy it could be!

CeAnn looked at Jenny in appeal. "You honestly think I should?"

Jenny strolled over and affectionately draped her arm about CeAnn's neck. "My dear, if it were me, Officer Steven Hayden would see nothing but a blue streak blowing down the highway for the next few mornings, and that blue streak would be none other than little ole me trying to attract little ole his attention."

"But he might think I'm crazy."

Shrugging, Jenny said impishly, "Once you gain his attention, he's bound to find that out anyway."

CeAnn smiled and good-naturedly shook Jenny's arm from her shoulders.

"You really think I should go after him, huh?" That was a scary thought, but then how would she ever attract any man's attention if she didn't put forth a little effort?

"Definitely. And if you decide it's too much trouble, and if he really looks like Jess, I'll do it myself," Jenny volunteered brightly.

"Oh, no, you won't!" CeAnn put in quickly, then frowned as Jenny burst out laughing. "It may kill me, but at least I'm going to give it a try."

"Look out, Steven Hayden." Jenny giggled.

"Yeah, look out, Steven Hayden," CeAnn echoed. But her voice didn't hold the expectation Jenny's did.

CHAPTER TWO

The early-morning traffic was just beginning to taper off as Officer Hayden watched a fellow patrolman pull his car in beside his and brake to a halt.

"How's it going, Steve?" The new arrival got out of his car and walked over to lean in at Steve's open window, a broad grin splitting his dark, swarthy features.

"All right. How are things with you, Kirk?"

"Can't complain." Plucking off his hat, Kirk wiped his brow and squinted up at the bright sun. "Looks like it's going to be another warm one."

"Yeah, but I'm not complaining. I love Indian summer. Billie feeling any better?"

"Not really. The doctor said she's probably going to be one of those unlucky ones who has morning sickness during her whole pregnancy," Kirk replied.

"Well, she only has a couple of months to go."

"That's what I told her at breakfast this morning, but she practically took my head off and went into this blistering tirade about how it was all my fault she was in this miserable state!" he said, mimicking a female voice. "You know, I'll be as glad as she is when this thing's over. She's as touchy as an old bear with a sore paw lately."

Steve chuckled at the look of distress on his brother-in-law's face. Kirk had been quite a rounder in his day, but a little over a year ago he had chosen to give up the single life and marry Steve's younger sister. In spite of all the complaining they both tended to do, they had a good marriage. But Billie's pregnancy had been a difficult one from the start, and the strain was beginning to show on both of them now.

"Don't laugh," Kirk grumbled. "That woman can be hell on wheels when she takes a mind to be. I still can't believe you two are related." While Steve was mild-mannered and rarely lost his cool, Billie was volatile and hot-tempered, leading Kirk a merry chase most of the time.

Steve laughed again. "I warned you before you married her what it was going to be like."

A begrudging grin showed on Kirk's face as he thought of his temperamental but very loving wife. "Well, I may complain a lot, but I wouldn't trade her for a farm in Texas."

Their conversation was interrupted by the sound of an unusually noisy car coming down the highway. As it approached it seemed to pick up speed, and then, in a burst of power, roared by them at breakneck speed. The motor backfired twice, then the old muffler sent a puff of blue smoke rolling over the officers' heads as the car sped on down the road.

Steve and Kirk looked at each other quizzically.

211

"What the hell was that?" Kirk exclaimed.

Steve quickly started his car, flipping on the red emergency light at the same time. "I don't know, but I'm going to find out."

Kirk stepped back as Steve wheeled out onto the highway, made a U-turn, and headed in the direction of the speeding motorist. As he began to gain on the other car he had a strange feeling that he had seen it before, but he couldn't remember where. As he got closer he turned on the siren. The old sedan immediately pulled over to the side of the road and waited. He pulled in behind it and stopped.

Climbing out of his car, he walked to the back of the vehicle and wrote down the license plate number, then ambled to the driver's side.

"Hi! I have my license this morning," a woman's perky voice said in greeting.

A flicker of surprise crossed his features as he came face to face with the woman he had encountered the morning before. She was smiling brightly at him, seeming not the least bit concerned that she had just been caught speeding for the second morning in a row.

Leveling a stern gaze at her, he said calmly, "I'm glad to hear that. May I see it, please?"

CeAnn let out a small, inaudible sigh of relief. Good! This could be an encouraging sign. He was obviously doing his duty, but perhaps he was also thinking about the marvelous opportunity he had missed the day before and was now eager to learn more about her.

"No problem, I have it right here." She handed

him the requested item and waited while he quietly studied it.

CeAnn Rebecca Masters, he read thoughtfully, five foot one, one-hundred-five pounds. Black hair and gray eyes. Birthdate: May twenty-fifth, 1959. He glanced up, then quickly looked again at the license. They had the same birthday.

CeAnn felt the butterflies gather in her stomach as she let her eyes scrutinize him once again. He looked even better than she remembered . . . if that were possible. Come to think of it, she believed he was even better-looking than Jess. She decided he must be an outdoors person, since his smooth skin still had evidence of a deep tan. His dark coloring made his eyes arrestingly blue, and she felt her pulse flutter as he leveled them once more on her.

"You realize you were speeding again," he said curtly.

"Yes." Since she had no good excuse, CeAnn could only hope Jenny had been right in surmising that it would be worth one ticket to get his attention. "And I forgot to buckle up again," she found herself foolishly confessing, for lack of anything else to say.

His gaze grimly assessed her. "I noticed that."

Darn! This was going to be hard. How in the world was she going to strike up a personal conversation when he seemed intent on keeping strictly to business?

"Nice morning, isn't it?"

"Yes, it is." He was calmly writing on his clipboard and paying absolutely no attention to her.

She tried to think of what Jenny would do at this point, but decided that whatever it was, she wouldn't be able to do it. If only he would look at her instead of avoiding her gaze.

"Are you married?" she found herself blurting out somewhat tactlessly.

He glanced up. "Beg your pardon?"

"I asked . . . if you were married." She wanted to play it very cool and nonchalant, but she was positive he could see her lips beginning to quiver.

If he did, he gave no indication of it. His eyes dropped away from hers once more and he continued to write the citation. "No, I'm not married," he answered in a voice so low she could barely hear him.

Steve really wished she would make this easier and stop trying to come on to him. It had not been easy for him to ignore the fact that he had felt an unexpected surge of excitement at seeing her again this morning. He wasn't sure why she had that effect on him, but the realization annoyed him.

"You're not married? What a coincidence! I'm not either," CeAnn returned brightly.

Ripping the ticket off the pad, he handed it to her and tipped his hat politely. "Yes, it is. Have a nice day."

CeAnn glanced at the paper he had slapped in her hand, and grimaced as he walked back to his car and got in. Have a nice day, indeed! This little episode was probably going to cost her an arm and a leg. Still, he was awfully good-looking, and she had found out for sure he wasn't married, so maybe it would be worth the money.

She mustered up a brave grin and gave him a friendly wave as he pulled the patrol car around hers and headed out on the highway.

She sighed and restarted her car. Well, tomorrow was another day and she would try again. After all, he couldn't go on ignoring her forever.

"I'm telling you, man, she's after you," Kirk declared after work the next day. He and Steve sat drinking cold beer in the local bar. "Why fight it? If she's as eager as you say she is, go for it."

"Ah, come on, Kirk, you know I don't go in for that kind of woman," Steve protested. "And even if I did, I'm certainly not her type. She'd probably be bored to death with a guy like me."

"Sure sounds to me like she thinks you're her kind," Kirk argued.

"I can guarantee you it isn't me she's interested in. She has this crazy idea I look exactly like some guy she used to go with. If she didn't think I looked like him, she wouldn't give me the time of day."

Kirk let out a low whistle. "I wouldn't bet on it. I think the woman is after you and she's getting desperate. Why, if she keeps this up, she's going to lose her license."

Steve took another sip of his beer and stared thoughtfully at his reflection in the dingy mirror behind the bar. "No, that's the funny thing. She doesn't go more than ten miles over the speed limit, so there won't be any points coming off her license. I haven't even given her that many tickets

215

so far. But I could swear someone's pushing her to do this," he mused.

"Why even bother to stop her if you know what she's doing?" Kirk cajoled. "You know, no matter what you say, I'm beginning to suspect you have an interest in this mystery lady. After all, you could always turn your head in the other direction if she's bothering you."

Steve peered at his brother-in-law solemnly. "I did look the other way when she sped by me this morning. But would you believe she turned around and sped past me again?"

Kirk sat up straighter, definitely impressed. "No kidding? What did you do?"

"Stopped her and fined her," he admitted with a fatalistic shrug.

"Listen, buddy. Take my word. If she's willing to go to this extent to get your attention, then she's got it bad," Kirk coaxed. "You'd better strike while the iron's hot."

"I told you, she isn't trying to get *my* attention," Steve argued. "She's chasing a fantasy. Besides, even if I was interested in her, you know I'm not very good when it comes to making a pass at a woman."

"Look, I hate to sound callous about this, but it sounds to me like the lady is asking for it. Why should you care what she's chasing? If she's offering a little action, all you have to do is grin and take her up on it. She'll do the rest!" Kirk punched Steve in the shoulder knowingly. "If it were me, I wouldn't question the hand of good fortune. Live it up a little, my boy. You're too strait-laced. If she's

216

the kind you think she is, you'll have a quick little affair, then she'll be moving on to greener pastures, leaving you with enough sweet memories to send you to a cold shower every night for a month."

"I don't know, Kirk . . . I don't like any of this. . . ."

Steve knew he should discard Kirk's advice and stick to his gut feelings about this woman. Although he knew his brother-in-law had been faithful to Billie since their marriage, Kirk's way of viewing the opposite sex was entirely different from Steve's.

CeAnn Masters was not worth the time or the effort, he kept trying to convince himself. Why even waste the energy on a brief, meaningless, completely inadvisable affair?

Then again, a demonic voice would inevitably argue, maybe he was all wrong about her. Was it possible she was merely outgoing and vivacious, instead of what he was beginning to fear, promiscuous and easy? Maybe she didn't realize what a negative impression she was making on him. That was entirely plausible. Maybe he should just ride this thing out. With any luck at all, she would give up and save him from wrestling with the difficult decision of whether or not to take the bait she had so temptingly thrown out to him. But if she persisted . . . no, she wouldn't. Before long she would tire of whatever game she was playing, or run out of money, and then she would leave him alone. The thought did little to sweeten his disposition.

CeAnn's disposition was not exactly sunny of late either. The tickets in her glove compartment were stacking up and she had decided that her ego, not to mention her purse, could no longer stand the strain of pursuing the elusive beast called man.

After three tickets and numerous not-so-subtle hints, it had finally become clear to her that Steve Hayden—unmarried and unattached though he was—was simply not interested in starting a relationship. She really didn't see much future in continuing the pursuit. It had taken a while, but she was now of the firm opinion that it was time to call it quits. Surely there had to be a man somewhere in the world who would be more appreciative of her attention, and she proceeded to tell Jenny so in no uncertain terms over the phone Friday evening.

"I quit, I quit!" she stated emphatically. "I'm bankrupt, not to mention the fact that he isn't the least bit interested in me, and I'm tired of making a complete fool of myself!"

"I just can't understand it," Jenny mused. "Is the man blind?"

"No, he isn't blind. He just makes it crystal clear he is *not* interested in furthering our acquaintance. Four miserable days of forcing myself to be overly friendly to that jackass and what do I have to show for all my trouble? Nothing but a fistful of summonses, that's what!"

"He has to be interested! He's a man, isn't he? Maybe you're doing something wrong."

"It wouldn't take a genius to figure that out.

218

Wait a minute, Jenny, the dogs are barking." CeAnn laid down the receiver and went to let the animals outside. How she'd ended up with five dogs and four cats was still a mystery to her, but she supposed it was because of a tender heart. The small house she rented was on the outskirts of town, and when anyone wanted to get rid of an unwanted animal, he would dump it on her secluded gravel road. Invariably, the animal would find its way to her house. Loving animals the way she did, CeAnn always took them in, promising herself she would find them a new home. That was not always an easy task, and she usually ended up with far more strays than she could find homes for. She even had an Australian chicken that laid blue eggs. But the eggs came in handy, so she really couldn't complain about that.

"Maybe you're just not coming on strong enough to him," Jenny speculated when CeAnn got back to the phone.

CeAnn shook her head in exasperation. "Are you kidding? I've come on stronger than ten pounds of onions and he merely looks at me with that baffled expression on his face and hands me another ticket!"

"Hmm . . . obviously he doesn't know what he's run into."

"Well, I'm sure *he* thinks he's run into an over-sexed tart the way I've been acting!"

"Nonsense! If he thought that, he'd be the one chasing you. If anything, I'd say you're too tame for him and he senses it." Jenny found it hard to believe that a normal, unattached man could dismiss CeAnn so easily.

"I don't think so. He just isn't interested in me, period." CeAnn slumped down on the sofa, cradling the phone against her shoulder as she stared up morosely at the ceiling. "I've tried all that witty banter and those flirty moves that you say work so well on other men, but they roll off him like water off a duck's back. Instead of sounding suave and sophisticated, I end up sounding like a three-dollar-a-night hooker who isn't even very good at what she does!"

"I think you're only imagining things," Jenny scoffed. "I still say he can sense the type of woman you really are and he probably prefers the swinger type."

"I'm telling you, Jenny, he couldn't possibly be mistaking me for a shrinking violet!" Her cheeks flamed anew as she thought of some of the really strange and out-of-character things she had said and done to get Steve's attention.

"This would all be much simpler if I could meet him," Jenny fretted. "I'd be able to tell you in a minute what sort of woman he's looking for. Then we could transform you into that woman before he knew what hit him."

"Well, just speed down the highway Monday morning and I guarantee you'll get the opportunity to make his acquaintance," CeAnn replied. "Along with a ticket to mark the occasion."

"That might not be a bad idea," Jenny mused. "If I can get his attention, then I'll be able to see what we need to do." Her voice sounded a little more predatory than helpful for CeAnn's taste.

"No, that *is* a bad idea," CeAnn protested. She had no doubt that Jenny would be able to catch Steve Hayden's eye, thus accomplishing what she so far had been unable to do. And after the horrendous week she had put in trying to attract this man, she wasn't about to turn him over to someone else that quickly.

"Oh, do I still detect a note of possessiveness in your voice, despite your vow to give up on him?"

"I may have been a little hasty in my decision," CeAnn hedged. "It's possible I'll give it a little more time . . . but whatever I decide, I think you should let me handle it my way."

Jenny laughed. "Whatever you say. But if you decide to give up on him, by all means let me be the first to know. He sounds more intriguing every day."

Deciding it was time to change the subject, CeAnn said, "Are we still on for racquetball tonight?"

Jenny was still mulling over the possibility of trying to meet the man who was giving her friend such a hard time. He was fast becoming an enigma she was anxious to unravel. "Oh, sure," she murmured absently. "Just give me time to change."

"I'll meet you over at the club in half an hour. Have you eaten yet?"

"No. I thought we might have a sandwich later."

"That sounds good. I'll see you there around seven."

As CeAnn replaced the receiver she was still

undecided as to how she was going to handle Steve Hayden. Very carefully or—as Jenny would—full steam ahead. The only thing she was sure of was that she wasn't quite ready to give up on him . . . yet.

CHAPTER THREE

Why she would continue to give Steve Hayden a
second thought was beyond her comprehension,
but for some reason she did.

After all, there are other men in the world,
CeAnn reminded herself twenty minutes later as
she drove to the racquetball club. Men who could
see her as more than another source of revenue for
the city! Granted, she didn't have an overabun-
dance of suitors trying to beat down her door, but
she could honestly say she could have had her fair
share of the available male population if she
wanted. And from now on she was going to center
her attention only on those who were worthy of it!

As she pulled her car into the parking lot of the
club, a smile tugged at the corners of her mouth.
She saw a familiar sight, that rascal Ruffe Sennett,
just getting out of his car. Now there might be the
perfect place to start my new campaign, she
mused. Any woman would be crazy to pass up a
chance to know that man better, and he had asked
her out on a number of occasions. It just so happened that she had always had other plans, but
maybe the time was right for her to start accepting

his invitations. Giving him a friendly wave, she pulled in next to his red Corvette and he waited for her to get out.

"Hi, Ruffe."

"CeAnn, it's good to see you." Ruffe Sennett was one of those men who made a woman feel she had his undivided attention, no matter where they were or what they were doing. His classical features, sultry coffee-colored eyes, and thick black hair bordered on the beautiful rather than the merely handsome. It was no wonder women flocked to him by the dozen. He had a reputation as a ladies' man. Not only was he an excellent hairdresser, but he had a certain way of making a woman feel like a woman, simply by the way he looked at her or spoke in that deep, totally masculine voice. Feeling wistful, she honestly wished she could feel like all those other women. But no matter how dynamic Ruffe might be, she still didn't feel that lurch of excitement she felt when Steve Hayden appeared on the scene.

Ruffe leaned down to open her car door and extended a helping hand as she got out. "How are you? It seems I haven't seen you as much lately as I'd like." He smiled down on her attentively as they started up the walk to the club.

She smiled back and thought once more how nice he always made her feel. "Thank you, but I've been staying late at the store most nights. One of the other ladies has been sick, so we've all been filling in for her."

They had reached the entrance of the club and

he courteously held the door and let her enter first. "Are you alone tonight?" he asked.

She hesitated a moment, sensing this would be a golden opportunity for her to become better acquainted with him. But seconds later she found herself apologizing for the fact that she wasn't available.

"Ah. That's too bad. I was hoping we could play a few games and then have a glass of Pripps," he said.

CeAnn wrinkled her nose in distaste at the mention of the nutritional drink the club served to replenish the body after rigorous workouts. "I'd really love to. Maybe next time," she said.

Actually, she knew that Jenny would encourage her to accept his offer and forget all about their date. She felt a nagging tug of guilt, knowing she really should take advantage of his offer this time. But somehow she just wasn't in the mood for male companionship.

His dark, compelling eyes caught and held hers momentarily. "I'll be here early tomorrow evening. May I buy you a drink then?"

"Well . . . I don't see why not." She smiled at him and felt her pulse increase in tempo under his intense scrutiny. She was uneasily aware that her shorts were a bit too tight, as his eyes continued their lazy perusal of her shapely legs and buttocks.

"Good. Until tomorrow?" He bowed slightly and picked up her hand to bestow a courtly kiss on the back of it.

To her mortification CeAnn found herself laughing nervously.

He glanced at her and smiled in puzzlement. "Did I say something funny?"

"No." She tried to straighten her face. "I'm just not used to such . . . courtesy from a man."

"Ah. But you should be, my dear, and I hope you'll allow me the supreme pleasure of giving it to you." The smile on his face was completely innocent, but his tone had changed almost imperceptibly to a suggestive one. For a moment it gave her pause to wonder just exactly what he hoped to "give" her.

"Oh . . . yes. Well, I guess. . . ." She hated to sound like such a dolt, but the insinuating comment had caught her off guard. Perhaps she had misinterpreted what he meant. Ruffe Sennett is a complete gentleman, she reasoned. He would never be so crude as to mean what she thought he did.

He winked and whispered in a sexy manner, "Around seven tomorrow night?"

"Yes, seven will be fine."

Her grin was slightly stupefied, not to mention downright silly, as she watched his tall form stride away. She glanced around for Jenny and the smile died an instant death on her lips.

Leaning against the refreshment bar, wearing white tennis shorts and a perspiration-soaked polo shirt, was none other than Steve Hayden. It was apparent by the look of cool disdain on his face that he and the man standing with him had watched the exchange between her and Ruffe.

Managing a weak grin, she then caught sight of Jenny hurrying toward her. "There you are. I was beginning to wonder what happened to you!" She paused and took note of CeAnn's flushed face. "What's wrong?"

"Over there at the bar . . . it's him."

"Who?" Jenny started to turn around to see who was causing her friend's distress.

"Don't look!" CeAnn hissed.

Jenny's head snapped back obediently. "What's the matter? Who is it?"

"Would you believe it? Of all the people in the world to run into, why did *he* have to be standing there when I walked in?"

"Who?"

Jenny thought she had the go-ahead to look, but found out she didn't when CeAnn grabbed her by the shoulders and abruptly whirled her back around.

"Don't look!" she warned frantically.

"But you said—"

"What is he doing here? I've been coming here for the last six months and he's never been here! What's he doing here now? Oh, gad, Jenny. What should I do? Ignore him or just walk right up to him and make an ass out of myself again?"

Once more Jenny tried to find out who was causing all the trouble, but was instantly jerked back around.

"How many times do I have to tell you? Don't look! He'll know I'm talking about him!"

"Who will know you're talking about him?"

"Oh!" CeAnn suddenly realized she wasn't giving Jenny much of an opportunity to help. "Steve Hayden. He's standing over there at the bar."

"Steve Hayden?" For a moment Jenny's features were blank. "Oh! Steve Hayden!" Her voice brightened at the prospect of finally meeting the man who had CeAnn's libido in such a dither. "Oh, good. Take me over and introduce me," she ordered.

"I can't just waltz over there and introduce you," CeAnn exclaimed. "I hardly know the man!"

"Sure you can." By this time Jenny had been able to maneuver enough to get a brief look at the two men standing at the bar. "My gosh, he *does* look like Jess," she whispered excitedly. "I can see why you've been so persistent. And his friend isn't bad either. Take me over there and introduce us, then let me do all the talking."

"Not so fast." CeAnn didn't like the sparkle that had suddenly appeared in her friend's eye. "I don't think we should—"

"Why not? Look, that's your problem, CeAnn. You don't come on strong enough. Do you see a ring on either one of those men's fingers?"

"No, but—"

"Then what's to stop us?"

"My shorts are too tight," CeAnn pointed out.

"Good thinking. That's bound to work in our favor."

"Jenny! The only reason I'm wearing these shorts is because they were the only pair I had clean, and I really don't think we should do this," she pleaded.

"Relax and just leave everything to me if you're so worried."

"I'm not worried," CeAnn protested in vain. "I

just don't think it's a good idea to go over there. If he were interested, he would come up to me first."

"But we can't leave matters like this to chance. He might not make the first move and I want to meet him. Just relax and make the introductions. I'll take it from there."

"I really don't feel like I know him well enough to be introducing him to anyone."

"You do. Take my word for it." Jenny nudged her gently in the direction of the bar.

It was hard to believe that she would allow herself to become a part of this ridiculous plan, but a few seconds later CeAnn found herself lamely trailing Jenny over to where the two men were standing.

Though he was out of uniform, Steve still looked forbidding and ominous to her. CeAnn tried to force a lump of nausea down her throat, praying Jenny knew what she was doing. Her only hope now was that the matter *would* be handled with finesse.

"Look at that, Kirk, didn't I tell you?" Steve muttered irritably as he watched the two women make their way toward the bar. "She's coming over here. She no more gets in the door with one man than she's after another one."

Kirk glanced over his shoulder to see an attractive dark-haired woman wearing a pair of shorts that would send any man's blood pressure soaring, following in the wake of a rather flamboyant redhead. "Please, Steven ole man, tell me it's the dark-haired beauty who has you in such a tizzy."

"It's the dark-haired one," he confirmed glumly,

trying to tear his eyes away from the expanse of shapely leg she was showing. Her shorts were too tight! "And she doesn't have me in a tizzy, Kirk! I wish you'd stop saying that."

"The hell she doesn't," he teased. "She's been on your mind for the last week and you might as well admit it."

Steve finally willed his eyes back to the mirror hanging over the bar. "You have a great imagination," he accused.

Though Kirk was a married man, he could still appreciate the beauty of the situation. "You mean to tell me that little dark-haired temptress is the one you've been trying to avoid all this time? Now I really am getting worried about you, my boy."

"Remember Billie, Kirk," Steve warned, noting the way Kirk's appreciative eyes were taking in the slender bare legs coming toward them.

"Not to worry, friend," Kirk said in a reassuring voice. "I have no trouble remembering my wife."

Both men straightened and turned as the women approached. CeAnn swallowed nervously and then seized the advantage by extending her hand to Steve in a friendly greeting. "Hi, Steve. What a pleasant surprise to see you here!"

Steve accepted the well-manicured hand graciously. "Hello . . . CeAnn, isn't it?"

"Yes, that's right. I was wondering if you would remember me."

His smile was still a bit on the cool side. "Yes, I remember you," he assured her.

She smiled back weakly. "Well . . . it's nice to see you again."

"Yeah. Real nice."

"Oh, this is Jenny Cochran, a good friend and co-worker. Jenny, this is Steve Hayden."

Steve accepted Jenny's hand politely. "Hi, Jenny."

"And I'm Kirk Mallard," Kirk intervened playfully. "Jack of all trades, master of none."

They all laughed and shook hands.

Eyeing the tall, dark-haired man interestedly, Jenny evinced the famous smile that was guaranteed to catch a man's eye. "How nice to meet you, Kirk." Then to Steve she said, "And Steve." She put her hand against her chest as if to say what an honor. "CeAnn has told me so much about you . . . all good, of course!"

Closing her eyes in disbelief, CeAnn vowed to take the woman's life when they were alone once more.

Jenny was surprised to see a faint blush touch Steve's already tanned cheeks. His only other response to the compliment was a detached glance in CeAnn's direction, and perhaps his hand tightened a bit around the glass of juice he was holding.

"Well, gentlemen," Jenny said brightly, aware that CeAnn was not going to be any help at all in getting the action rolling. She was standing back, acting as if the two men were going to bite her at any moment. "We were just getting ready to play racquetball. If you're not busy, would you be interested in playing doubles?"

Steve and CeAnn glanced at each other uneasily.

"I think that would be great," Kirk accepted readily. "Don't you, Steve?"

"I don't know, Kirk. . . . We've been playing for the last couple of hours and I'm about worn out."

"Jenny, I'm sure they wouldn't want to play with us . . . we're not that good." CeAnn had finally mustered up the courage to speak. It was perfectly obvious that Steve Hayden didn't want to be bothered.

Jenny shot her a dirty look. "Oh, I'm sure they wouldn't mind. Would you, fellows?" Once more her most beguiling smile was turned on full force for the benefit of both men.

"If CeAnn wants to play a game, one more won't hurt you, Steve," Kirk encouraged pleasantly.

CeAnn wants to play? "Oh, no . . . it isn't me who wants to play," CeAnn blurted out, feeling the warm blood rush to her cheeks.

But before she could protest further, Kirk continued. "I can assure you, ladies, neither one of us is that good either. But first I think I should clear it with my lovely wife," he conceded, glancing in the direction of the ladies' room, from which a petite brunette, who was obviously in the last months of pregnancy, had just emerged.

"Oh . . . your wife?" The announcement definitely took the lilt out of Jenny's voice as the four turned to watch Billie's approach.

"Hi, honey." Kirk stepped over to wrap his arms protectively about her thickened waist. "This is CeAnn Masters and Jenny Cochran." Kirk and Bil-

232

lie exchanged a meaningful look before he continued. "Steve and CeAnn are . . ." To the dismay of both Steven and CeAnn, he laughed devilishly before finishing his sentence. "Good friends. Would you mind if we play a quick game of doubles?"

Steve shot a frosty look at his brother-in-law as CeAnn took a deep breath and shut her eyes again. Oh, no, he thought, good friends!

"Really, Kirk, I'm sure Billie's tired," Steve protested.

"No, I'm not," Billie assured him brightly, her interest perking up at the mention of CeAnn's name. Kirk had been telling her about the colorful woman who had been shamelessly chasing her brother for the past few days and she was excited about this accidental meeting. "Actually, I feel pretty good." She smiled encouragingly at the two couples standing before her. "Go ahead and play. I'll watch."

She proceeded to lead the way to the court Steve and Kirk had been playing on previously. A few minutes later the game began, Billie watching CeAnn with unusual interest from the loft above.

Although all four had denied any expertise in the game, they soon proved they were only being modest as a fast and lively exchange of the ball developed. After getting over the initial disappointment of finding out that Kirk was married, Jenny relaxed and kept up a witty conversation with him, trying to cover the fact that CeAnn and Steve were saying very little.

Steve would respond when spoken to directly,

233

but like CeAnn he tended to keep his eye on the ball and ignore everything else.

Once they both ran to hit the ball and collided as they lunged. Since both their faces were flushed from the exertion of the game, it was hard to tell which one blushed harder as Steve jumped quickly to his feet and then, almost as an afterthought, hesitantly offered CeAnn a helping hand. Kirk and Jenny caught each other's eye, trying hard not to laugh at the obvious shyness of the two. At this rate, CeAnn Masters and Steven Hayden were a hopeless case.

A few minutes later their laughter could not be held in check. CeAnn slammed the ball and it ricocheted straight back, hitting Steve smack in the middle of the forehead. A not-so-very-nice word escaped his lips as he dropped to one knee and rubbed the ache.

CeAnn didn't know whether to go over and try to assist him or stay where she was. She was saved the decision when Jenny and Kirk went to check on him. A few minutes later she was so embarrassed she wanted to cry: she saw a knot the size of a goose egg swell up on his forehead.

"I'm sorry," she murmured as he came to take his stance beside her.

"Don't worry about it." Then, wonder of all wonders, he actually effected a shy grin and said jokingly, "I'm always looking for a place to hang my coat."

Her grin was as contagious as his. "Well, thanks to me, you now have your own private coathook."

The competition proved so enjoyable that after

the first game they decided to play another one, and then another.

After an hour and a half of rigorous activity the men went in search of something to drink while Jenny disappeared into the ladies' room.

CeAnn plopped down on the bench next to Billie and let out an exhausted sigh. "I've surely sweated off ten pounds!"

Billie laughed and patted her rounded stomach. "I used to love to play racquetball," she revealed in a friendly voice. "But when I became pregnant, that all had to stop."

CeAnn smiled, wishing she could be as outgoing with a stranger as this woman was. "When is the baby due?"

"The doctor says in about eight weeks. I can't wait until it gets here," she said candidly. "I've been sick a lot and I'm driving Kirk up the wall with my nasty disposition."

CeAnn laughed. "I've heard pregnant women can get that way."

"Believe me, they can!" They fell into an easy conversation for a few minutes. Then Billie smiled and said, "So you and Steve are good friends?"

"Oh, not really," CeAnn clarified hurriedly. Her heart still was wont to skip a few beats every time she thought of him. It didn't matter that he had barely talked to her all evening. His continued indifference couldn't keep her from being aware of what an attractive man he was.

Billie paused, disappointment clouding her face. "Oh? Kirk and I were sort of hoping you were. Did you know Steve was my brother?"

"No." CeAnn was surprised by the announcement, yet pleased. For some reason she felt she knew Billie, even though they had just met.

"Yes, he's older than me, but I still worry about him," she admitted in a maternal voice.

You shouldn't, CeAnn thought dismally, he can certainly take care of himself, especially when it comes to women!

"I was hopeful when Kirk said you two were friends." Billie sighed. "I should have known it was too good to be true. I swear, as shy and picky as he is, he's going to be a bachelor all his life," Billie prophesied, as if she and CeAnn had known each other forever.

"He's shy?" CeAnn's ears perked up at this new bit of information.

"As an old maid on her wedding night," Billie informed her. "You'd never believe it to look at him. I mean, as handsome as he is, you'd think he wouldn't have any trouble with women. But he does. Ever since he was a little boy, girls have scared the daylights out of him."

CeAnn looked at her skeptically. "Surely not." Somehow she had never stopped to consider that possibility. But now that she thought about it, perhaps Steve wasn't merely the conceited person she had been tempted to believe he was. If he did have a hard time relating to women, then that would explain why he couldn't look her straight in the eye when they talked. And the way his tanned features got that soft, rosy blush about them when she tried to gain his attention by flirting with him. All those things seemed to indicate a person who

236

was shy. She didn't know why she hadn't thought about that sooner. After all, until she had met him, she had been exactly the same way.

Somehow the idea that he wasn't the aloof man she had thought made her want to try all the harder.

"Yes, I'm afraid it's true," Billie conceded. "That's why when Kirk mentioned Steve had been stopping you . . . well, I had sort of hoped there was some reason for it."

"There was. I was speeding." CeAnn winced at her words. "But if you're hoping he was using his job to corner me, he wasn't," CeAnn noted wearily. "It was the other way around."

Billie brightened visibly. "Oh! You're trying to gain his attention?"

"I was, but I'm about ready to give up," she confessed. "I can't afford another ticket."

Shifting on her seat, Billie faced CeAnn, a bright sparkle in her eye. "Don't! At least, don't give up yet. Like I said, he's a little shy, but Kirk and I both have this crazy feeling he *has* noticed you, even though he denies it. In fact, he and Kirk have discussed it several times lately, and Kirk always comes home laughing at Steve's obvious dilemma."

Billie wasn't at all sure why she was encouraging CeAnn to pursue her brother, except that she had liked CeAnn immediately. The woman was not at all what she had expected; actually, she was quite the opposite. Instead of being forward and pushy, she had hung back and let her friend do all the talking. Billie's teeth toyed with her lower lip as her eyes scanned the skimpy shorts, and the gray eyes peering hopefully back at her. In all honesty, she didn't look like the sort of woman who would throw herself at a man. CeAnn's shorts were a bit tight, but not indecently so. She really was a very attractive woman.

"You don't really think he would be interested in me . . . do you?" CeAnn inquired hesitantly. She knew it was probably only wishful thinking, but she felt her spirits soar in spite of herself.

"Yes, I think he might." Billie felt a twinge of guilt at stretching the truth somewhat. Actually, she was aware that Steve had denied to Kirk on more than one occasion this past week that he was interested in this woman. But she looked so . . . hopeful, and Billie and Kirk had decided long ago that if Steve was ever going to do something about his personal life, he was going to need a gentle nudge from those who loved him.

"I hope you like cola." Steve's voice interrupted the women's conversation as the men returned with their drinks.

CeAnn glanced up guiltily and took the cup Steve was extending to her. "Thanks. Cola's fine."

"Where's Jenny?" Kirk handed Billie one of the three drinks he was carrying.

"She's still in the ladies room—oh, here she comes now," Billie noted. The drinks were distributed and the five sat quietly, savoring the cool refreshments.

"Thanks, that hit the spot." Billie took a final sip from her cup and smiled at her brother affectionately. "Well. This has been fun tonight, don't you agree? We should all do this more often now that we've gotten to know each other."

Steve eyed her distrustfully, praying she wasn't about to pull one of her matchmaking schemes on him again. "Yeah, it's been great, but I'm going to have to be running along. It's getting late."

"Oh, do you have to? It's not really all that late," she protested.

"It is for an old man like me," Steve quipped as he gathered up his gear. "I'll see you and Kirk tomorrow night." He paused and turned to face her once more. "We're still on for dinner, aren't we?"

It was pitiful the way men could be so easily taken in, Billie thought. "Tomorrow night?" She purposely made her face go blank. "Did we have a dinner engagement for tomorrow night?"

"Yeah, at least I have it marked on my calendar," Steve replied thoughtfully. "Why? Something come up?"

"Oh, how thoughtless of me," Billie fabricated. "I told Jack and Harriet we'd have dinner with them tomorrow night."

"Jack and Harriet?" Kirk's ears perked up. "When did they get back in town?"

"Oh . . . last week. Didn't I mention it to you?"

"No kidding? Jack's job on the oil well must not have worked out. That's strange. . . ."

"Well, no problem. We can get together one night next week," Steve offered.

"You sure it was Jack and Harriet you saw?" Kirk

pressed. "I could have sworn someone told me he was crazy about his job—"

"It was Jack and Harriet, dear," Billie said sternly. "Now be quiet. I can tell Steve is disappointed because we can't be with him tomorrow night and I feel terrible. Maybe we can think of something he can do." Her eyes wandered angelically to where CeAnn stood.

Steve glanced at his sister sharply, dread crawling up his spine like a spider. Good Lord. Surely she wasn't about to suggest that he have dinner with *her* tomorrow night!

But she did.

"I really feel bad about this," Billie said. "Hey, wait a minute! Just because Kirk and I can't go doesn't mean that the rest of you can't get together for dinner tomorrow night. Wouldn't that be fun?"

She had an uncanny knack for making it sound as if that *would* be the most natural thing in the world for all of them to do.

"Gee, that sounds like fun, but I already have a date," Jenny apologized.

"Oh, sorry. Maybe next time." Billie turned to CeAnn and grinned. "What about you, CeAnn? You're not busy tomorrow night, are you?" she prompted.

"Well, sort of . . ."

"Billie!" Steve warned under his breath.

Billie ignored him and shot CeAnn a meaningful look. "Nothing you couldn't cancel, is it?"

CeAnn was well aware of what Billie was trying

240

to do, but she didn't want her to do it. "Well, no, but—"

"Good! That settles it. Steve and CeAnn can have dinner together." She let out a sigh of relief and tried to ignore the murderous glare her brother was sending in her direction. "I feel much better now that I know you won't have to eat alone," she exclaimed brightly. She hesitantly lifted her gaze and gave Steve a guilty grin. "Don't you?"

"I still can't figure out what Jack and Harriet are doing back here," Kirk fretted.

Billie punched him in the ribs and kept the smile plastered on her face.

Absently rubbing his still smarting forehead, Steve continued to shoot daggers at his sister. "Maybe CeAnn would rather keep her other appointment," he pointed out. He was far too much of a gentleman to refuse the date in front of CeAnn, but he still held on to the hope that she would have enough sense to back out of the obvious setup herself.

. It was on the tip of her tongue to refuse, but something held her back. It would be a rotten trick to pull on him, but maybe, just maybe, if he were able to see her in a different light than he had previously, she would be able to make some progress with him.

"Oh, no . . . it isn't that important. I mean I wouldn't mind if you really wanted to have dinner together," she clarified meekly.

Spit fire and save the matches! He was trapped!

"Are you sure?" he inquired politely, trying to

keep his voice steady. He hated being a patsy, and Billie was going to hear about this when they were alone!

Lowering her eyes from his steady blue gaze, CeAnn softly acquiesced. "If you're sure you don't mind."

"You'll have to give me your address so I can pick you up. I don't know where you live."

Seeking to make it easier on him, she smiled. "Why don't I meet you?"

"Okay. Would the Grove be all right with you?"

"Yes. I love seafood."

"About eight o'clock?"

"Eight o'clock would be fine."

Shifting his racquet to his other hand, he barely glanced at his sister as he started for the doorway. "See you in the morning, Kirk. Jenny, it's been nice meeting you."

"It was great to meet you, Steve," Jenny returned, then winked knowingly at CeAnn. "I have to be running along too."

"I'll see you Monday. Drive carefully," CeAnn said.

"I'll pull the car around to the front, honey," Kirk offered as he turned to follow Jenny and Steve through the doorway, leaving CeAnn and Billie alone.

"This is great!" Billie took her hand and squeezed it reassuringly. "I know you and Steve will have a wonderful time tomorrow night."

"I don't know, Billie. I probably should have refused."

"Nonsense. Where's your sense of adventure?"

242

"The same place your brother keeps his." She grimaced.

"Trust me. I know what I'm doing . . . but, CeAnn, I want only the best for Steve, so be careful with him. I have a feeling he'll bruise easily."

CeAnn nodded in sincere agreement, wondering why Billie would feel inclined to issue such a warning. Be careful with him? What did she think she was going to do to him?

Billie hated the idea of scheming against her own brother, and the thought continued to nag her later that evening as she fixed herself a cup of hot tea before bed. Maybe she was literally throwing the poor man to the wolves. After all, he had warned her on numerous occasions to stay out of his personal life and she knew without a doubt he was going to be upset by all of this.

She didn't know one thing about this CeAnn Masters other than the fact that she seemed overly eager to get something going with her brother.

Billie knew she should refrain from being a busybody and leave it to fate. If it were meant for Steve and CeAnn to get together, they would do so with no help from her. She paused in her thinking and tapped her index finger against her two front teeth. Still . . .

Steve is such a dear, she thought fondly. He didn't eat right and he didn't do his laundry as often as he should, and his apartment had been an absolute mess the last time she had dropped in on him unexpectedly. He really needs a woman to take care of him, she reasoned. If he accused her of scheming again, well . . . she could always use the excuse that pregnant women were not always responsible for their actions.

Yes, she decided, some things are better formed by meticulous planning rather than unpredictable destiny.

CHAPTER FOUR

Why was she so intent on making a fool of herself? That question kept running through CeAnn's mind as she drove to the restaurant the following night.

The thought continued to plague her: her date with Steve was not his doing. If it hadn't been for Billie, Steve would have left the club last night with barely a polite good night in her direction.

It isn't as if I'm desperate for male companionship, she defended, as her old car weaved in and out of traffic. She could hardly say that when she had just broken a date with Ruffe Sennett. Ruffe would probably never ask her out again and she couldn't blame him. The excuse, that she had to sit with a sick dog, *was* pretty weak.

Well, she might not have the heart to give up on Steve yet, but she was going to quit pretending to be someone she wasn't. All this forced flirting was going to stop. From now on she was going to be the same CeAnn Masters she had been for twenty-seven years. And if that didn't get her anywhere with Mr. Hayden, *then* she would think about giving up.

It irritated her to realize that she was acting like a teenager in high school instead of a grown woman trying her best to start if not a sophisticated then at least a mature relationship with a certain man whom she happened to find unusually attractive.

Why should that be so unreasonable?

She might not be the most beautiful woman in the world, but she certainly wasn't the ugliest. She was neat and thoughtful, and even kind when the occasion called for it. Various people had commented that she would make some lucky man a wonderful wife someday. Her brow furrowed worriedly. If all that were true, then what was it about her that turned Steve Hayden so totally off?

As she pulled into the circular drive of the elegant Grove Restaurant and stopped behind a shiny black Rolls-Royce sedan, CeAnn suddenly wished she had taken a taxi tonight. As a rule she never thought about the appearance of her car, but the old Chevy looked out of place in such luxurious surroundings.

One of the young red-coated male attendants came to help her out of the car as soon as she stopped.

He jumped in and took her place behind the wheel as she put the ticket in her wallet.

She glanced up uneasily then. The motor began to vibrate loudly. The attendant looked bewildered for a moment, then nearly jumped out of his seat as the car heaved one loud belch of blue smoke, backfired twice, and died.

"Wow. What did I do?" he exclaimed.

"Oh, you didn't do anything," CeAnn assured him. "It's that darn carburetor again. I have trouble with it all the time."

"You want me to see if I can fix it?" the attendant offered.

"Thanks, but I think I know what the problem is. It'll only take me a minute."

Walking around to the front of the car, she tried to ignore the other cars that were pulling in behind her. She unlatched the hood and jerked it open. In a few moments she had the top off the carburetor and her fingers were busy making the necessary adjustments. "Okay," she called out. "You can try it now, but you'll have to pump the gas pedal a couple of times before it will start."

The attendant obediently did as she said and the sound of the old motor laboring and straining to start filled the air.

"You may have to pump it several times," she yelled above the noisy racket.

The attendant pumped away, but the old car still refused to start.

By now the newly arrived dinner guests were growing fidgety at the delay and some began to sound their horns impatiently.

Shooting the driver directly behind her a rather impatient look herself, CeAnn tried to work faster, but all the racket was making her nervous.

"Try it again!"

He did, and it didn't.

The sound of tires screeching agitatedly on the pavement joined the ruckus. One of the cars waiting in line shot around the stalled vehicle. In a burst of anger the driver called out his window, "I suggest you push that wreck to the nearest dump, lady!"

CeAnn's head jerked out from under the hood and only the sound of the attendant trying to start the car saved the rude observer from hearing *her* suggestion.

Another few minutes and CeAnn was ready to admit defeat and call a tow truck. But the attendant decided to give it one more try. Just as it seemed this effort was doomed too, the car unexpectedly sprang to life with a series of deafening backfires. A rush of air wheezing through the carburetor blew CeAnn's hair straight up in the air. Though she was relieved to hear the old car finally cooperating, she was dismayed when the attendant continued to gun the engine loudly, causing the tailpipe to shoot up another plume of blue smoke. It smelled like old tires burning.

The dinner guests turned up their noses in distaste as they rushed for the safety of the restaurant's entrance. One of the snootier-looking women pulled out a lace handkerchief and slapped it across her nose as if she were being subjected to mustard gas instead of simple exhaust fumes.

"Hey, now that I got it started, you want me to go ahead and park it?" the attendant shouted.

By now all CeAnn wanted to do was crawl into a hole and pull a cover over it.

"Yes, I'd appreciate that," she managed. "But do you think it will start again?"

248

"Smells to me like we have it flooded," the boy speculated.

"Oh, well, if that's all it is, I'll be able to start it again. I flood it all the time," she said with a sigh of relief.

With a squeal of what rubber she had left on her tires, the attendant gunned his way around the building and, thankfully, out of sight. She lifted her head proudly and cast an imperious look at the guests still waiting for the parking attendant. Brushing a stray lock of hair out of her eye, she winced at the grease on her hand and hoped it wasn't all over her face as well. But with her luck, it would be.

Turning swiftly to the entrance, she hoped she would be able to get most of the grime washed off before Steve arrived. Thank goodness he hadn't been here to witness the latest fiasco!

"Strange. It always seems to run so well in the mornings," a familiar male voice noted dryly.

At the sound of his voice CeAnn felt the same old thrill of excitement. It never failed to make her pulse increase in tempo. She stopped her hurried entry into the restaurant and self-consciously raised her eyes to meet the blue noncommittal gaze of Steve Hayden. The unexpected joy of seeing him again was immediately replaced by the sickening realization that he had been standing there watching every moment of the event that had just taken place. And, as usual, she had come away looking like a fool.

He was casually leaning against a pole of the

restaurant's awning, his eyes taking in her now disreputable appearance.

"Oh, Steven," she greeted, less than enthusiastically. "I was hoping you hadn't gotten here yet." She felt her cheeks grow very warm as she took a deep breath and started to walk past him, determined to retain her composure in the face of this most recent catastrophe.

"I started to come over and ask if you needed any help, but you looked like you had everything under control."

"Driving a car like mine, I'm forced to be a mechanic whether I want to or not," she replied with just a trace of defensiveness in her voice.

"Yes." He looked at the traces of blue smoke still lingering in the air. "I would imagine so."

"Is there anything wrong with a woman being able to fix her own car?" she challenged. She didn't care for the superior tone his voice had taken on.

"Oh, no. I think it's nice. It's not often I meet a woman with such knowledge of a carburetor. I'll know where to go the next time mine acts up," he joked, then instantly regretted his poor choice of words, realizing she might not view them as the compliment he meant them to be. He had hoped to ease her obvious embarrassment by making light of the situation, but he sensed he had gone about it the wrong way.

When he had walked up earlier and seen her working under the hood of her car, her derriere sticking out invitingly, he had been surprised. He had also been a little irritated to feel immediately that old rush of excitement at seeing her again.

He still found it hard to believe a mature woman would go to such lengths to chase a man—and that he would foolishly allow himself to be turned on by her.

Apparently she had managed to get his own sister on her side, and together they had hatched up this hair-brained scheme, getting him to take her to dinner tonight. And he wouldn't be a bit surprised if she tried to throw herself at him again. Well, maybe he'd just do an about-face and intercept the pass this time. Maybe Kirk was right. Why shouldn't he let down his hair a little and flow with the tide?

Suddenly the idea took on a great deal more appeal than it had originally.

Yes. Why not? Maybe a wild woman was exactly what he needed to help him get over his timidity around women. And who could be wilder than CeAnn Masters?

"I'm not a mechanic by profession," she pointed out as they fell in step, strolling up the walk of the restaurant. She resented the fact that she had finally caught his eye—but not quite in the way she had intended. "What else was I supposed to do? I had traffic backed up. I had to fix it."

"Oh, I thought you did the right thing," he agreed quickly. Now that he had made up his mind to let himself be captured, he thought it best to stop antagonizing her. It was sort of thrilling to speculate on what she might do to him now that he was willing.

CeAnn kept her eyes fixed straight ahead as they walked, willing herself not to look at him any more than she had to. No matter how hard she tried, though, it was impossible to ignore the fact that he was breathtakingly handsome tonight, in a pair of gray slacks, a navy sport coat, white shirt, and burgundy-and-silver-striped tie. The faint aroma of a clean masculine aftershave drifted pleasantly to her nostrils as they walked side by side. For one brief moment she let herself pretend that she was actually his date for the evening by choice rather than by coercion. Momentarily he would turn those lovely blue eyes solely on her and comment on how nice she looked.

By all rights, he should be nice enough to do that anyway, she reasoned, since she had taken such special care in dressing tonight. The Chinese-blue sweater and skirt she was wearing was one of her favorite outfits, and she felt she always looked her best in it.

"It's nice out tonight," he commented pleasantly. "Not too hot, not too cold." He smiled politely down at her, trying to make casual conversation, but feeling he should have come up with a better line than that one.

"Yes, very nice," she murmured self-consciously, racking her brain for something cute and witty to say. But, as usual, cute and witty had fled her vocabulary.

"I hope you were able to cancel your plans tonight without any problem. I want to apologize for my sister. I mean . . . Billie really put us both on the spot, didn't she?"

"Oh, I didn't have any problem. Ruffe was very nice about it." She knew her answer had come too quickly when she saw the startled look on his face. She cleared her throat and spoke more calmly this time. "I mean, it was a very informal date and we're going to try it again some other time."

"Oh?"

He sounded skeptical.

"Yes," she continued, trying to affect an air of sophistication that was totally foreign to her. "Ruffe Sennett and I were going to have a drink together. Do you know Ruffe Sennett?" Let him stick that in his little pipe and smoke it!

"You mean that fruitcake who wears lavender shorts around the club?" He laughed in disbelief. "Yeah, I've seen him around."

CeAnn stiffened with resentment at his description of Ruffe. "He is *not* a fruitcake."

"Well, he sure looks like one to me," Steve contended.

"I don't care what he looks like to you," she said crossly. "Ruffe Sennett is one of the nicest men I know. Other men are just jealous because they can't attract women the way Ruffe does."

"Jealous? That's a hoot. Who would be jealous of a man who wears lavender shorts and—"

"Let's just drop the subject, okay?"

Realizing that they were about to become involved in an argument, Steve quickly set aside his own observations and smiled down at her congenially. "Of course." He held the outer door open for her courteously.

Giving him her most superior, dismissive look,

CeAnn quickly stepped around him and went in. "Excuse me, but I'd like to freshen up a bit before we eat."

Breezing unconcernedly through the open doorway, she then deliberately let the heavy wooden inside door slam shut in his face.

Oh, she fumed under her breath. "I've never met a woman who knew so much about carburetors. . . . Ruffe Sennett, the fruitcake who wears lavender shorts?" she mimicked as she marched toward the ladies' room. And they most certainly were not lavender shorts! They were . . . sort of pinkish.

Steve had jumped back quickly before the door could rearrange his nose, surprised at her abrupt departure. It belatedly occurred to him that no matter how eager she had been to go out with him before, she could be getting a little annoyed that he had so successfully resisted her charms this long. She probably wasn't used to that sort of treatment from a man. Not if she dated that Sennett guy. He frowned. No doubt, all the other men in her life had immediately taken her up on her offers when she had been as persistent as she had with him. He smiled knowingly. Yes, she had probably decided that she had been a little too easy, and since he hadn't been overly eager to fall into her little trap, she would now try the old hard-to-get approach. He shrugged. Well, he probably deserved that. Still, letting her know that he was now willing to accept her offer might get a little embarrassing . . . but as hot as she had been to get him, it surely wouldn't be an impossible task.

He pushed the door open and stepped into the restaurant. As his eyes adjusted to the dimly lit interior, he located CeAnn across the crowded room.

She was sitting quietly in a dark corner next to a large saltwater aquarium, trying to look as inconspicuous as possible for someone with dirt on her face and a spot of grease on her sweater.

He took a deep breath, trying to quell the new surge of shyness threatening to engulf him as he made his way over to the row of chairs.

When she saw him coming, she groaned inwardly. If the ladies' room hadn't been so crowded, she would've been in there trying to make herself presentable, instead of perching out here like a sitting duck. She frantically searched her mind for something stimulating to talk about, but found she couldn't remember one solitary subject Jenny had suggested. So she decided to handle it the only way she knew how.

She would simply ignore him.

"Through already?" He paused and looked at her as if to say "You've wasted your time and effort if you are."

"The ladies' room was too crowded. I'll have to wait until it clears out a little," she muttered.

"Oh?" He looked around uneasily, noting that there were a lot of empty seats. For a moment he toyed with the idea of blissfully sitting across the room from her. That way, neither one of them would have to make conversation. But he couldn't do that. She would probably expect him to sit next to her. "Is this seat taken?" He motioned to the empty chair beside her.

Begrudgingly, she scooted over and gave him enough room to sit down.

"Thanks." He sat down and for the next few minutes there was an appalling silence between them as they stared glumly at the fish swimming around in the tank.

Finally, the maître d' came over and asked if they had reservations, which Steve assured him they did.

"I'm sorry, but we've had a mix-up in reservations tonight and it's going to be a while before your table's ready. Please be our guests at the bar while you wait." He bowed politely and left them to their silence once more.

They looked at each other helplessly.

"You want a drink?" Steve offered. At least that would kill a few minutes while he went to get them.

"No, thanks. I'll wait."

"Oh. Well, if you change your mind, let me know."

Ten wordless minutes later Steve stirred uneasily. "They usually aren't this slow. I hope you're not too hungry."

"No, I'm fine," she assured him.

Glancing nervously at his watch a few minutes later, Steve frowned. "Our reservations were for eight. It's eight forty-five already."

"I'm sure our table will be ready anytime."

Moments later he was still fidgeting, looking at his watch again. "I think I'll go see what's holding them up." He moved away to the reservation counter and in a few minutes he came back with a worried frown on his face. "It's going to be another thirty minutes."

"Look . . . if you want, we can just skip dinner," she suggested meekly. "I'm really not all that hungry."

"No," he shot back hurriedly. "We're already here. We might as well see this thing through."

See this thing through? She seethed silently. Their date was something to be endured like a dental appointment!

More agonizing moments of silence dragged by, then she felt him staring intently at her.

"Is there something wrong?" she asked curtly.

"No . . . I just thought that the ladies' room might be empty now and you'd want to freshen up while we waited. . . ." His voice died away lamely.

Her hands flew to her face self-consciously. She had been so intent on her immediate problem of how to get through this horrible night that she had completely forgotten all about going back to the ladies room and trying to scrub off the grease. "Oh . . . yes. I believe I will. If you'll excuse me?"

"Certainly. Uh, are you sure you don't want a drink?" Steve prompted. "I'll be happy to get you one while you're gone."

"Thank you, but that won't be necessary," she answered politely. "I'll be back in a few minutes."

CeAnn was beginning to panic as she started for the powder room, wondering how she was going to get out of this embarrassing predicament. The night was turning out to bé a total disaster, not only for her but for Steve as well. She knew he would welcome a reprieve from the still-to-be-endured dinner as much as she would.

How were they going to sit across the table from each other and eat without both of them ending up with an ulcer? What she needed was a good old fashion emergency that would rescue her from this mess. . . . An emergency! Why hadn't she thought of it before!

A white-coated waiter was walking past her carrying a tray of drinks. With a pleasant smile frozen on her face, she latched on to his coattail and literally jerked him around the corner with her.

Trying to balance his wobbling margarita glasses without spilling their contents, the waiter asked in a startled but courteous voice, "May I help you, ma'am?"

"I certainly hope so." She rummaged around in her purse as she talked in a hurried whisper. "You see that man sitting out there next to the fish aquarium? When I come out of the ladies' room I'll be going back over there to sit next to him again. Now, I want you to come over and ask me if I'm Ms. Masters. I'll say I am, and then you tell me that I have a phone call." She handed him a ten-dollar bill. "Okay?"

"Yes, ma'am. Telephone call for Ms. Masters. I've got it."

"Good! Thank you very much."

Relieved that this nightmarish evening would soon be over, she ducked into the bathroom, and the waiter continued on his way.

Oh, brother! He had had miserable dates before, but this one took the cake. Steve tried to figure out what to do. It was obvious he was boring the poor woman to death. And the idea of spending another two hours with her was scaring *him* to death. For someone who had been so eager for his company, CeAnn had suddenly turned as cold and uncooperative as an iceberg. He couldn't get her to say anything she didn't have to say. What was he going to do to get them both gracefully out of their misery?

As the waiter CeAnn had stopped walked by, Steve abruptly stood and stopped him, causing the man to balance his tray of drinks precariously once more.

"Excuse me. Could you do me a big favor?"

"Yes, sir." The waiter straightened and drew a deep breath, relieved that he had again managed to save the contents of the tray.

Steve drew a ten-dollar bill from his pocket while keeping a nervous eye on the door leading to the ladies room. "In a few minutes a lady is going to join me again. When she does, will you please come over and ask if I would happen to be Steve Hayden? I'll say yes, then you say that I have—"

"A phone call," the waiter finished dryly.

"Yes . . ." Steve eyed him suspiciously. "How did you know what I was going to ask?"

"Just a lucky guess, sir."

"Oh. Well, can you do it?"

"Yes, sir. I'm to come over and ask if you happen

to be Steve Hayden. You'll say yes, and I'll say you have a phone call."

"Right . . . just as soon as she comes out."

"Right."

Steve sank back down on his seat, tickled pink with the plan that had suddenly occurred to him. He might be a little dull, but CeAnn would have to hand it to him if she ever found out what he was doing. He could be as crafty and cunning as a wolf when the occasion called for it. Not to mention original. Not many people would be able to fabricate an emergency just at the right time. Too bad, he thought with a fleeting pang that felt suspiciously like disappointment. Now that he had been around her a bit, she wasn't all that bad. In fact, if circumstances were different and she would try a little harder, they both might have enjoyed the evening.

Five minutes later CeAnn emerged from the ladies' room looking much more presentable, and took her seat next to Steve.

Steve glanced over apologetically. "Sorry. No table yet."

She smiled brightly. "Well, I'm sure it won't be much longer now."

Why was life so unfair? she thought wistfully as they both resumed watching the fish. For the past week she had been beating her brains out trying to get a date with Steve, and now that she was actually out with him, she was sitting around acting like a tongue-tied idiot.

"Pardon me, would you happen to be Ms. Masters?" the waiter asked as he walked up to them.

"Yes." She put on her most convincing puzzled look. "Why?"

"There's a telephone call for you, ma'am."

Steve glanced at her in surprise, then at the waiter with distrust. Ten dollars and the guy couldn't get the message straight.

"For me?" She heaved a resigned sigh. "It must be Jenny. She's the only person who knows I'm here."

"Jenny? I thought she had a date tonight."

She crossed her fingers behind her back. "She did, but she had to cancel because she didn't feel well and I told her to call if she needed me. Excuse me for a moment?"

"If you'll follow me, ma'am." The waiter led the way and it was but a few minutes before she returned for her purse. "Jenny's really not well. I'm sorry, but I'm going to have to leave."

Steve rose to his feet politely. "That's too bad."

Suddenly the same waiter was back, grinning like a sly fox. "Excuse me, sir, but would you happen to be Steve Hayden?" he parroted in a monotone.

"Uh, yes." Steve tried to signal that the fake summons would no longer be necessary, but with CeAnn standing right there, it was impossible.

"You have a telephone call, sir."

"Oh. You sure it's for me?" he asked lamely.

"Yes, sir. It's for you."

He looked at CeAnn sheepishly and shrugged. "Excuse me."

He ambled away guiltily, thinking about the ten dollars he had just blown. Moments later he was

261

back. "What a coincidence. That was Kirk. There's been an emergency and they're calling in extra help."

"Oh? I hope it isn't anything serious."

He grabbed the first thing that entered his mind. "Train derailment."

"How awful. Well, it's been nice visiting with you," she murmured. "I guess I'll be running along."

"Yeah . . . uh, listen, I'll walk you to your car," he offered hesitantly.

"Oh, you don't have to."

"That's okay," he insisted.

He fell into step with her as she walked out the front door into the cool night air.

"Strange, isn't it? I mean, we both get called away for an emergency," she mused as she pulled out her parking ticket.

"Yes, I was thinking that myself." He lowered his eyes and pretended an unusual interest in the shine on his shoes. "What's wrong with Jenny? She seemed fine last night."

"Some kind of stomach virus. Were there many people hurt?"

He looked at her vacantly. "When?"

"In the derailment?"

"Oh. The derailment . . . well, Kirk didn't say. Hopefully not."

"Yes . . . hopefully not." She took a long, cleansing breath of the crisp night air and glanced up into the clear, autumn sky, ablaze with stars. "It seems much cooler than when we went in. I should have brought a jacket."

Handing the attendant her parking ticket, she was surprised to find that Steve was going to wait with her until they brought the car around.

"Yeah, this time of year you always need a jacket," he agreed. Shrugging out of his sport coat, he quietly draped it around her shoulders. His delicious male smell assaulted her senses as she closed her eyes and snuggled down into the warmth that had been his a moment earlier. Even if he hadn't reminded her so much of Jess, there was a certain something about him that attracted her.

"CeAnn . . ." It wasn't in Steve Hayden's nature to be dishonest with anyone, and his conscience was already bothering him. Common sense told him it would only be a matter of time before she found out there was no train derailment, so he might as well tell her the truth and get it over with. "I have a confession to make."

Glancing up at him, she smiled. "What?"

"I . . . there is no emergency. I made that up."

Her lower lip began to quiver. "You did?"

"Yes. I'm sorry. But I just thought that I was boring you to death and you would be happier if you could go home."

Now it was her conscience nagging at her. "That's not true. . . . I was having a nice time. I thought it was you who were bored and wanted to go home."

"Me?"

"Yeah . . . you."

"No, I wasn't bored," he said. "I just thought I was making you miserable."

"Then I have a confession to make too."

He looked at her warily. "What?"

"Jenny isn't sick. She's on that date."

He put his hands on his hips. "Then you don't have an emergency either?"

"Nope." She grinned impishly.

They both burst out laughing. "And I thought I was being so clever," Steve confessed.

"Well, you know what they say. Great minds work in the same channels, or something like that."

Now that the tension between them had eased somewhat, Steve let his basic good nature shine through. "I'll tell you what. I'm hungry. How about you? And it just so happens I know a little place not far from here that isn't very fancy, but it has great hamburgers and chili."

She would've dearly loved to go with him, but CeAnn knew he was only being polite again. No matter what he said, after spending the last two hours with her he had undoubtedly discovered she was not the exciting, outgoing woman she had pretended to be. Now he knew what a true drip she really was and he had to be bored to death. "Oh, no. That would be too much trouble. I think I'll just go on home."

Steve eyed her in confusion, finding it hard to believe this was the same woman who had been so feverishly chasing him for the past few days. Was she actually going to play hard to get now, when he had decided to give in? "It wouldn't be any trouble," he persisted. "I'm starved."

He was being polite again. "Thanks, maybe next

time." There would be no next time and she knew it, but he was being gracious about it, so she could be too.

He looked at her again, trying to figure out what he was supposed to do next.

The attendant came back around the corner with a frown on his face. "Your car won't start again, ma'am."

CeAnn groaned. "I was afraid of that."

"You're welcome to leave it here overnight," he offered. "You can send a tow truck for it tomorrow morning."

"Thank you. It's getting so late I think that's what I'll have to do," she accepted gratefully.

"Can I call a taxi for you?" the attendant asked.

She started to give her consent when Steve interrupted. "No, I'll take the lady home." He handed the attendant his parking ticket. "It's a white Riviera."

"Yes, sir. I remember the one."

"Steve, I can't impose on you to take me home," CeAnn protested as the attendant left to get the car.

"It's no imposition," he said. He was determined not to let the night end this soon. A faint whiff of her earthy perfume drifted enticingly on the night air, subtly recalling to mind what pleasures awaited him if he played his cards right. He suddenly found his male instincts aroused as they stood waiting for the attendant to bring his car.

There was no doubt about it, she was beautiful.

And inviting.

And, up until a few hours ago, perfectly willing.

Well, maybe he wasn't the kind of man she was used to, but now that he had made up his mind to stop fighting her advances, he would just have to swallow his timidity and be the kind of man she expected him to be.

Now that he had come to grips with himself and admitted she did arouse a certain excitement in him that no other woman had managed quite so easily, he would be able to bluff his way through the next few hours as well as the next guy.

He hoped.

CHAPTER FIVE

"It's the second dirt road on the left."

The sound of her voice breaking the silence was startling for a moment. They hadn't exchanged a word since leaving the restaurant, each one racking his brain for something to talk about—but failing. For a few moments outside the restaurant they had finally let down and enjoyed themselves, but the ride home had brought on that ominous silence once more.

The Riviera made the turn and bounced along the gravel road for a few minutes before she spoke again. "It's the yellow house on the right."

The headlights swept over the small clapboard house as the car pulled into the drive and stopped. The pleasant sounds of night creatures filled the car as they sat for a moment, listening.

"You like living way out here?" he asked.

"Yes, I love it." She took a deep breath and leaned her head back, closing her eyes. "I especially love the sounds out here. It's so peaceful and comforting."

"Yes, they are nice," he agreed. "How long have you lived here?"

"Three years. I used to live with a friend. We had a small apartment in town, but when she got married I decided that, with my life-style, I needed a place of my own. When I found this house I fell in love with it immediately."

"Then you don't get lonely out here by yourself?"

"Goodness, no!" She laughed, thinking of all the animals she had to keep her company. "I usually have all the company I can handle."

Steven felt a surge of jealousy shoot through him as he thought of the other men in her life. Why he should care, he didn't know. After all, wasn't he here to take advantage of her . . . generosity himself?

"You have a lot of male companionship, huh?" he asked pleasantly, letting his hand casually drop to her knee.

CeAnn froze for a moment. Was that his hand? Cautiously, she opened one eye and stared at the weight on her knee. It *was* his hand. She sighed. And Billie thought her brother was shy! Ha! She'd always heard you had to watch the quiet ones.

"Yes, they're mostly male," she conceded hesitantly, keeping her eye trained on his hand. "I try to arrange it so I only keep five of the healthiest to take care of myself, and I pass the rest on to whoever wants them. But it's getting harder all the time to get rid of them once they've gotten a taste of my hospitality," she admitted. "I'm afraid I spoil every one I come in contact with."

At the rate people were dumping their animals, she often accumulated as many as six males and seven or eight females before she could find them new homes.

"The healthiest?" he questioned with a distasteful lift of his brow.

"Well, none of them have been unhealthy," she corrected, "but I'm sort of selective about what jumps up on my bed and sleeps with me." She grinned.

His lip quivered and he reluctantly withdrew his hand from her leg. "Yeah, I'd feel the same way." His blue eyes narrowed suspiciously. "You never, um, picked up anything from them . . . did you?"

There's still plenty of time to back out of this, he reminded himself. He had never kidded himself that she was a one-man woman, but he had never thought of her as being *that* . . . loose either.

"Nope! I guess I've been lucky, but they've all been fairly clean. Oh, a couple have looked pretty shaggy and one smelled like a rotten goat, but it's amazing what a good bath will do for them." She smiled, somewhat encouraged by his interest in her animals. "Would you like to come in and meet my animals?" she asked expectantly.

"There's some of them here—right now?" he asked incredulously.

"Sure." She looked at him warily. Where else would she keep them? "I have five dogs, a chicken, a canary, and three cats."

"Oh!" He let out a sigh of relief. Somewhere along the way she had switched subjects on him, as all women had an unnerving way of doing. She was talking about her pets!

"Well, sure. I'd like to see them," he agreed. Since he had never been with a woman like CeAnn before, he didn't know what to expect. Apparently this must be her way of getting the ball rolling. Instead of seeing her etchings, he would see her menagerie. A most unusual approach, if he did say so himself.

They got out of the car and walked to the door. She fished around in her purse for the key. Grumbling about the fact that she was going to have to get around to cleaning the thing out someday, she handed him assorted paraphernalia to hold while she continued. Steve was just deciding she wouldn't be able to find a hotel in that mess, let alone a tiny key, when she finally produced the object of her search.

Steve could hear a bunch of dogs barking as she unlocked the door. It sounded more like a kennel in there than only five animals. As they walked in, CeAnn's full entourage met them, including the three cats and a strange-looking chicken. A large Doberman jumped up on him and he staggered, eyeing the dog fearfully. "I hope he doesn't bite."

"Oh, Blackie is a good dog," CeAnn assured him.

Blackie was licking the side of Steve's face when a large collie decided to join the gathering.

"Get down, Goldie," CeAnn scolded, dragging the overly friendly dogs from him. "Go over there and sit down next to Brownie and Whitey," she ordered. She turned to Steve and smiled. "The dogs' names aren't very original. It's just much

270

simpler for me to name them whatever color they happen to be. Blackie! I mean it! Get off him!"

The Doberman, in his exuberance at having company, had nearly knocked Steve to his knees. CeAnn rushed over to remove the dog a second time. "They're all very friendly," she said. "You'll have to forgive their manners."

Steve took out his handerchief and wiped his face. He had never particularly cared for overly affectionate dogs, and he had seen nothing in the past few minutes to make him change his mind.

"Just take a seat and I'll get us something to drink," CeAnn said. "Will coffee be all right?"

"Coffee's fine." He replaced his handkerchief in his pocket, his eyes darting uneasily about the room to see where the dogs had gone. They were all sitting in the corner, neatly lined up watching him as hawks watch a chicken. Brownie, Blackie, Goldie, Whitey, and a little Heinz fifty-seven the color of mud stared back at him with their tongues hanging loosely out of their mouths. The cats had disbanded, the Siamese draped comfortably over the television set while the calico sprawled out on an arm of the sofa and the yellow one, whose breed Steve couldn't immediately ascertain, occupied the only other empty chair in the room. There were other chairs in the rom, he noted, but they had so much stuff on them it would take a week to clean one off so he could sit down.

Giving the dogs another wary look, he cautiously started over to the frayed footstool in front of a frazzled, overstuffed chair. He suddenly sucked in his breath and his eyes widened as he felt his foot slide in a pile of something slick. He groped in the air for support, then went to his knees once again.

"You'll have to pardon the house," she called from the kitchen. "I'm afraid I'm not much of a housekeeper."

"Oh, it looks fine," he lied. He got back to his feet, trying to refrain from profanity, and ripped a page from the old newspaper lying on the floor. Seconds later he was grimly trying to scrape the animal feces off the bottom of his shoe. Since he had always had an extremely weak stomach, he found himself trying to keep from gagging as he shot the dogs a series of dirty looks. To his dismay, the odor was stronger than his determination. When CeAnn returned to the room a few minutes later, he was embarrassedly wiping tears from his cheeks with his handkerchief.

"Is something wrong?" She paused and looked at his sickly features.

"Uh, I just stepped in some . . . uh . . . over there by the sofa." He hated to be rude and point it out, but he sure as hell didn't want to step in it again either!

CeAnn slapped her leg in exasperation and turned to level a stern gaze at the dogs. "All right, guys. Which one of you is guilty this time?"

By their angelic expressions, none of them could be guilty of such a crude and unsociable act. It had to be the cats' fault. The cats looked up at the sound of her stern voice and it was plain to see *they* were innocent.

"You're *all* going to be banned from the house if

you don't stop doing this," she warned, going to the kitchen for a wet paper towel. She returned seconds later and cleaned up the remaining mess. "I'm terribly sorry. Did you get it off the bottom of your shoe?"

"Yes, I think so. . . ." It didn't really matter. Steve planned on throwing the shoes away when he got home anyway.

"Well, just have a seat. I'll have our coffee ready in a few minutes."

She disappeared back into the kitchen and he could hear her rattling dishes around as he took his place on the footstool.

He sat quietly looking around the cluttered room, trying to decide if he should make his excuses and leave now or have coffee and then go. He supposed he should be polite enough to stick around for the coffee, since she had gone to all the trouble of making it. But as far as staying for anything else, he was having second thoughts. Somehow the thought of having an affair with her had dimmed considerably since he'd entered the front door.

His eyes roamed the room absently. There was a large cage hanging in the corner and he noticed a small yellow canary sleeping on the perch. How he could do that despite all the ruckus was a puzzle to Steve, but the bird seemed to manage without any trouble at all.

From the corner of his eye he saw a black streak shoot out of the kitchen and race across the room to duck behind the sofa. He wasn't sure if his eyes had been playing tricks on him, but the damn thing looked like a skunk.

Dismissing the idea as preposterous, he let his gaze once more roam the room. It was furnished sparsely with mismatched pieces, odds and ends. Unless he missed his guess, CeAnn had furnished the entire house out of a used-furniture store.

A noise caught his attention and he glanced down at his feet. His eyes widened, first in disbelief then outright terror, as the black animal, a white stripe running down its back, leaped up on his lap and stared straight into his eyes.

"Oh, hell . . . CeAnn," he muttered sickly.

"Did you say something?" CeAnn walked to the kitchen door and peered into the living room. She froze when she saw him staring eyeball to eyeball with the skunk.

"Oh, that's Little Stinker." She sighed. "I forgot to tell you about him."

"Is he safe?" Steve was afraid to move a muscle: the standoff continued.

"Sure. I mean, I guess so. I found him when he was a baby and he's never done anything . . . yet." Her face clouded momentarily. "I guess I really should have him checked to see if he's been descented." She shrugged, deciding to add that little chore to her list of things to do next week. "Just push him off your lap if he's bothering you."

He was bothering him, so Steve took a deep breath and gave the furry animal a gentle shove. Deciding the new visitor wasn't all that interesting, the skunk soon disappeared into the kitchen where CeAnn had gone back to work.

Trying to settle his nerves, Steve took a deep breath and ran his hands through his hair. This place was a madhouse! As he gradually relaxed, his gaze fell on an eight-by-ten family portrait on a round wooden whiskey barrel serving as a table. Curiosity made him go over for a closer look at what he assumed was CeAnn's family. He picked up the picture and studied the people who smiled back happily. She had two sisters and a brother, and he saw that she bore a striking resemblance to her mother. Studying the handsome, youngish-looking couple standing beside their children, he quickly decided neither one of her parents looked old enough to have kids that age.

Replacing the picture carefully, he walked over and sat back down. He couldn't imagine why it was taking so long to make two cups of coffee. A low clucking sound caught his attention and his gaze fell on a chicken standing at his feet.

The hen tilted her head sideways and studied him intently with two beady eyes.

For a moment they tried to outstare each other, then Steve finally broke. "Shouldn't you be in your nest?"

"Did you say something?" CeAnn hollered from the kitchen.

"No, I mean . . . I was talking to this chicken."

"Oh, that's Ms. Cluckie."

"I would have been disappointed if her name had been anything else," Steve grumbled underneath his breath.

"What?"

"I said that's nice!"

"Someone told me she's an Australian chicken, whatever that is. I found her wandering along the road one afternoon during a thunderstorm. She was nearly drowned so I brought her home to dry out and she's just hung around ever since." CeAnn came back in the room carrying a tray. "I decided since you were starved, I'd fix us a sandwich to go with our coffee. I hope you don't mind."

He wasn't sure if he did or not. But after careful inspection of her house he had come to the conclusion that, despite the earlier, unsanitary incident involving the animals, it was a fairly clean cluttered mess she lived in.

"I hope you like tuna. That's all I had," she apologized.

"I like tuna," he verified readily. His gaze drifted down inquisitively to the two soup bowls on the tray. They were filled with coffee.

"You'll have to excuse my dishes too," she said embarrassedly. "I'm afraid I've broken all my coffee cups and I keep forgetting to replace them when I do my shopping." She handed him a napkin with his sandwich on it. "I have some potato chips if you want them, unless the dogs got into them while I was gone today."

"No. No, this will do fine."

At her mention of them the five dogs came to hover around the couple, hoping for a handout.

"Go away, guys," CeAnn said. "You've already been fed." She bit into her sandwich and shooed the dogs away with her free hand.

"Would you care if I washed my hands?" Steve asked suddenly.

"No, not at all. You can use the kitchen sink or the bathroom; it's off my bedroom."

"The kitchen sink will be fine," he said hurriedly.

The kitchen was in perfect harmony with the front room, he noticed as he picked up the bar of soap in the sink and vigorously lathered his hands, the thought of his earlier harrowing encounter still troubling him. There were dirty dishes on the counters and stove, and at least eight bowls of cat and dog food on the floor. There was an empty cardboard box filled with straw next to the refrigerator, and in the nest was one blue egg. Ms. Cluckie's pad, no doubt, he thought, wondering how the devil she had managed to lay a blue egg.

Turning off the water, he searched for the paper towels, but found only an empty cardboard cylinder. The lady might be beautiful and willing, but she is definitely a lousy housekeeper, he concluded as he shook the remaining water off his hands and wiped them dry on his pants.

He had to sidestep a large aluminum basin in the center of the room, filled with water. Various doggie treats littered his path as he carefully made his way back to the living room.

"Would you care to bring the milk for our coffee?" CeAnn called.

Crunching his way back through the dog biscuits, Steve went to the refrigerator and opened the door. He stood for a moment, his puzzled eyes blinking at the monstrous plastic sack confronting him. He wasn't sure if she was making her own penicillin or if it was her neglected ironing molding away in there. Reaching for the carton of milk, he shut the door and returned quickly to the living room.

"Thanks," she said. He handed her the carton, then sat down opposite her. "I didn't know if you used cream or sugar."

"No, I drink mine black." For a moment he was undecided on how to begin his meal. He had never drunk coffee from a soup bowl, but he reasoned there would only be one way to do it. Picking up the bowl with both hands, he took a cautious sip, then smiled at her politely. "It's very good."

"I hope I didn't make it too strong."

"No, this is fine."

She picked up his sandwich and handed it to him again. "I hope you don't mind eating two heels. I'm afraid I'm out of bread too."

He looked at the two thick slices of bread in his hand. "No, I don't mind."

She must be out of lettuce and mayonnaise too, he thought a few minutes later as he tried to swallow a wad of dry tuna. It was the driest sandwich he had ever tried to eat.

"Would you like more tuna?" she inquired eagerly. "I have plenty. I always keep it around for the cats."

To his chagrin a thin spray of dry bread crumbs came out of his mouth as he hastened to refuse her offer. Grabbing for a napkin, he fought to keep from choking, and shook his head wordlessly.

"Oh, dear. I'll get you a glass of water." CeAnn

278

jumped up and was back in a minute, holding a glass out to him.

After she administered a few helpful pats to his back, he managed to draw a deep breath and feebly return the remainder of his sandwich to the tray.

"Are you through?" she asked disappointedly.

"I think I'll just drink my coffee," he said hoarsely, groping blindly for the soup bowl.

While she placed the remains of their dinner on the tray, he finished his coffee and set the bowl back on it too.

"I think there might be some old cookies in the kitchen," she suggested. He doesn't eat much for a man of his size, she thought.

"I'm fine, really."

Shoving aside a stack of magazines on the sofa, she tucked her feet in under her and leaned back to enjoy the rest of her coffee. With dinner over there was nothing to make the conversation flow as it had, and once more they found themselves searching for something to say to one another.

During a moment of silence Steve supposed he should be making some sort of move, but he couldn't decide what it should be. What would Kirk do in this situation? No, he couldn't do that!

She picked up an emory board and became unusually absorbed in her thumbnail. Billie's words kept ringing over and over in her mind. He was shy. That was why he wasn't paying any attention to her. Studying him through lowered lashes, CeAnn remembered the feel of his hand on her leg in the car earlier. It hadn't particularly been doing anything, just lying there, yet it was the closest he had ever come to touching her personally. What would Jenny do in this situation? She continued to eye him discreetly. No, she couldn't do that, even though she was sure it was what a man of his experience would expect her to do!

Or was he that experienced?

Maybe Billie had been right and he wasn't a man-about-town at all. Well, the only way to find out was to ask. Maybe if she did, that would clear the air. If he admitted to being shy, then they both could have a good laugh when she confessed that she was too, and maybe they could start anew.

Taking a deep breath, she summoned up every ounce of courage she possessed, trying to keep the color from flooding her cheeks.

"Steve . . ."

"Yes?" He glanced up guiltily.

"I have the feeling . . . you don't care for me. Is that true?"

"No." He sat up straighter. "Why do you say that?"

"Well, I mean you are single, and I have been coming on rather strong to you with no success. Could it be . . . maybe you're shy?" The telltale color spread across her cheeks. She felt as though she were coming down with a fever.

She was torn between hoping he would adamantly deny the fact and help her out, or else confess he was shy, and thus alleviate once and for all her fear that he was not attracted to her.

"Me? Shy?" He laughed nervously. "Of course not." Swallowing a lump that threatened to cut off his air supply, he edged forward on his stool and reached for her hand. "Haven't I been moving fast enough for you?"

"Oh, yes . . . I mean . . . no." She felt herself blushing clear to the roots of her hair. What was she supposed to say now?

He edged a little closer, feeling a small surge of confidence. "Well, I was just thinking you might want to go in and slip into something more comfortable," he suggested lightly.

She laughed weakly. Her heart was beginning to pound uncomfortably in her chest at the touch of his hand on hers. "I'm very comfortable. Besides, I haven't done the wash, and everything I have is dirty."

"Oh." He lifted a brow in indecision. "You haven't got anything?"

She shook her head nervously. "Nothing."

He took a deep breath and looked around for a moment. "Well, I suppose you wouldn't need to change." He reached over and tried to take her in his arms, to kiss her, but one of the cats had jumped on her lap and was looking up at him with adoring green eyes.

"Can you get the cat off your lap?"

"Oh, sure." The cat hit the floor on all four feet as she smiled pleasantly and slid closer to Steve.

Suddenly he lunged at her, and before she knew what was happening, he was giving her a searing kiss, pushing her back into the couch. His unexpected ardor thrilled and frightened her at the same time. His hands soon grew as bold as his kisses, and a few minutes later she was forced to slap one of them in its lusty wandering, and to push him off her rather roughly.

"What's the matter?" he asked in surprise.

"I . . ." She laughed shakily. "Whew. Let's slow down a little bit."

Steve was instantly contrite. He sat back and let her regain her shattered composure. "Oh, sure. I'm sorry. I thought . . . you were ready."

Ready! she thought resentfully, eyeing him as she sought to straighten her tangled clothing. For what, the Saturday-night wrestling matches?

They sat for a moment in uneasy silence as he graciously allowed her to catch her breath. She glanced at him shyly and her pulse increased in tempo once again. Here she was acting like an idiot when he was actually trying to make an honest-to-goodness pass at her. And she realized if she were ever to have a prayer of attracting him, she would have to swallow her own shyness and be a little more accommodating.

Her hands slowly trailed around his neck and she waited breathlessly as his mouth slowly descended to meet hers.

"You asked me a while ago if I liked you," he said in a husky whisper, brushing his lips tenderly across hers. He realized as he spoke the words that he *did* like her—very much—and he was ashamed for coming on to her so strong a minute ago. He had always been a gentleman where women were concerned, and from now on he would treat her with the respect he'd show any other woman. "I like you very much," he finished softly.

Her eyes grew warm and limpid as she stared at

his handsome features and tried to still her erratic pulse. "You know something? I was afraid you were never going to notice me," she confessed shyly.

"I hardly see how I could have failed." He chuckled.

"I was afraid I might scare you away with all my . . . flirting. I don't usually do that with a man."

"Scare me away?" he bluffed. "No, I've decided you're just the kind of woman I need right now." His lips touched the tip of her nose affectionately.

She sighed, hardly daring to believe his words. "You're just what I want in my life right now too," she whispered.

"Then I don't think we should waste any more time, do you?" he murmured suggestively.

Their lips touched gently and she heard his soft intake of breath as he pulled her tighter against him. Moments later their mouths willingly melted into each other's in a long, satisfying kiss. He tasted as wonderful and as marvelous as he looked. And at that moment she seriously doubted if Jess McIntosh could ever have held a candle to Steve Hayden.

"Do you want to go to bed now?" he whispered hesitantly when their lips parted a few moments later.

She hated to see the evening end, but there would surely be many more to look forward to now that the ice had been broken. "Yes, I hate to, but I really think I should. It's been a long day, and I'm visiting friends in the city tomorrow. I'll have to get a ride from them after I get my car taken care of." She stood up regretfully to walk him to the door. "Will you call me Monday?"

He blinked and stared at her. He might not be the most experienced man in the world, but unless he missed his guess, he was being dismissed!

"Uh . . . yeah. I suppose I can." He stood up and shuffled halfheartedly after her, wondering what in the world had gone wrong.

"Good." She paused and smiled at him pleasantly. "I'll be home from work around seven."

"Okay."

Opening the door, she waited to see if he would kiss her again, but he didn't. He's a strange man, she thought, hot one minute, cold the next.

But she liked him regardless, she realized a few minutes later as she turned out the porch light and locked the door.

She liked him a lot.

CHAPTER SIX

"Dispatch, this is car twenty-three."

"Car twenty-three. Go ahead," a pleasant female voice said over the crackling radio.

"I'll be out on foot patrol in the seven-hundred block of Chanccy Street for the next couple of hours," the officer said.

"Clear, car twenty-three. Have a nice day."

Steve was still smiling when he replaced the mike in its holder and switched on his portable radio. Sandi Weller was one of those fellow employees who made the workday a little easier. Divorced, the mother of three small children, she was still always bubbly of spirit and never failed to have a sympathetic ear for anyone who needed it. More than one co-worker, male and female both, had been guilty of pouring out their troubles to Sandi over a cup of coffee after their shifts had ended.

For one brief moment Steve toyed with the idea of asking Sandi's advice about his own personal dilemma, then quickly discarded the idea.

Just the thought of CeAnn Masters made him a little edgy. Because of her little teasing games he had spent two long, miserable nights and the whole day Sunday fretting, and he still hadn't been able to figure out what had gone wrong. Everything had seemed to be moving along fine until he'd asked her if she wanted to go to bed. Maybe that *had* been a little direct, but she had certainly been acting as if she were more than ready to get on with things. He still had a nagging sense that he'd handled the situation badly. He had been banking on her taking the lead after the ice was broken, but the only place she'd led him was to the front door for a polite good night.

He shook his head disgustedly and stepped out of the patrol car. Who could figure a woman?

The downtown traffic was bustling along as he hurriedly crossed the street and walked into Mayfields, one of the largest department stores in Donovan. He continued to tell himself he hadn't picked this store to make his rounds in today for any particular reason other than that he hadn't been in for a while. And I certainly didn't pick it because CeAnn mentioned that she worked behind the cosmetic counter here, he insisted as he sauntered through the store. He paused to exchange small talk with the floor managers and various employees, seeking to assure them that the police department was within easy reach should the need arise.

Well over an hour after he'd entered the store, Steve found himself drifting in the direction of the cosmetic counter. It isn't really necessary to go by that department at all, he reasoned, but since I'm here, I might as well stop by for a few minutes. If

286

he should happen to see her, it would save him the trouble of making the promised phone call, something he wasn't all that comfortable about doing. It was quite possible at this hour she would be gone to lunch; if she was, then he might call her tonight, and then again, he might not.

The sultry smell of perfume and powder drew him closer to his goal. He tried to look interested in the products displayed. From the corner of his eye he tried to locate CeAnn without being obvious, but the only lady standing behind the counter was Jenny Cochran.

When Jenny glanced up and saw him standing there, her face brightened and she rushed over to join him.

"Steve! What a surprise to see you," she exclaimed.

Steve's smile bordered on the guilty. "Hi. I was just walking my beat and thought I'd stop by and say hello."

"I'm so glad you did! Listen, CeAnn and I really enjoyed ourselves at the club the other night. We'll have to do it more often," she encouraged, hoping to boost his lagging relationship with CeAnn. "If Kirk can't make it, maybe we can pick up a fourth person at the club."

"Yeah, that sounds like a good idea."

"Listen to me babble on! I'm sure you didn't stop in to say hi to me," she apologized. "Does CeAnn know you're here?"

"No, I—"

"She's with a customer right now, but I know

she'll want to see you," Jenny assured him. "I'll send her over as soon as she's free."

"Yeah, thanks." By then he had managed to locate CeAnn, who was at the opposite end of the counter talking with a good-looking guy. He seemed to be enjoying the conversation a bit too much for Steve's taste. His pulse quickened at the sight of her and he felt a familiar tightening in his loins. She looked unusually pretty today, but then, he was beginning to think that every time he saw her lately.

The lilting sound of her laughter reached him as he forced himself to turn his attention back to the bottle of perfume he had picked up. He tried to ignore the surge of jealousy suddenly overwhelming him. Whoever the guy was, she was having a good time with him.

As the couple continued chatting, a man wearing a florist cap walked up and handed CeAnn a bouquet of a dozen long-stem American Beauty roses.

For a moment he could tell she was speechless, but after hastily reading the card, she squealed and threw her arms around the neck of the man smiling down at her with affection.

Steve stiffened with resentment as Jenny ran over to join in the excitement. The two women examined the flowers. Moments later several employees from other departments joined the festivities and it was a good ten minutes before the department settled down to normal.

Steve watched the exchange going on before him with a growing disgust. Apparently this was another of CeAnn's acquaintances. Steve eyed the stranger with growing animosity, then slammed the perfume bottle down on the counter.

He spun around and started to leave the department. Then he heard his name being called. Glancing resentfully in the direction the female summons had come from, he saw CeAnn waving at him, a friendly, expectant smile on her pretty face.

"Steve . . . wait! Hi!"

Tossing her a halfhearted wave, he continued his departure, and would have made it if she hadn't scurried from behind the counter to intercept him.

"Hi," she said again in a breathless voice, blocking his path.

"Hi."

"I didn't know you were here," she explained.

"You were busy," he noted curtly.

"Were you looking for me?" she prompted, hardly daring to believe he was.

She gazed up at him hopefully, trying to still her heart as it pounded like a jackhammer.

He towered above her, solemnly returning her gaze. "I was walking my beat and thought I'd stop by and see . . ." His voice faltered as he gazed into her sparkling gray eyes. She has eyes a man could drown in, he thought longingly. Then he managed to regain control of his tingling senses. She also has an unnerving way of looking so damn innocent when she wants to, he reminded himself sharply. "To see if you wanted to call off our date this evening," he finished.

Her gaze widened at his suggestion. "Call off our date? Why?"

"I thought you might have made a change in your plans." His gaze drifted involuntarily over to the man still standing at the counter where she had been working. Roses didn't come cheap, and the guy would probably expect her to cancel any previous plans she might have had to go out with him. The thought tore at his insides painfully. Why? Why was he falling for a woman like CeAnn Masters?

"No, I haven't made any change in plans." Her heart sank. He wants to break the date, she realized, but I'll be darned if I'll give him any help. She had fought long and hard to get to where she was with him and she wasn't about to let him off this easy.

"You haven't?"

She managed a brave smile. "No, I haven't." She noticed they were having one of their "witty" conversations again.

"That man over there. Who is he?" he demanded suddenly, praying that she would laugh and say, Oh, that's my brother. Come on over and meet him!

He had changed the subject so abruptly it took a minute for her to grasp the question. She turned around to see whom his eyes were impaling. "Oh, him?" She laughed. "That's Palmer Jarvis. He's a good friend."

Steve's face fell like an underbaked cake. "Oh." He knew he shouldn't have asked.

"Would you like to meet him?" she offered

brightly. "He just sent me the most lovely bouquet of flowers in repayment of—"

"No!" he exclaimed, before she could finish telling him she'd been helping Palmer select gifts for his wife for the past three years. The couple had sent her the flowers as a gesture of their gratitude.

He shuddered inwardly. Roses . . . This woman sure knew how to pick boyfriends. "I don't want to meet him. I was just wondering who he was."

"He's very nice," she insisted.

"I'm sure he is." He took a deep breath, trying to decide if she was actually worth all his misery. It would be so much better for him to walk away now . . . before he got in one inch deeper.

She continued to gaze up at him, the smell of her perfume tantalizing his senses. He felt his knees getting weak with temptation. *It's not as if I want to marry the woman,* he rationalized. *One night . . . that's all he wanted* and then he would have her out of his system. "Well, I suppose if you're still agreeable, then our date's still on," he concluded.

She felt herself going limp with relief. "Good." She resented the fact that he acted as if he were talking about his execution instead of a simple date, but she'd take whatever she could get.

He cleared his throat and nervously ran the rim of his hat along his hand. "Is seven-thirty too late?"

"No, seven-thirty would be fine."

His gaze finally met hers and held for a moment. The clear, arresting blue of his eyes was deep and oh-so-inviting as she gazed wistfully back at him. *Why do we seem to have such a hard time getting* together? she agonized. She might not be his type, but she was certainly going to try her very best to keep from boring him to death again.

"Well, I guess you'd better be getting back to your . . . friend," he said. "I should be getting back to work myself."

"Yes, I see Ms. Harrison giving me the evil eye." She hesitated for a moment, then extended her hand and they shook politely. It was as if they had just concluded a grueling business negotiation. "I'll be ready at seven-thirty."

Men!

CeAnn watched him walk away, still shaking her head in bewilderment. Saturday night she would have bet her last dollar she was finally making progress with him, but today he seemed as aloof and unapproachable as he had ever been. Well, she was going to force herself to be bright and witty and totally captivating tonight. Her eyes grew steely with determination. She *was* going to gain ground with him this evening or know the reason why.

It seemed as if seven-thirty would never come. Then CeAnn finally heard Steve's car pull up in the drive, and she quickly smoothed the nonexistent wrinkles out of the magenta shirt-dress she was wearing. She paused before the mirror to check her appearance one last time. She was still apprehensive about it. When the time came to apply fresh makeup after her shower, she just hadn't had the heart to put all those creams and blushers and eyeshadows back on. Instead, she had used only a soft rose blusher and just a touch of burgundy lip gloss. Her thick black hair was not disorganized and windblown as usual, but styled instead in one neat French braid that barely reached her back.

Critically studying the image before her, she had to admit she didn't look a thing like the CeAnn he was used to seeing, and she didn't know what he would think. He always looked so together and urbane, and she wanted him to be proud of her this evening.

The dogs began to bark and gather around the door in anticipation of company as the doorbell sounded. Little Stinker and Ms. Cluckie came out of the kitchen, and CeAnn shot them a warning look as she went to let their guest in. "I want all of you to behave. And don't jump on him, Blackie."

The forewarned dog hunkered down on the floor and wagged his tail innocently. CeAnn nervously rechecked her braid. "And you stay off him too, Little Stinker. I love you, but I think you make him nervous."

She took a deep breath and opened the door, smiling her welcome as Steve stepped in. Blackie instantly jumped on him, pinning him to the wall with his large paws.

"Blackie!" CeAnn hurriedly dragged the dog off her date and apologized profusely for his behavior. "I'm so sorry. I don't know why he insists on being so friendly with you." Actually, that wasn't quite true. If she had been a dog and could have gotten away with it, she'd have been all over him too.

There was a loud, protesting squawk from Ms. Cluckie. In trying to avoid Blackie's affectionate greeting, Steve had accidentally stepped on the inquisitive bird. Chicken feathers flew around as Steve groped for CeAnn, trying not to step on the chicken again.

All five dogs decided to voice their opinions and Poops, the canary, raised his voice in protest at all the racket.

CeAnn finally managed to steady Steve, and he looked down at her, smiling in disbelief. "This place is a madhouse. You know that, don't you?"

"I know." She grinned back at him, happy to see he was taking all the confusion in stride. "And it gets worse."

She snapped her fingers authoritatively, demanding obedience, as she ordered the animals to quiet down and disperse. When calm prevailed, she drew a deep breath and apologized again for their behavior.

"Why do you keep so many animals?" he asked, helping her into the jacket she had just picked up from the sofa.

"Oh, I don't know. I suppose it's just my promiscuous nature," she quipped, then could have bitten her tongue. She hoped he wouldn't take that feeble attempt at humor seriously! *Indiscriminate* would have been a much better choice of words.

Her eyes narrowed as he looked at her. "Have you ever thought about trying to change your nature?"

"No." She sighed with weary resignation. "I've always been that way. I realized a long time ago that I'm just a soft touch for whoever wants or needs my attention, so I just try to put up with all the traffic." She smiled encouragingly at his worried frown. "But thanks for being concerned."

Steve wasn't the first to be mortified by her weakness for animals. Many of her friends felt the same way, but she just couldn't turn any of the animals out on the street.

With a defeated sigh, Steve decided to forget it and just concentrate on having a nice evening. As they walked out to his car, they both commented on what a lovely night it was. Although it was cool, the air had an exhilarating crispness to it.

"I thought we might take in a movie," he suggested. They got in and he started the engine. "There's one playing at the Cinema that sounds pretty good."

She knew the movie he was referring to. "That sounds great. I love Harrison Ford."

That didn't surprise him. It seemed as if she loved everyone.

The evening passed much more quickly than either of them expected. They managed to get past their initial shyness, and an easy and relaxed conversation developed. After the movie they went to an ice-cream parlor and had hot-fudge sundaes and coffee, finding endless subjects of mutual interest to discuss.

It was growing late when CeAnn glanced up at the clock and noted the hour. "Oh, gee. Look at the time."

"Yeah, it's late. I should be getting you home." He reached for the check as they slid out of the booth. She waited while he paid the cashier and then they started for the car.

The temperature had taken another drop and with the added chill of the ice cream, her teeth were chattering as they got in the car.

"It'll take a few minutes for the heater to warm up," he told her. He glanced at her hesitantly, then shyly reached over to pull her next to him. "In the meantime, maybe this will help."

She nestled against him as he started the car and pulled out of the parking lot. Closing her eyes contentedly, she drank in the pleasant scent and feel of him as his arm closed more tightly about her.

They didn't make an attempt at conversation during the ride home. Each was lost in his own thoughts and pleasure.

Steve pulled into the drive leading to her house and killed the motor. Then he turned to gaze at her thoughtfully.

"Are you warm yet?"

"Mmm . . . I'm almost asleep," she confessed quietly.

It felt good to hold her in his arms this way. CeAnn was smaller than he'd thought, small-boned and delicate.

The light of the bright harvest moon streamed through the windows. His eyes ran hungrily over her slender curves, and lingered on her dress and makeup. There was something different about her tonight. He'd noticed it the moment he picked her up, but he hadn't been able to pinpoint the change. She was as beautiful as ever, but she also had a pure, wholesome look about her. That's it, he realized. The heavy makeup and wild hairstyle were gone, replaced by a sweet simplicity that left him breathless.

Aware of his close scrutiny, she blushed and modestly lowered her lashes. "Do I have ice cream on my nose?" she bantered.

"No . . . I was just thinking that you look different tonight." His voice had grown husky, almost reverent, as he gazed down at her.

"I hope I meet with your approval," she said sincerely. She knew he probably preferred her more flamboyant style, but he had to see the real CeAnn Masters sooner or later.

"I approve . . . very much so." His hand reached out hesitantly to touch her face, his fingers gently grazing the silken skin. She closed her eyes and let herself feel his heavenly touch. "And you're wearing your hair differently. I like it this way."

"Thank you. I was hoping you would." Her voice was barely a whisper. She opened her eyes and met his blue gaze.

Slowly, they moved closer, until their mouths were only inches apart. "I like everything about you," he confessed.

"Excuse me if I find that hard to believe." She laughed softly. "But it seems to me that I've noticed a definite lack of interest on your part."

His mouth touched hers lightly, sending shivers up her spine. "It isn't that I wasn't interested. I just wasn't sure how to approach you," he admitted.

"I don't know why," she murmured, feeling every bone in her body melt. "I'm not unapproach-able. . . ." Her words dissolved like cotton candy as his mouth closed over hers possessively. There was no trace of shyness as he pulled her closer and continued to deepen the kiss. It could have been moments or it could have been hours, neither was sure, but the kisses grew more intimate, lingering. There was an increasing hunger between them as their hands began to explore and tease. Tongues touched and passion grew to painful intensity, and CeAnn's mind whirled with indecision.

If she let this continue, there was no question where it would end. Normally, there would be no need for a decision. She would say good night and send him on his way. But Steve Hayden did not make her act normally. He made her go a little crazy.

"CeAnn . . ." He paused, his lips barely touch-ing hers. "Could I come in with you?"

"Yes." The decision was made without a second thought.

Steve knew he wasn't good at this sort of thing. He was going to sound like a fool, but he wanted her so very much. "I know this is rather sudden, but . . . oh, hell, CeAnn. I want you." He buried his face in the warmth of her neck, hoping she would forgive his lack of sophistication. With other women, sex had been something he could detach himself from, simply enjoying the moment. But with her, it was going to be different. He knew that as clearly as he knew his own name, and for a brief moment he thought about the Pandora's box he was about to open. But he knew he had come too far to back away now. Though she was far more experienced than he, still he felt a closeness to her that he had never felt with any other woman.

"I'm very honored you would want to stay with me," she whispered lovingly.

"No, I'm the honored one," he returned sincerely.

As they left the car and walked toward the house, a thought nagged him. He wished she wanted him to stay because she wanted Steve Hayden, not just a man . . . or more particularly, a man who reminded her of an old flame.

Forget it, Hayden! he scolded silently. She's just a woman. One night and you'll have her out of your system. One night, that's all it will take.

But the next few hours proved that one night would not be nearly enough to assuage his hunger for her.

She melted willingly into his arms when they entered the bedroom. She gazed up at him so trustingly, whispering his name almost reverently, as their mouths tenderly grazed one another's.

"CeAnn . . . you're so very special to me," he whispered, his eyes filling with adoration. There was not the slightest hesitation as he helped her slip out of her clothing. "I want you to know that."

"Mmm . . . and you're so sweet," she sighed, laying her head on his shoulder, letting the tips of her fingers graze his neck affectionately, as he continued efficiently to disrobe her. The light beside her bed glowed, but she felt no reserve as his eyes devoured her hungrily.

"Sweet?" His hands paused and he withdrew a bit, a look of predatory maleness in his features now. "Sweet?"

"Well, you are," she replied, unbuttoning his shirt and letting it slide to the floor. "You're the sweetest man I know and you should be proud of it. Not many men can claim that trait." His trousers joined the shirt, and moments later he was in the same natural state as she.

"Sweet is not exactly how I hoped you'd view me at this moment," he protested as he brushed her hair aside and touched the tip of his tongue to her ear.

Shivers of desire raced up and down her spine. She gasped softly and her hands tightened on his firm, bare shoulders. "You know what I mean. . . . I don't think of you as just sweet . . . but you are."

"Well, we'll see if you have the same opinion of me an hour from now," he drawled lazily, shifting his weight and pulling her down to the bed with him. "Maybe together we can come up with something a little more exciting to add to your vocabulary, just for when you think about me."

"If I got any more excited thinking about you, I'd be disgraceful," she confessed. Her hands smoothed the silken hair on his chest as their thighs brushed against each other's.

"Good. I think I'd like to keep it that way," he whispered. His hands slid provocatively over her soft curves and his tongue forcibly parted her lips.

The night turned magical as Steve began a virile

assault on her that left her weak with longing for the ultimate.

"The light . . ."

"Leave it on," he replied in a husky voice. "Leave it on. . . ."

Her desire for him was so complete that she forgot all her inhibitions and strove only to match his fervor, which was stunning in its power.

He groaned and rolled over, pinning her beneath him. His mouth found hers again, his powerful need for her pressing tightly against her fevered flesh.

She could feel his body trembling with the wonder of it all. They exchanged long kisses that sparked the banked fires of their passion to an almost frightening intensity.

"Special . . . you're so very special," he murmured as he moved to make her finally his own. It was almost as if the thought were an agonizing one to him, as if he didn't want it to be. But it was, and he could no longer control his feelings.

And you are so very special to me, she returned silently, blinded by the tears that suddenly sprang to her eyes. I love you, Steve Hayden, her heart cried out. I love you! But the depth of her emotions made it impossible to speak. Her body willingly accepted his, and their ardor began to build and soar, eventually blocking out the entire world.

CHAPTER SEVEN

"I think you were being a little modest," she said timidly as they sat across from each other in a restaurant the next morning. It was barely six o'clock, but Steve was scheduled for the early shift and they had decided to have breakfast together before he went to work.

He glanced up from the menu. "About what?"

"About . . . not being very good at certain things. I thought last night was wonderful." Her face had a radiance about it this morning. She shyly picked up his hand and held it gently between her small ones. For some reason, while making love to her last night, he had found it necessary to apologize repeatedly for some imaginary inadequacy.

A momentary look of discomfort crossed his face. Then his grasp tightened and he smiled at her candidness. "I didn't mean I wasn't very good at . . . that," he clarified, a typical male response. "I only meant I wasn't good at telling you what I was feeling."

"I thought you did fine," she assured him, her pulse still racing at the memory of his tenderly

302

spoken words of passion. "But if you want to tell me again this morning, I won't object," she prompted.

The blue of his eyes darkened seductively as their gazes met and lingered. She had been so different from what he expected. Instead of the experienced woman of the world he had thought to find, Steve had found only an incredibly desirable lady, giving herself in a way that left him longing for more of her touch. He had thought one night was all he would ever want with her. This morning, he knew that one night, or one month, or even one year would not be enough to satisfy him. And he felt a fear he had never before experienced, realizing he had let himself fall in love with a woman who would never be able to give the love or loyalty he would expect in return. In a way it was pathetically funny. For a man who prided himself on being levelheaded and, according to Billie, irritatingly detached when it came to women, he had plunged head first into a situation that would leave the most open-minded man in the world wondering what to do next.

Placing her hand back on the table, he patted it awkwardly, then turned his attention back to the menu. "I'm hungry this morning. What are you going to have?"

Those were not exactly the words she had been hoping to hear, and CeAnn was sure her face revealed her disappointment. She dragged her hand back across the table and tried to focus her jumbled thoughts on breakfast. Why wouldn't he take the opportunity she had just so indiscreetly flung in his face to tell her he'd enjoyed last night too? She had no doubts whatsoever that he *had* enjoyed it, every bit as much as she had.

"Let's have the Harvest Hand breakfast," he suggested. "I'm starved."

"That's a lot of food," she exclaimed. "Pancakes, eggs, biscuits, sausage, gravy, and fruit is a little more than I usually eat in the morning."

"What do you usually eat?"

"Nothing. I hate breakfast," she confessed. "I think I'll just have juice and coffee."

"You sure?"

"Positive."

"How about a roll with the juice and coffee? It says here they bake their cinnamon rolls fresh every morning."

"No, really. I couldn't eat a thing."

The waitress came and took their order, and they went back to holding hands across the table, talking about their plans for the day. After skirting the subject several times, they finally decided they would see each other again that night.

"Would you like me to fix dinner for us?" CeAnn offered, leaning over for another bite of the sausage he was extending to her. So far, she had eaten half his biscuits, three forkfuls of scrambled eggs, one pancake, the bowl of fruit he insisted he wouldn't touch, and two spoonfuls from the gravy bowl, just for a small taste.

"No, we can go out," he replied, trying to contain his amusement as they shared the last biscuit and she licked apple butter from her fingers.

She sighed and pushed her half-full glass of orange juice across the table. "That's okay with me. You want this? I told you, I'm never hungry this early in the morning."

They left the restaurant and he walked her to her car, still holding her hand. "Is this thing giving you any more trouble?"

"No, the man at the garage worked on the carburetor after they towed it in. It seems to be running fine now."

Casting an uneasy glance to see if anyone was watching, he pulled her to him and quickly kissed her good-bye. But she wasn't willing to settle for such a short, to-the-point kiss. Wrapping her arms tightly around his neck, she leaned closer. Their second good-bye kiss was much more satisfying.

"We're making a scene," he murmured as their lips finally parted long moments later. His lips came down to graze the curve of her neck. Then he whispered in her ear, "Maybe we should plan on a late dinner this evening."

"Mmm . . . I was thinking the same thing. A real late one."

Steve gave her one more hug, then opened the car door for her. "I'll see you around six."

As he watched her drive off, he warned himself again that he was getting in too deep. But when she turned around to smile and wave as she pulled out of the parking lot, he ceased all thought of prudence. He was in over his head as it was.

The next several weeks were a succession of late dinners, early breakfasts, warm showers together, long nights of making love, and endless daylight hours of longing for the moment they could be in each other's arms once again.

Steve was fairly certain that CeAnn wasn't seeing anyone else at this point. In the first place, he was allowing her little time for anything but work. Never before had he pursued a woman with such dedication and zeal. It was a driving power within him that both puzzled and annoyed him. CeAnn Masters was in his blood like a virus, making him burn with feverish delight both day and night. At times he was so possessive that he knew he was making her miserable, demanding an accounting of every hour she spent away from him. But though he knew they had no verbal commitment to each other, he couldn't bear the thought of her being with another man.

CeAnn was viewing their puzzling relationship with mixed emotions. Steve was a considerate, exciting man and she was head over heels in love with him. The only blemish on her happiness was his seeming inability to profess his feelings about her. Even at the height of their passionate moments, never once did he tell her he cared for her. Her frustration was so complete that one night, in an effort to coax the words she longed to hear out of him, she teasingly asked if he was as crazy about her as she was about him, to which he promptly replied in the testiest of voices that he wouldn't be in her bed if he didn't care for her.

He had hurt her feelings deeply, and after that she never tried to force the issue with him again. By this time her love was not a teasing matter. She was beginning to grow resentful because he wasn't showing any signs of returning that love. As the weeks passed, she felt she wasn't any closer to Steve emotionally than she had ever been.

It was as if he wanted her . . . but didn't want her.

"I hope you weren't planning anything special tomorrow night," she told him one night as she cleared away their dinner dishes. Steve was lying on the sofa reading the evening paper, trying to keep Blackie out of his face.

"Will you call this damn dog into the kitchen?" he grumbled, irritably snapping the sports page of the paper open in front of him.

"Blackie, get in here." CeAnn walked to the door and ordered the dog out of Steve's domain. "I'm sorry. Was he bothering you?"

"He's licking my face again! You know I can't stand him licking my face."

"I'm sorry."

"There's always a chicken or a bird or a cat or a dog or *something* under my feet," he complained. "I don't know why you insist on living in a zoo."

She sighed without comment and turned back to her work. Because she knew her laxity in housekeeping annoyed him, she had made a conscious effort to improve the appearance of the house. But it was hard with the animals around. She had redoubled her efforts to place them in new homes, but so far she hadn't been able to find a new residence for one of them, let alone *all* of them. It seemed he was complaining more than usual about them lately. Come to think of it, he was complaining more than usual about everything lately.

A few minutes later he came into the kitchen and opened the refrigerator for a cold drink. "What did you say about tomorrow night?"

"I said I hoped you didn't have anything special planned. It's Jenny's birthday and several of the women at the store want to take her to dinner and over to Rosco's."

"Rosco's?" Steve slammed the refrigerator shut and turned to face her in disbelief.

CeAnn winced at his abrupt movement. "Yes, Rosco's. Anything wrong with that?"

"Nothing other than the fact that no self-respecting woman would be caught dead in that rat hole!"

Turning back to the sink, CeAnn struggled to keep control of her temper. He was spoiling for a fight tonight and she was not going to oblige him. "I don't know what makes you say that. Rosco's isn't all that bad and they do have the best margaritas in town. Jenny loves margaritas. That's the only reason we're going there," she said defending herself guiltily.

She was aware of the atrocious reputation the small bar and grill had, but she was getting a little tired of his telling her what to do. It would be different if he professed to *care* about what she did, but it seemed he went out of his way lately to let her know he was keeping himself coolly detached from anything remotely close to a personal commitment.

"You are aware of the sort of crowd that hangs around that dump, aren't you?" he demanded.

"Not really. I haven't been there in years," she replied.

He moved to stand next to her, his eyes sparking angrily. "Is it going to be all women in the party or will there be men involved?"

She turned to face him, her expression growing even more defensive than his. This was not the first time he had implied that she was seeing other men, and she resented his indirect accusations. "I really don't know, Steve. The guy Jenny's been dating said he might drop by and have a drink with us. If you're not doing anything, you're certainly welcome to join the party."

"I change shifts in the morning," he snapped. "I'll be working from two in the afternoon until eleven tomorrow night."

"Too bad. You're always such a delight to have around," she snapped back. Taking off her apron, she flung it over the back of a chair and marched into the living room, tripping over the cat in her anger.

"What's that supposed to mean?" He followed and towered over her ominously as she flopped down on the sofa and picked up a magazine. She really couldn't understand why this was going to lead to a fight, but she knew that's exactly where they were headed. If he had honestly cared about her safety or reputation and asked her in a nice way to cancel her plans, she would have considered his feelings and gladly bowed out of the party tomorrow night. But the way he was acting, she would go come hell or high water! "It means I'm getting tired of your attitude!"

"What attitude? I simply asked you if you're aware of what a hole in the wall you're going to."

"That is not what I'm talking about."

"Then what *are* you talking about?"

"I'm talking about the way you keep implying I'm seeing other men. Frankly, it's getting on my nerves." She thumbed angrily through the magazine. She had never even looked at another man since Steve Hayden entered her life, and it angered her to think he thought she would.

"Are you seeing anyone other than me?" His voice had lost a lot of its anger now, growing almost uncertain and boyish in his anxiety. When the conversation began, he'd had no intention of confronting her on the issue. On the contrary, it was something he tried to forget. But over the past few weeks the thought had plagued him until it had his nerves on a ragged edge.

She glanced up at him through gathering tears, feeling herself grow more and more stubborn in the face of his persistently annoying attitude. "Does it matter whom I see as long as I give you your fair share of my time?"

It was her attitude that angered him now.

"Not if it doesn't matter to you!" he announced curtly.

It hurt to hear him voice so clearly what she had suspected all along. He didn't care one way or the other. "While we're on the subject, Mr. Hayden, are *you* seeing other women?" she countered heatedly.

His mouth dropped open in indignation. "What sort of stupid question is that? Of course I'm not seeing other women. I'm not that kind of guy!"

"Meaning that I *am* that type of woman?"

"How should I know? That's what I just asked you," he snapped. Since they had never openly discussed her earlier personal life, he thought he'd give her ample opportunity now to confess her past indiscretions. At this point, he loved her enough that it no longer mattered what she had done in the past. But he'd be damned if he would stand by and let her continue along the same path, and the past was no doubt the key to her current behavior.

If he couldn't see the terrible hurt in her eyes, it was because he wasn't looking for it.

"Do you honestly think I would do such a thing?" she asked.

"I don't know, CeAnn. That's what I'm asking." His obstinate gaze locked with hers, begging her to be honest with him.

"*No!* I'm not seeing anyone but you. Is that what you want me to say?"

"If it's the truth, yes, that's what I want you to say," he relented, feeling a swift rush of relief at her apparently honest denial.

"Whether or not I'm telling the truth is something you'll have to decide yourself," she challenged in a frosty tone, causing his earlier surge of elation to deflate like a pricked balloon. "And I think we'd better change the subject before this turns into a full-blown argument."

"Who's arguing?" His voice grew almost pleasant now.

"You are. And on second thought, I think you should just go home before it gets any worse." It irked her to think he could suddenly become so nice after being such a fool earlier.

"I was not arguing. I was only trying to point out that you're going to get yourself in a peck of trouble if you go over to that bar tomorrow night. There's a rough motorcycle gang that hangs out there and you'll end up in a pinch."

"I'm perfectly capable of taking care of myself when it comes to other men," she replied dryly. "But if you're so concerned about my welfare, why don't you drop by the bar and see for yourself what I'm doing?"

"Not on your life, lady. If you insist on going over there, you'll have to do it without my protection," he retorted.

"I don't *need* your protection," she returned sullenly. She needed his love, not his protection!

"Of course not. For a moment I almost forgot." He reached over and peevishly scooped up his jacket from the arm of the sofa. "Well, since I've been invited to go home, I guess I will. Have a nice time at your party!"

"Thanks! I certainly plan on it," she flung back.

The tears cascaded down her face as he slammed out the front door. She heard his car start a few moments later. The big dummy! She *would* have a nice time, even if it killed her!

The following evening she had to keep reminding herself that she was having a nice time. It took a concentrated effort on her part. From the moment the five women entered the dingy bar located in the cellar of one of the oldest buildings in the worst part of town, Steve's warning about the establishment kept running through her head.

No doubt about it. The bar was a dive and a half.

Squinting through a thick haze of smoke, she tried to adjust her eyes to the dimness as they walked to the only available table and seated themselves.

"Lordy! This place is worse than I remembered it," Jenny confessed, her gaze wandering hesitantly around the crowded room. "Just look at those guys over there at the bar," she whispered.

All eyes turned in that direction, and they all had to smother nervous laughter. The burly, rough-looking subjects were leaning insolently against the bar, watching the new arrivals with suggestive leers.

"Wow. Dibbies on the one in the neon-pink shirt," Joyce Bartlett bantered.

"And I'll take the one with the cigarettes rolled up in his shirt sleeve," Meryl Hazens joined in playfully.

"Gads. Don't encourage them," CeAnn warned, hiding her face behind a menu. It had samples of every dish smeared across the front and back.

"Look at this," Neva Garrison mused, intently studying the drink selections. "The specialty of the bar is something called a Black Widow. I wonder what that is?"

"It sounds lethal," Joyce said. "I think we'd all better stick to the margaritas. Here comes Rosco, girls. Hold on to your heartstrings," she teased.

The proprietor, who also served as waiter and bartender, came to take their order and the women looked up at him with apprehension. Rosco was wearing a white sleeveless T-shirt, a pair of camouflage pants, and red tennis shoes. He weighed at least three hundred pounds, and had a thick patch of black hair at the back of his neck that made him look remarkably like an ape to CeAnn.

"What'll it be, ladies?" The room was hot and stuffy and Rosco was sweating profusely. Rivulets of perspiration rolled down his fat cheeks as he waited impatiently for the women to make their selections.

Five margaritas were quickly ordered and he lumbered off to fill the order.

"Have you noticed we seem to be in the minority here?" Joyce pointed out. "Whose idea was it to come here anyway?"

CeAnn had been looking over the shady-looking clientele, and had noted with despair that they were the only women present.

"It was mine!" Meryl confessed. "Listen, you guys. Loosen up. This place isn't as bad as it looks. I come here all the time." She was beginning to sway to the music coming from the jukebox in the corner. "Look, here comes Brass Knucks and a few of his buddies."

"Brass Knucks?" CeAnn glanced at her friend apprehensively.

"Oh, I don't know if that's really his name, but that's what everyone calls him. He's probably pretty rough," Meryl warned needlessly. Anyone with eyes could tell he wasn't exactly the Pat Boone type. "But he's always been polite to me. They're probably going to ask us to dance."

The other women at the table sincerely hoped not. The men coming toward them all wore black motorcycle jackets, dirty jeans, black boots, and looks of grim determination on their faces that struck immediate terror into the women's hearts. All except Meryl, who was wearing a most disgustingly inviting smile.

The four men reached the table before anyone could voice objections and run. "Hiya, Meryl." Brass Knucks paused and looked at the pretty blond. There was a long, ominous-looking chain hanging from the shoulder of his jacket.

"Hi, Brass. What's happenin'?"

"Not much. Me and my friends were just thinking it was a shame to let all this good music go to waste." His eyes ran suggestively over the other women peering up at him. "We thought your friends might like a little company."

"I don't know about them, but I sure don't want to let all that beat go to waste," she accepted brightly. She was on her feet, hurriedly claiming Brass Knucks's arm. "Take your pick, ladies," she said over her shoulder.

"All right, girlies. "No fighting, now. Who wants to be first?" The three men leered down at them hopefully.

A rash of nervous smiles broke out at the table.

315

"Oh, not me, thanks," Jenny refused. "I'll just wait here for my drink."

"Oh, go ahead," Joyce urged. "It's your birthday, and we all know how much you love to dance."

"No, I couldn't . . . really! Besides, there are only three of them and there are four of us. I'll be happy to sit this one out. You go ahead and dance, CeAnn."

"Oh, not me. I'm content to sit here and listen to the music." CeAnn cast a dirty look at her. "You go ahead, Neva."

"Well, I would," Neva hastily excused herself, "but I was just about to go to the powder room."

The men watched the exchange with bland looks on their blunt-featured faces. Finally, one of them broke the impasse. "We told you not to fight, ladies. There's enough of us to go around."

Before the women could utter another word, a fourth man was summoned from a nearby table. Seconds later they found themselves out on the dance floor.

Mercifully, CeAnn's companion was not a talker. He was just short and stinky. He merely pulled her up against his chest, plopped his head on her chest, and started to waltz her around the room, holding her like a rag doll in his arms. When that first number was over, it was decided among the men that they would switch partners, which they did. The next hour was spent trying to discourage the overzealous group of men, who insisted everyone was having a good time. More than once, CeAnn wished she had taken Steve's advice and stayed home.

The thought of him made her heart literally ache. He hadn't called today as he usually did. She supposed he was still angry with her, and her pride had prevented her from calling him. Being pressed up against these other men's unwashed bodies made her long even more for the comforting feel and smell of him. She had a frightening realization of just how much she loved him, and it hurt even more to know he didn't return that deep love.

"Say, baby. How would you like to see my tattoo?" her newest partner offered in a drunken slur. The staggering number of drinks he had consumed was beginning to tell in his speech.

"Thanks, but I don't care much for tattoos," she refused politely. She had noticed during the course of the evening that several of the men had shed their jackets so they could display the various serpents and symbols emblazoned on their arms. The last thing she wanted was to upset this rowdy group, but neither did she want to look at their works of art. All she wanted was to get out of here alive and go home.

"But . . . baby." He paused and pulled her closer, peering defiantly with small reptilian eyes into hers. "My tattoo's different," he tempted. "Women are crazy about it."

"Oh," she returned lamely, "that's nice."

"You wanna see it?"

"No, not really."

"You're making a mistake," he warned, his eyes

narrowing resentfully. "I bet you ain't never seen one in the place mine is."

"Well, thanks anyway, but I'll pass—"

The grip on her arm tightened painfully. "But I want you to see it," he insisted.

Her heart sank. She was going to have to see the dumb tattoo, like it or not. "Well, okay. Where is it?"

He grinned devilishly. "Right here." He unceremoniously unsnapped his pants and let them drop to the floor. CeAnn gasped. Her mouth fell open as he turned around and dropped his shorts, bending over to proudly display a nude hula girl dancing on his right buttock. While CeAnn was still staring speechlessly at the expanse of flesh revoltingly displayed before her, a hand reached out to prevent the man from setting the dancing girl into action.

"Okay, fella. I think she gets the picture. You want to pull up your pants and go with the nice man out to the squad car?"

CeAnn turned and almost fell into Steve's arms as the officer with him stepped forward to take the culprit into custody.

"Oh, Steve," she cried, throwing her arms around his neck gratefully. "I'm so glad to see you!"

"Really? Aren't the margaritas as good as they used to be?" he asked dryly.

As mad as he was at her for getting herself in this mess, he still couldn't keep his arms from tightening around her affectionately, pulling her against him. Because he was officially on duty, he moved her out of the crowd to a secluded corner where they could have a few moments of privacy. Burying his face in her neck, he held her closely and whispered in a relieved voice, "Are you okay, sweetheart?"

"Now I am. Oh, Steve." She pulled away so she could look into the blue eyes she loved so very much. "I'm so glad to see you. What made you come by here tonight?"

She wanted to hear him say that he was so worried about her he couldn't stay away. She longed to hear him tell her he loved her and was sorry about the disagreement they'd had the night before . . . even though he had been totally right about her not coming here.

"You're just lucky I did," he scolded, trying to evade her question. "Five more minutes and this place would have been in a riot."

"I know. You were absolutely right about it," she admitted. Her arms tightened about his neck. "I've had a perfectly miserable evening. I promise I'll listen to you next time."

"Sure you will." He chuckled dubiously. "Agreeing to see his tattoo! Damn, CeAnn. Surely you're not that naive?"

"I'm not naive," she defended meekly. "I told him I didn't want to see it, but he insisted. . . . It *was* a little unusual," she said breathlessly. "It was this hula girl—"

"I saw it!" he snapped. "You mean to tell me you liked it?"

"Oh, no. It was horrible," she said soothingly. She could see by the look on his face that she'd better change the subject. "You really came over here to see about me, didn't you, you big faker?" she challenged, breathing in the marvelous familiar smell of him. She kept pressing closer, stirring him to arousal by rubbing against him suggestively.

"CeAnn . . . I'm on duty," he protested as her lips teased his seductively.

"Answer my question." Her tongue touched his lightly.

"I forgot what it was."

"You did not!"

"I'm on duty, CeAnn. If I'm here, it's only because I'm doing my job," he hedged, growing weak in the knees at her sensual onslaught. No matter what she did, he wasn't about to admit he had worried himself sick about her all night and had finally convinced his partner that they should drop by the club as a precautionary measure.

She sighed softly at his refusal to admit he was worried about her. "There are times, Steve Hayden, when I think you don't even like me."

He moved against her, letting her feel the firm effect of her on him. "Does that feel like I don't like you?"

No, that didn't feel as if he didn't like her. But she wanted more. She wanted him to love her.

"I have to get back to work," he announced with one final kiss. He set her back from him gently. "I hope you and your friends are ready to go home now."

She laughed nervously. "I believe we are. Will you kindly escort us to the car?"

"I'd planned on it." He leveled his gaze on her.

It lingered longer than he wanted it to. "I thought if you didn't have any objections, I'd come by after I get off tonight."

"No objections," she said softly.

"I'd like to spend the night with you."

"You can spend a year, if you want to."

They kissed again unhurriedly.

"CeAnn . . . I *was* worried about you," he couldn't help but confess when their mouths finally parted. "I know you can take care of yourself when it comes to men, but you sort of feel like mine. I hope you don't mind."

"No, I don't mind," she said lovingly. "You sort of feel like mine too."

CHAPTER EIGHT

It seemed hours before Steve arrived that evening, yet CeAnn only had time to take a quick shower and slip into her new negligee. Kitty Bledsoe, who worked in lingerie, had guaranteed it would make a man's blood boil.

She stood before the full-length mirror in her bedroom and nervously modeled the sheer, icy green creation. The material clung to her slender hips and shapely thighs in a most alluring and provocative way. Although she wasn't as well-endowed as she wished, she still had enough to hold a man's interest. A soft smile curved her lips. At least one man's interest, she corrected. And that was all she was worried about. Funny. Before meeting Steve she would have gasped at the thought of wearing such shockingly revealing attire. Her smile turned into an outright grin as she tried to visualize his reaction to her latest purchase. But it wasn't shocking anymore. He managed to bring out in her all the wild and crazy things she had always wanted to do, and she felt not the slightest trace of shyness.

Now all the little naughty things were downright fun.

A little after midnight she finally heard his car pull into the drive. She dropped her hair brush on the bureau and eagerly ran to meet him.

He glanced up as she came out of the bedroom, his pulse quickening. The light from the doorway accentuated her slender curves.

"I was beginning to worry about you," she scolded, wrapping her arms tightly about his waist.

"Why? I didn't get off until eleven."

"I know. I think I've just been eager for you to get here," she admitted, impatiently leaning closer to steal a kiss.

He chuckled softly as he pulled her closer, letting his mouth trail soft kisses along her neck and into the creamy hollow of her throat. "What have you got on?" he murmured, his hands exploring under the silken material of her negligee.

"Practically nothing," she said, temptingly.

"I can see that."

"You like?"

He sighed and touched his tongue seductively to hers. "I like," he confessed. Tenderly, his eyes held hers as his mouth slowly descended for a long and lingering kiss. The kiss continued to deepen as they molded their bodies closer and closer to one another's.

Her hands moved slowly from his waist to toy with the buttons of his shirt. He was still in uniform, and she couldn't remember when he'd ever looked more handsome. She heard his soft intake of breath as, one by one, the buttons opened to reveal a mat of silken hair her fingers could not resist.

"You still like?" she parried.

"I still like," he assured her, pressing against her to show his appreciation. Once more their mouths met, his tongue parting her lips and delving into the sweet warmth of her.

In the beginning, CeAnn had felt that their lovemaking was a little stilted. Although Steven was devastatingly male, she had sensed a certain uneasiness in him . . . at times almost a timidity when he made love to her. But that no longer was the case. Now he had an assurance that left her breathless, longing for more.

His shirt peeled away and discarded, her hands reached for his belt buckle. Her newfound boldness surprised her. But with Steve, courage came easily. She couldn't get enough of him no matter how hard she tried, and she had tried very hard the past few weeks. It was becoming more difficult to quell the hurt she felt every time she thought about their relationship; it seemed almost nonexistent except in the bedroom. He seemed very content in her company, but she always had the feeling she wasn't to cross some invisible line he had drawn at the perimeter of his heart. And because she valued what little she did have with him, she had not dared to cross that line.

"I'm not complaining," he said in a husky tone, "but you were serious when you said you were a little eager, weren't you?" He pulled away from her slightly, allowing her hands room to continue their pleasant task.

A soft blush colored her cheeks as their gazes met and held lovingly. "Very serious, Mr. Hayden." She reached out to trace the outline of his face. "All I've been able to think about all evening is the way you make love to me . . . the way you whisper my name and the look you get on your face when you tell me how good it's been for you." Her fingers paused to smooth away the tired lines at the corners of his eyes.

"CeAnn . . ." Steve caught her hands and pressed them to his mouth, trying to still the emotion threatening to choke him. There were so many things that had been left unsaid. He longed to tell her how very, very much he loved her, but for a man who had never found it easy to express his true feelings, the words were hard to find.

"Yes?" She held her breath and gazed at him in complete adoration, sensing the struggle going on within him.

Closing his eyes against a swift stab of pain in his stomach, he took a deep breath and pulled her face to his chest. "Are you sure you want me to make love to you, or is it just the memory of the guy I happen to remind you of?" he managed in a shaky voice.

The question took her completely by surprise. "Why . . . Steve Hayden! What a rotten thing to say."

"Rotten or not, is that why you're sleeping with me?" he demanded. All of a sudden it was very important for him to know.

"Of course that isn't why I'm sleeping with you! Whatever in the world gave you such a ridiculous idea?" She didn't have the slightest inkling of how important that particular question was to him. She stood on tiptoe and blew playfully in his ear.

"CeAnn . . . I want to talk about this," he said shakily, the tip of her tongue sending hot shafts of desire through him.

"So? Talk."

"I can't talk with you doing that," he groaned.

"Okay, how's this?" Her hand made him even more miserable than her tongue had.

"That's worse. Cut it out."

"Oh, all right, grouchy. What's so important that you feel you just have to talk about it right now?"

"I want to know if you're sleeping with me because I remind you of Jess," he said again.

"No. Now can we continue?" She hungrily drew his mouth back down to hers.

"No, I want an answer," he returned stubbornly, pulling away while he still had the strength.

"Steven, this is ridiculous. Jess McIntosh happened a long time ago in my life, long before I even knew you existed. Why in the world would you be worrying about him now?"

"Because it just seems to me you'd probably never have given me the time of day if I hadn't looked like that guy you used to go with. I mean . . . like you said, we are as different as night and day."

"Well, you're wrong. And I don't think we're all that different from one another. I wish you'd stop saying that. Even if we were, I'd still care very much for you, Steve." Her arms tightened about his neck once more. She breathed deeply of his familiar scent, knowing full well she shouldn't have confessed that to him. But the words had poured out before she could stop them. Maybe they didn't exactly see eye to eye on every subject, but she was willing to give ground at times, just as he had been. He puzzled her with his continuing insistence that they lived such different lives. Actually, she thought that, other than her shyness, they had a great deal in common. And as far as her timidity went, hadn't she proved to herself she could overcome that obstacle and go after the man she wanted if she really had to? What greater example of how far she had come in that area than what she had just confessed so openly to him? It hadn't been pleasant pretending to be the aggressive one in this relationship, but in the end it would be worth it if it enabled her to keep him. Someday she would confess that, in her effort to win his love, she had done things she would never have thought of doing for another man and they would both have a big laugh about it—if she ever managed to get him at all.

In a persuasive whisper she urged him toward her bedroom. "Come with me, Mr. Hayden, and I'll show you who I think I'm sleeping with."

"Where are we going?" he asked, innocently letting her lead the way.

"Guess."

"You want to see if I have a tattoo?"

"You don't have one."

"Oh, but I might. At least I would have if I knew you liked them so much."

"That's not funny . . . but come to think of it . . ." They had reached her bedroom door. She paused to grin impishly at him. "That guy did have the cutest set of . . ."

"Of what?" He cocked a dubious brow.

"Buns."

"Buns? Now wait a minute. I thought you said they were horrible."

"I didn't say *they* were horrible. I said his hula girl was horrible. Actually, his tush wasn't all that bad."

"CeAnn Masters, you should be ashamed of—" Her marauding mouth prevented him from chastising her further.

"Never fear. I'm sure I will be by the time I get through with you," she predicted happily, pulling him into her room and hurriedly slamming the door.

Later, much, much later, she rolled over in his arms and let out a long, contented sigh. Their lovemaking had been intense and very emotional at times. She could not remember when he had been more attentive or more exciting than in the past few hours.

"Mmm." She nibbled at his neck affectionately. "I trust everything was to your satisfaction, sir."

"Mmm," he replied sleepily.

"You hungry?"

"Mmm."

"Does that mean, mmm, you're hungry, or mmmm, you're not hungry?"

"It depends. If I have to eat blue eggs again, I'm not hungry."

"What's wrong with blue eggs? They taste just like white ones," she protested.

"I don't know. There's just something about eating a blue egg that turns me off."

"Ms. Cluckie is going to be hurt. She's very sensitive."

"Tell her my cholesterol level is up. Surely she'll understand."

CeAnn chuckled and kissed him long and leisurely once more. "Well," she murmured a few moments later as her hand brazenly explored his body. "If you don't want to eat, what do you want to do?"

"I don't know. What are my choices?"

"We could go to sleep, or watch television, or talk . . . or"—she nuzzled her nose against his playfully—"try for a third time."

He groaned and opened one groggy eye to peer at her, begging for mercy.

She laughed. "Talk?"

"Yeah, let's talk," he agreed. He rolled over on his back and propped the pillow behind his head. Then he drew her tightly to the curve of his naked thigh. "What do you want to talk about?"

CeAnn paused, then replied softly, "Could we talk about us?"

His face clouded for a moment. Then his expression grew tender as he gazed down at the mass of shiny curls spread across his chest. Gently reaching out to stroke the perfumed silkiness of her hair, he sighed and gradually let himself relax in the downy softness of the bed. "All right. What about us?"

"That's what I want to know," she coaxed in a small voice.

For a moment he didn't answer. He just lay there absently stroking her hair, his eyes focused on the ceiling.

"Steve?"

"Yes?"

"I—I know you don't want me to say this. . . . I mean, I can sense that for some reason you don't want to talk about our personal feelings for one another. But I just feel like I'm going to burst if I don't say this. I love you. I can't help it, but I do." There. She had said it and it was out in the open.

Again there was only silence. He continued to stroke her hair gently, still staring thoughtfully at the ceiling.

"Well?"

"Well, what?"

"Aren't you going to say anything?"

He struggled to find the right words. "I don't know what to say."

She propped up on her elbow and studied him quietly. "It's what you're not saying that bothers me," she confessed.

"If you want me to say that I love you in return . . . then consider it said," he advised softly, and she could've sworn he blushed as he said it.

"You do? You love me too?" She sat up straighter and peered at him hopefully.

"Of course I do. Very much."

The sudden swell of elation in her heart was tempered by his maddening reserve. "You don't sound as if you do," she complained, willing him for once to let down his barriers and tell her what he was really feeling.

"You know I'm not very good at this sort of thing, CeAnn. I love you . . . okay?"

"Okay." She lay back in the circle of his arms and couldn't help but feel a nagging sense of disappointment. This was the moment she had waited for all her life. The moment when the man she loved told her he returned that love in full measure. But somehow it had come and gone as undramatically as hanging out the wash.

"Oh, good grief. I was afraid of this! Does the skunk *have* to sleep with us?" he grumbled. A ball of soft black fur jumped up on the bed and scurried across their naked bodies.

Steve sucked in his breath painfully. "Damn! He has sharp claws." He frantically tried to shield a certain vulnerable part of him from the tiny feet clawing their way across the bed. But the animal was undeterred in his quest and in a few moments had tunneled under the blanket at the foot of the bed.

With a dirty look on his face Steve settled back down. Then both of them just stared up at the ceiling. Finally he broke the silence. "Have you ever really been in love before?"

Although the question caught her completely off guard, she saw no reason to be anything but honest with him. "Yes."

"Who?"

"Jess McIntosh. What about you? Have you ever been in love before?"

"No. You're the first." The softly spoken admission made her heart skip a beat.

"Come now, I'm not that naive," she bantered. "There had to be women in your life before you met me."

"I didn't say there weren't any women in my life, I just said I had never been in love with any of them."

"I think that's nice." She grinned. "So I'm the best, huh?"

"I don't know about the best, but you're the strangest," he allowed with a cocky grin. "Why didn't you marry Jess?"

She sighed and let her fingers run adoringly through the curly hair on his chest. "I don't know. At the time I felt like I wasn't ready to settle down. We had both just gotten out of college and at that time I had a lot of big dreams. I wanted to make my mark in the world before taking on the responsibilities of a husband and children. Jess was so possessive of my time and attention that I knew he would never let me be just me. I would always be Mrs. Jess McIntosh and I didn't want that." She laughed ironically. "Now look at me. I'm twenty-seven and haven't made my mark in the world. In fact, I haven't even made a tiny dent yet. I love my job, but it isn't exactly where I'd hoped to be at this point in my life. Did you know I majored in English? I was going to be a school teacher."

"What happened?"

"I taught junior high for a couple of years. To be honest, the students got to me. They were not quite children and not quite adults, and I soon found out I wasn't cut out for that type of work. So now I devote my time to making the women of the world more lovely for you men to look at," she finished wistfully.

"On behalf of all the men in the world, I thank you for making our lives a little easier," he teased. "We need all the help we can get."

"Don't be so smug," she warned. "I have a lot of men customers too."

He seemed to wilt before her very eyes. "Yeah, I know. . . . I think we should talk about that."

She propped up on an elbow again and grinned at him. "I hope this means you're jealous?"

"Well, hell, yes. I'm jealous," he admitted rather heatedly.

"Good!"

"I thought you didn't like possessive men."

"I don't. But being possessive and being jealous are two different things . . . sort of."

"Well, I'm not possessive, but now that we have our feelings for each other out in the open, I expect you to give up the other men," he warned.

She frowned. "Give them up? Why? That would cut my wages nearly in half." And the loss in commissions would be staggering, she thought.

"Why? You have to ask me why?" Steve suddenly sat straight up in bed, angrily threw the sheet back, and stood. "Why? The woman has the audacity to ask me why!" he grumbled as he stalked to the window. There was a loud, protesting squawk as he inadvertently stepped on Ms. Cluckie, who was nesting on a blanket beside the bed. Feathers and profanity abounded as man and bird tried to separate themselves. The dogs in the other room set up a howl at the unexpected disturbance. CeAnn jumped out of bed and protectively gathered the chicken and the skunk into her arms.

Steve was still vehemently threatening every animal in the house as she hurried out to quiet the dogs, returning Ms. Cluckie to her box in the kitchen and Little Stinker to the sofa.

When she returned, he was dressed, standing by the window and peering out at the moonlit yard.

"There. They're all quiet and tucked in for the night again," she soothed. "Steve? Why are you dressed?"

"I'm going home," he stated flatly.

"Home?" She glided swiftly across the floor on bare feet and stood beside him. Placing a hand on his shoulder, she carefully turned him around to face her. "Please don't. I want you to stay."

"I don't think that's such a good idea," he said almost curtly.

"Well, for heaven's sake, why not? I know the animals upset you, but—"

"It isn't necessarily the animals, CeAnn . . . it's all of this . . . this mess!"

"What mess?" Her tone was somewhat guarded. Her hand hesitantly dropped from his shoulder. For the life of her, she couldn't understand his moods. A few minutes ago everything had been fine, and now he was on edge and testy again. "We were having a simple conversation when all of a sudden you stormed out of bed and then blew up like a time bomb! What happened?"

Letting out a sigh of exasperation, Steve jammed his hands into his pockets and turned back to the window. "I just don't know if I can handle this," he confessed in a weary voice.

"Handle what?" By now she was losing her patience.

"All of this! You, the other men, the animals, the . . ." He shuddered, running his fingers agitatedly through his hair. "My life was perfectly sane before I met you, and now I find myself crazy in love and I don't know how to express my feelings in words. I know I should be telling you how much I love you and how I don't think I can live without you . . . but at times I don't think I can live with you either. And to be honest, CeAnn, I don't know if my nerves will be able to survive a relationship with you," he finished helplessly.

"Steven! Who are these men you keep referring to?" she demanded.

"The other men you're dating and sleeping with," he shot back angrily. "I don't know their names, and I don't want to know them, but if we're going to continue seeing each other, you're going to . . . stop that. Immediately!" he added firmly.

"The other—" Her eyes narrowed angrily. "I think you'd better explain that little crack."

"What's to explain? I'm not saying I didn't step into this relationship with my eyes wide open. At the time, maybe I only wanted . . . I don't know, but I love you now and you say you love me, so the time's come for you to make up your mind about what you want out of life. Your freedom or me."

To say she was flabbergasted by his accusation would have been an understatement. "You think I've been seeing—no, *sleeping* with—other men while I've been dating you?"

His gaze locked with hers obstinately. "Yes."

A sharp slap stung his face. "Well, I'm not."

He flinched. His cheek smarted painfully. "CeAnn, you've never tried to hide it from me. I know you have."

She slapped him again. "I have not," she returned stubbornly.

"You mean to stand there and tell me that I'm the only man you've slept with?" he taunted, reaching up to rub his cheek, which was turning bright red.

"I have slept with two men in my life: Jess McIntosh and you."

"What about that man who sent you flowers?" he challenged.

CeAnn had to think about that one. "You mean Palmer Jarvis?"

"I don't know his name! The guy who sent you all those expensive roses."

"Jarvis and his *wife* sent me those flowers for helping him select her gifts for the past few years," she returned evenly. "You listen to me, Steven Hayden. Until I met you I barely had the nerve to speak to another man, let alone go to bed with him! You may not want to believe this, but I happen to be a very shy person!"

"Excuse me if I do find that hard to believe. The

way you went after me was hardly the way a shy woman would go after a man."

"Well." She took a deep breath and straightened to her full height, which was only to the middle of his broad chest. "If you have such a low opinion of me, perhaps we're both wasting our time seeing each other."

"Now, look, CeAnn." He began to back off a little at the look of determination in her eyes. "I told you, I love you. I don't care what you did before you met me, but now that we've found each other, I don't think it's too much of me to ask for your . . . loyalty." He strove to phrase it so he wouldn't upset her again.

As dearly as she loved him, she would never stay with a man who had so little respect for and trust in her.

"I'm sorry, Steve, but I think you were right. You should go home. Don't bother to come back." She swept by him angrily, trying to blink back her tears. She walked over and sat on the bed. In all honesty, he probably had every right to feel that she had been a woman on the make by the obnoxious way she had gone after him. But at the moment that did nothing to alleviate the pain closing in around her heart.

"CeAnn." His voice was tender with concern as he knelt down beside the bed to take her hand in his. "You can't mean that. I know I'm not a man to express his feelings the way I should, but I do love you, no matter what."

"You don't love me or you would never think

such an awful thing about me," she pointed out with a sob.

"Okay, okay. Maybe I've been wrong," he conceded, inclined for the first time to believe she was telling the truth. He noted the tears running down her cheeks with growing distress and he reached up to gently touch one of his fingers to the salty wetness. "If I've offended you, I didn't mean to . . . I don't know where I got the crazy idea that you were seeing other men. . . . I'm sorry for my stupidity. I suppose it was a bad first impression and then, as time went on, I never saw anything to change my mind."

"You thought I was a—a loose woman?" She could barely get the words out.

"Not loose in that sense, just not necessarily a one-man woman."

Her eyes sparkled with fury. "I can understand what made you feel that way at first, but after you began to know me, you should have realized I wasn't that sort of woman."

"I'm sorry. I made a mistake. The only excuse I have is that I haven't had that much experience with women." He reached in his pocket and withdrew his handkerchief to hand to her. She took it and wiped at the tears still streaming down her cheeks. "Look, I'm sorry I misjudged you. Can we start all over?" he pleaded in a husky whisper.

"I don't think so, Steven. I guess you've been right all along. We have absolutely nothing in common. I'd never think such an ugly thing about you without confronting you on the matter." She blew her nose and tried to hide her red-rimmed eyes from him. "You've said it yourself . . . many times. We are different and I just don't think it will work out. You dislike my animals and my life-style . . . and I don't know if you'll ever really trust me. Trust is important, Steve. I'm me and I always will be. I don't want to change."

"CeAnn." He groaned, his hand tightening on hers. "I don't want you to change and I'll admit I've been the world's biggest fool. We're not all that different—not really. Why, I haven't ever told you this, but we even have the same birthday . . . isn't that something?" he asked in desperation. He just couldn't lose her now.

"Having the same birthday does not erase what you've thought about me," she insisted in glacial tones. "That is unforgivable."

"Don't say that," he pleaded. "We can work this out. And as far as your zoo's concerned, we can surely reach a happy compromise about—"

"No. I mean it, Steve. I don't want to see you again." The painful realization that he could think such a thing about her was still so fresh in her mind that it clouded any thought of the future.

He stood up slowly, realizing she was not to be reasoned with at the moment. "Just like that, it's over between us?"

"Just like that," she affirmed, lying across the bed on her back and letting the tears flow freely. "It's over."

"I don't want to believe that."

"You better make yourself," she sobbed, "because I mean it."

With a tired sigh he ran his hand through his

hair. "All right. If you won't listen to reason, there's nothing else I can say . . . except I do love you, CeAnn. I always will. Call me if you ever change your mind."

Without another word he rose, staring at her for a moment, then turning. He heard her cry out his name. "Steven?"

"Yes?"

"You want to hear something funny?"

Somehow, he couldn't think of a thing he'd find amusing at the moment. "What?"

"I *am* a one-man woman. I just have an uncanny knack for picking the wrong man every time."

Steve's eyes clouded with pain. "I know you can't believe this right now, but you didn't pick the wrong man this time, sweetheart. Only a very human one who's made a very stupid mistake."

CHAPTER NINE

CeAnn didn't care what Dr. Pierson said. She should have been over Steven Hayden by now. It had been one month since he'd left her house. He hadn't returned, or even called, for that matter, and instead of getting over him, she was getting more miserable every day.

She stepped out of the doctor's office into the corridor of the medical building, mumbling under her breath and scratching painfully at the red, angry rash on her arm. Urticaria! That's what the doctor said—in laymen's terms, she had plain old hives!

"Are you under any sort of stress, CeAnn?" Dr. Pierson had inquired as he wrote out a prescription for the discomfort.

"A little," she admitted.

The doctor peered sympathetically over the rims of his glasses. "Well, whatever's bothering you, I'd suggest you try to get it cleared up. This medicine will help, but it's up to you to get control of the situation."

Little does he know the situation is totally out of my hands, she agonized as she made her way to the adjoining pharmacy and handed the pharmacist the prescription. She had been the one to foolishly inform Mr. Hayden she never wanted to see him again, and he had taken her at her word. He never came back!

Many times in the past few weeks she had thought of calling him and retracting that thoughtless statement, but she always decided against it. She had already made a big enough fool of herself by shamelessly chasing him and she couldn't bring herself to repeat that mistake.

Although, she had to admit, his opinion of her couldn't possibly sink any lower.

"This is going to take a few minutes to fill," the pharmacist informed her pleasantly. "If you like, you can step over to the fountain for a cup of coffee.

"No, thanks, I'll just wait here," she replied glumly.

Taking a chair next to the door, she picked up a magazine and absently leafed through it, trying to resist the overwhelming temptation to scratch the inside of her thigh.

The door opened and a pregnant woman lumbered in, proceeding laboriously to the counter. "Excuse me, I was wondering if the prescription for Mallard was ready yet?"

Glancing up from the page, CeAnn's face broke into a friendly smile. "Billie!"

Turning at the sound of her name, Billie saw CeAnn sitting there and broke into a big smile of her own. "CeAnn! How nice to see you again."

"It's good to see you too." CeAnn stood as Billie

came over to give her a big hug. They had become very close during the time she dated Steve, and CeAnn had missed her lately.

"Whoa!" CeAnn laughed, trying to get her arms to reach around Billie's burgeoning waist. "I see Junior is really progressing!"

"Is he ever! And his mother's miserable," she confessed as she sank down on a chair with a weary sigh.

"How much longer?"

"The doctor thinks it will be another week, but I'm sure it's going to be any second."

CeAnn sat down next to her and smiled. "I know you can't wait."

"I think I'm doing better than Kirk. He's a real basket case. We've had I-don't-know-how-many mock rehearsals on getting me to the hospital when the labor pains start. He has it timed to precision, but I'll bet anything when the time arrives we'll be as disorganized as they are in all those comedies you see on television." She sighed wearily. "It can't come soon enough for me. The nursery is ready and everything is just waiting for Baby Mallard's appearance." Billie reached out and grasped her hand tightly. "Gee, it *is* good to see you. How have you been?"

"Fine . . . I guess."

Billie's gaze softened as she patted her hand reassuringly. "I was sorry to hear about you and Steve. I really hoped it would work out between the two of you."

"Yeah . . . I hoped so too," CeAnn admitted. "How is he?"

"Didn't you know? Well, no, of course you wouldn't. Steve's in the hospital."

"In the hospital! No, I didn't know—what's wrong with him? Oh, Billie, he hasn't been hurt on the job, has he?" It had been weeks since CeAnn had picked up a newspaper or listened closely to a news broadcast because she had been so immersed in her own troubles. Dear Lord! Had he been shot or hurt in a car accident or beaten up in an alley and left to die? The mere thought made her go weak with fear.

"Actually, they don't know what's wrong with him," Billie confided thoughtfully. "For the last couple of weeks he's been feeling terrible, so the doctor finally admitted him to the hospital yesterday for testing."

CeAnn's grip on Billie's hand grew almost painful as her terror continued to grow. "What do you mean, they don't know what's wrong with him? Do they think it's something serious?"

"As I said, we just don't know. He's been having some pain in his abdomen and vomiting, and the poor guy has lived on antacids since it all started."

"When do they think they'll know something?" CeAnn persisted. "Does he have a good doctor? If he doesn't, I'll call around and find one who—"

"No, no, that's not necessary," Billie said. "He has a marvelous doctor who's a specialist in stomach disorders, and by tomorrow or the next day we should know the results of the tests." Noting her concern, Billie patted CeAnn's hand reassuringly once again. "Listen. Why don't you stop by and

344

visit him? I know he'd like that. He's in room four fourteen at Bellview."

"Oh, no, I couldn't," she refused hurriedly. "I'd probably only make him worse."

"Now, why would you say that?" Billie chided. "I've always thought you were very good for Steven."

"Too bad he didn't share your feelings."

"I think he does, but he just doesn't know how to show it."

"He doesn't have any trouble expressing himself when he really wants to," CeAnn objected. But her mind seemed intent on torturing her with memories of the nights she had lain in his arms and they had talked and made love into the wee hours of the morning.

"Mrs. Mallard? Your prescription is ready," the pharmacist announced. He walked over and handed Billie a small package. "I just put it on your account."

"Thanks, Mr. Holman." Billie tucked the prescription into her purse and pulled herself up out of the chair. "I have to be going now. Kirk's come down with a cold and I want to stop by the hospital before I take this medicine to him. It's really been good seeing you again, CeAnn. I hope you reconsider about going to see Steve. I know he'll welcome your visit."

"I don't know, Billie . . . I'll have to think about that. But call me sometime and we'll have lunch."

"Sounds great, but it may be awhile." She

laughed, patting her stomach affectionately. "By then I hope I'm about thirty pounds lighter!"

"Billie." CeAnn caught the other woman's arm as she opened the door. "Will . . . will you call me and let me know what they find out about Steve?"

"No," she said kindly. "If I told you, then you would never go to see him. And I may be wrong, but I think he needs you more than anything in the world right now." Her arms encircled CeAnn's neck and she hugged her once more. "And I think it's only fair to warn you that I'm not wrong very often when it comes to my brother." She turned and walked out before CeAnn could plead with her further.

Billie's words kept ringing in her mind on the way home and all the following day at work. Steven needed her. Steven needed her. Was that really the truth or was CeAnn just desperately hoping it was?

The day seemed endless, and when she finally walked to her car that evening she felt drained and exhausted from the struggle within her.

After a tasteless meal and a hot shower, there was still a persistent nagging in her. At seven-thirty she finally admitted defeat, slipped on her clothes, and made the thirty-minute drive to Bellview Hospital.

She entered the large medical complex, her stomach tied in knots. She walked to the elevator and pushed the button. According to the signs, visiting hours would end in another thirty minutes. But that would give her plenty of time to stick her head in the door and ask how he was doing. She only planned on staying long enough to pay a respectful visit and inquire about his health. It would be hard to swallow her pride, but she knew if she didn't, she wouldn't sleep a wink all night. CeAnn had to see for herself if he was all right.

Walking down the fourth-floor corridor, her eyes noted the room numbers. Then she was standing outside room four fourteen. The door was partly ajar and the sounds of men's voices came from inside. She paused and took a deep breath. Then she tapped softly and the voices stopped.

"Come in," a man's voice called.

Pausing just long enough to gather up her courage, she pushed open the door and stepped in.

There was one bed, in the center of the room, with a single light over it. The light glowed on the tired and drawn features of the man lying beneath it. CeAnn's breath caught as her gaze locked with a pair of blue eyes she had gazed into so many times before.

"CeAnn?" Her name was a disbelieving whisper on his lips as she stepped closer to the bed.

"Hi . . . I hope I'm not disturbing you."

"No . . . no, you're not disturbing me." His eyes continued to drink in her unexpected presence. "Uh . . . CeAnn, this is Bryan Hollister. Bryan and I work together. Bryan, this is CeAnn Masters."

Bryan and CeAnn made the appropriate responses and a few minutes later Bryan announced that he had to be running along.

"Thanks for stopping by," Steve said. Bryan walked to the bed and shook his hand.

"Take care of yourself, buddy. I hope to see you on your feet and back at work before long."

"Yeah, thanks. I hope to be."

Bryan left, closing the door behind him, shutting the couple in a world of their own.

"Hi, again." Steve smiled shyly.

"Hi." She grinned back.

"Come over here where I can see you," he coaxed, moving to the middle of the bed to make a place for her by his side.

"I don't think they want visitors sitting on the beds."

"You can get up if anyone comes in."

Cautiously, she went over to him and settled herself comfortably in the spot he had made for her.

Reaching out, he took her hand in his and they both held on tightly, as if the other was liable to run. "To say that I'm surprised to see you would have to be the understatement of the year," he said. "How did you know I was in here?"

"I saw Billie at the pharmacy yesterday and she told me."

"What were you doing at a pharmacy?"

"Having a prescription filled."

Steve's face immediately showed concern. "Are you sick?"

"No, I just have hives." At the mention of the word, she immediately wanted to scratch, which she proceeded to do. He watched with growing concern.

"Do you want me to help?" he offered as she tried unsuccessfully to scratch in the middle of her back.

"Would you mind? Here." She jabbed at the spot that was driving her crazy. "Right there . . . I can never reach that particular spot."

Obediently, he rubbed and massaged until she finally heaved a relieved sigh. "Thank you. That's much better."

"That must be miserable."

"Yes, it is."

"Hives, huh?"

"Yeah, but they're nothing serious."

"What caused them?"

"I really don't know," she hedged. She certainly wasn't going to let him know *he* had caused her hives. "What about you? Have they found out anything yet?"

"Peptic ulcer," he announced glumly.

"No kidding? I hope that doesn't mean you have to have surgery."

"No, it's not that bad. I'll be on a strict diet for a while, until it's under control."

"Well, that sounds encouraging." She let out a sigh of relief. "I wonder what gave you a peptic ulcer."

You! he wanted to shout. But he contained himself, shrugging sheepishly. "The doctor asked if I had been uptight lately. Would you hand me the vial of white pills in the drawer?"

"Of course." She opened the drawer, extracted the item, and handed it to him.

"Thanks." He popped a couple of white tablets into his mouth.

"You're welcome. What was that?"

"Antacid."

She sat up straighter on the bed and peered at him anxiously. "Have . . . have you been nervous or upset about anything lately?" If he had, that could be a sign that their breakup had affected him as badly as it had her.

"Oh, no," he scoffed hastily. Too hastily in her opinion. "I think in my case it was something other than nerves that caused it."

"Oh." The expectant light in her eyes died as fast as it had blossomed. "Well, that's good to hear. It would probably be much harder to get over if it had been caused by nerves."

"Yeah . . . probably." They looked at each other for a moment, thirstily drinking in each other's features. "Gosh, it's good to see you," he reiterated.

"Thank you . . . it's good to see you too," she replied politely. She had no idea why they were finding it such a strain to talk to one another. Not when all she wanted to do was throw her arms around him and kiss him senseless.

He picked up her hand once again and she found herself glancing away shyly. "What about you? You haven't been upset about anything lately . . . have you?" he prompted hopefully.

"Me?" She laughed merrily. "Goodness, no. Everything's been going marvelously for me lately," she lied.

His face dropped somewhat. "Oh, well . . . good. I'm glad to hear that. Your hives must have been caused by something other than nerves, then."

"Oh, definitely. It wasn't nerves that caused them. I'm sure of that. It could simply have been something I ate."

"No doubt."

She frantically searched the room for a safer topic to discuss. "Your flowers are lovely."

"Yeah, they are. Everyone's been real nice since I've been in here."

"You're well loved," she returned, and her voice caught with emotion. Realizing her mistake, she sprang from the bed and walked over to the window, hoping to conceal from him the tears that had sprung up so unexpectedly in her eyes. "You know, it feels like we could get our first snow tonight," she observed, trying to speak past the thick lump in her throat. "The air really has a nip to it."

"Really? Well, I guess it's getting about that time."

"Well." She turned from the window and pasted a bright smile on her face. "I suppose I should be running along. Visiting hours will be over in a few minutes and I know you need your rest. I just wanted to pop in and see how you were doing."

"You don't need to go yet, do you?" He raised himself up in bed and eyed her anxiously.

"Yes, I think I should." As if to add credence to her hasty announcement, a nurse entered the room at that moment carrying a tray of medication.

"I'm sorry, Mr. Hayden, but visiting hours are over," she announced as she searched the tray for a small container with his name on it.

"Couldn't she stay just a little longer?" he implored. "She's only been here a few minutes."

"I'm sorry, I don't make the rules. I only enforce them." She handed him his medicine and watched as he obediently downed the three pills. "Do you need anything?"

He did, and it was standing at the window quietly watching as the nurse fluffed his pillow and made him more comfortable. He needed CeAnn in his life—permanently. But the nurse could hardly fulfill that need, so he grumbled a polite "No, thank you" and waited until she left the room.

CeAnn walked to the foot of the bed and stood gazing at him wistfully. "Is there anything I can do for you before I leave?"

"No, I'm doing fine." He smiled. "Thanks for coming. I appreciate it."

"Oh, my pleasure. Well, I guess I'll be going." Picking up her purse from the bed, she took a deep breath and started for the door. If only he needed something! Magazines, loose change—anything to give her an excuse to return the following day.

"Uh, CeAnn."

"Yes?" She whirled around expectantly.

"I was just thinking . . . I hate to ask you, but I

really need a couple of pairs of clean pajamas. Billie forgot to bring them this afternoon."

"I'll be happy to bring you some," she assured him, trying to keep the elation she felt from her voice. "Should I go by Billie's and get them?"

"No, she probably hasn't had time to do laundry yet. If you don't mind, I'll give you a credit card and you can buy me some and then bring them tomorrow night."

"I don't mind at all." She crossed the room again and waited while he searched through the billfold he had pulled out of the drawer beside his bed.

As he handed her the card, their hands touched briefly and she felt herself go weak inside.

"You sure this isn't too much trouble?" he prompted as their gazes met and held again.

"Not at all." His eyes continued to hold hers captive. She felt as if someone had shut off her air supply.

"Then you'll be back tomorrow night?" Their faces moved closer, almost as if a magnet were pulling them together. She could smell his familiar aftershave and it made her go even more limp with longing. Should she dare lean over just a fraction more and let her mouth touch his? She wanted to. Dear Lord, how she wanted to taste and feel and savor the sweetness she knew would be there.

"I'll be here," she promised softly.

He continued to drink in her presence. It might have been her imagination, or merely wishful thinking, but it seemed to her she could see a longing in his eyes that she had never seen before. "I'll be waiting," he said in a husky voice.

"My goodness, do you still have company?" The door had burst open and the nurse came back into the room. CeAnn guiltily sprang away from the bed and scooped up her purse. "I'm afraid I'm going to have to ask you to leave. Visiting hours are over," she informed her authoritatively.

"I was just going." CeAnn cast one last look over her shoulder at Steve and grinned sheepishly as she headed for the door. "See you tomorrow night."

"Come by as early as you can," he called after her.

"I will!" She disappeared out the door as the nurse closed the blinds and drew an extra blanket out of the closet to put on the patient's bed.

"Now, is there anything else, Mr. Hayden? Will you need a sleeping pill tonight?" she asked as she neatly tucked him in for the night.

"No, no pill, but would you get those three pairs of clean pajamas out of the bottom drawer and put them back in my suitcase?" He grinned. "I don't think I'll be needing them."

The following night CeAnn was back at the hospital thirty minutes after she got off work, proudly carrying the new pajamas. And it was again fifteen minutes after visiting hours when she left that evening.

They had walked down to the coffee shop and Steve kept her company while she ate a sandwich. They talked of everything but their severed relationship, both of them making sure the subject didn't come up.

When she walked him back to his room, the hour was getting late. "I can't believe it's eight-thirty already," she exclaimed as she glanced at the nurse, who already had a frown of disapproval on her face. CeAnn smiled and nodded pleasantly to let her know she was aware visiting hours were over. "I'm just leaving," she mouthed silently.

"I'll be glad when I get out of this prison," Steve said as they walked into his room.

"Do you know how much longer you'll have to stay?"

"Another couple of days."

Although she didn't want him ill, she didn't necessarily want him to go home either. If he went home, there would no longer be an excuse to see him. While they were in the coffee shop, he had mentioned that he had accidentally dropped a bottle of his aftershave that morning and broken it. She eagerly suggested that she come back the following evening with a new bottle, since she knew it was his favorite scent. Without a moment's hesitation, he had accepted the offer and even suggested that she plan on eating dinner at the hospital again.

"I know you'll be glad to get home," she sympathized. "Speaking of home, I suppose by the look on the nurse's face I'd better be getting out of here before she comes in and pitches me out into the street."

"I wish you didn't have to go." He sounded

lonely as he sat down on the bed and watched her prepare to leave.

She scratched her arm absently. "I wish I didn't either, but Poops will think I left the country."

"Yeah, not to mention the other animals. They'll have the house in a shambles."

"I don't have any other animals," she informed him quietly.

He glanced up. "Where are the dogs?"

"They all have new homes now."

"New homes? What are you talking about?"

"I decided that maybe you were right when you said there were too many animals in the house, so I got on the ball and found new homes for them. The cats too," she admitted reluctantly.

He let out a low whistle. "That must have been pretty difficult. What happened to the chicken?"

"Ms. Cluckie?" she asked unexpectedly.

His face paled. "Oh, come on, CeAnn. Surely you didn't—"

Realizing how misleading her question had been, she giggled. "No, silly. I wouldn't do that! You see, I found a nice old couple who live on a farm and they took Blackie and the chicken and extended an open invitation for me to come out and have dinner with them anytime and visit the animals. Maudie—that's the woman's name—said her specialty was fried chicken and I was welcome to bring a guest with me. I thought I might go some Sunday afternoon."

"And the skunk?"

She sighed. "No one wanted him, so one day I took him out in the woods and turned him loose. I haven't seen him since, so he must have met up with one of his own kind and I figure he's doing fine."

His smile was tender as he reached out and took her hand, pulling her down on the bed next to him. "You didn't give those animals away because of anything I said . . . did you?"

Her scratching increased in tempo. "No."

"Because if you did, you didn't have to. I know I was unreasonable about them at times, and those darn blue eggs really weren't all that bad."

"No, you were right. I had too many," she said. "I've even decided to sell the house and take a small apartment in town so I won't be tempted to take in any more strays. Besides, I'm sure they're all much happier now. I wasn't home enough to take care of them the way I should, but knowing they're happy makes me happy."

Reaching out, he stilled her busy hands lovingly. "So everyone's happy now."

"Yeah . . . I guess so." She smiled. "Looks that way."

His face suddenly turned very somber. "CeAnn . . . what about you? Are you happy?" Before she could answer, the nurse bolted through the doorway, war flags at full mast.

"I know, I know," CeAnn and Steve exclaimed at the same time as they sprang to their feet. "Visiting hours are over!"

"Right!"

They looked at each other yearningly as CeAnn gathered up her jacket and purse.

"Tomorrow night?" Steve prompted. "Early?"

"Tomorrow night," she assured him.

And the next and the next and the next, she vowed adamantly as she let herself out of his room and rushed down the quiet corridor.

As long as Steve Hayden wanted her to come to him, she would be there.

CHAPTER TEN

One day the following week, the sun just barely peeping over the treetops, Steve got out of his car and walked into the hospital.

"The baby is beautiful, Billie," Steve declared twenty minutes later as he stood at the foot of his sister's bed, beaming proudly. "I think I'm going to like being an uncle."

"She is gorgeous, isn't she?" Billie accepted the praise as her just due. "Kirk thinks she looks like his side of the family, but I think she has your eyes."

"Does she have eyes?" he asked innocently. "How can you tell? She had them all scrunched up when I saw her."

"No, she didn't! She was sleeping. My lovely daughter does not scrunch up her eyes!"

Steve laughed. "How are you feeling this morning after sixteen hours of hard labor?"

"Wonderful." Billie stretched like a lazy cat in the warm sun. "After the baby was born I had the best sleep I've had in months. You know, I think she's going to have a marvelous figure. She used to

359

do aerobics all night long while I was carrying her. She'll knock the men's eyes out."

"I wouldn't doubt it. Well, I'll go so you can catch another nap before they bring in your breakfast. I'm on the early shift this morning."

"Are you feeling better?"

Steve's face clouded momentarily. "Physically? Yeah, I'm doing better."

"Good. I worry about you."

"Don't. I'm doing okay." He walked around to the side of the bed and gave her a hug.

"I can't help it. If you're not happy, I'm not happy," Billie said.

Her words had a familiar ring to them. Steve straightened and tugged her nose affectionately. CeAnn had said basically the same thing about the animals she had loved and given away. "I'm happy, okay?"

"No, it's not okay. You're fibbing and you know it."

"I might be, but I don't have time to get into it right now," he said to pacify her. "Take care of yourself."

As he walked out of the hospital, a terrible sense of loneliness assailed him. It had been a week since he'd seen CeAnn. The truth was, when released from the hospital, he could think of no logical excuse to see her again, so he had gone home to his apartment and stared at the phone, that night and every night since, wishing he could think of one good reason to call her. If he had thought for one moment that she would welcome his call, he might have swallowed his timidity and made himself dial her number. But at this point he wasn't at all sure how she would react.

She certainly hasn't made an effort to call me and see how I'm doing, he noted sourly as he put on his sunglasses and got into the car.

As he pulled out into traffic, his mind went back to the hours she had spent with him in the hospital, and he tried to analyze what her feelings had been at that point. She had been friendly and helpful and pleasant, but nothing personal had passed between them. Other than the brief, impersonal touch of hands when he had handed her his credit card, they hadn't touched each other . . . but he had wanted to. Oh, how he'd wanted to. But once again he had held back only to regret it later. If only he could tell her all the things he kept so closely guarded in his heart, then he wouldn't be going home to face an empty apartment again tonight.

When night did come, he found he couldn't face the thought of another lonely evening, so he ate a hurried dinner at a local fast-food chain and then decided to go to the racquetball club for a vigorous workout. Maybe that would help him avoid another long, sleepless night.

The moment he stepped through the doorway of the club and saw CeAnn standing at the bar with that fruitcake Ruffe Sennett, Steve knew he had made a mistake.

She glanced up from her conversation with Ruffe, and her speech faltered at the unexpected sight of him. Before she could manage to regain her composure, her smile froze on her face. He looked like double-fudge chocolate cake with whipped cream and cherries to a starved dieter. She was so hungry for him it took all her willpower to remain tranquil. She tried to concentrate on what she had been about to say, and finally managed a friendly smile and a wave in his direction. Then she turned back to Ruffe and continued the conversation.

Suddenly, for the first time, it hit Steve squarely between the eyes that he loved this woman more than life itself, and if he didn't get on the ball and *do* something about it, he was going to lose her. It was as pure and simple as that.

Without a second thought he was striding across the room, oblivious to several friends who were calling out his name. He heard nothing but the pounding of his heart as he approached the man and woman at the bar.

"CeAnn." He wedged himself in between her and Sennett, his blue eyes filled with an unusual determination.

"Yes?" She could hardly believe what she was seeing. The nice, polite, never-stir-the-water Steve Hayden was shoving in on another man!

"I want to talk to you."

"Now?"

"Right now."

"Perhaps the lady doesn't want to talk to you," Ruffe interjected curtly.

"Shove off, Sennett. Go buy a pair of decent shorts!" Steve snapped without turning around. "Now, CeAnn. It can't wait." His courage was at a peak and he couldn't waste time.

"CeAnn, do you want me to get rid of this guy?" Ruffe inquired sharply.

"No, Ruffe . . . I think I'd better talk to him," CeAnn replied soothingly. But before the words were completely out of her mouth, Steve was dragging her toward one of the empty courts.

"Where are we going?" she demanded, not at all sure she approved of this new, forceful personality he was exhibiting. "You were downright rude to—"

"I told you, I have to talk to you."

"So talk and quit dragging me around like a rag doll," she protested as they entered the four-wall court. He pitched a racquet in her direction. She caught it and shot him a dirty look. "I thought we were going to talk. Besides, you can't just come to the club and waltz out on the first empty court you see!"

"They'll just have to make an exception this time. They're dealing with an emotionally distraught man."

"Emotionally distraught? What are you talking about?"

He wound up and hit the ball with such force it ricocheted off the walls for several seconds. CeAnn stood back to watch him, amazed at his mood this evening. Steve continued to hit the ball with such ferocity she sank against the wall and just stared at him.

Finally, when his shirt was soaked with perspiration, the struggle within him ebbed and he spoke.

"What were you doing with Sennett?" he asked in a bone-weary voice.

"Just talking. Why?"

"I don't like it."

She felt her hackles begin to rise. "Too bad. I wasn't aware I needed your permission to talk to another man. Since when does it matter to you whom I associate with?"

"Since when did you start associating with him again?" he fired back. "He's nothing but a rounder. Surely you know that."

"I've known Ruffe for a long time," she said in her defense. "He's a perfect gentleman."

"You mean to tell me you've actually gone out with him?" he asked disgustedly.

"No . . . not really. But I should have. Maybe *he* would be interested in deepening a relationship," she taunted. "I had a date with him one night, but I broke it to go out with you."

"When?"

"You know when! The night Billie set us up to go out with each other,"

Steve frowned and slammed the ball against the wall once more. "Damn fruitcake!"

"At least that 'fruitcake' treats me with a little respect," she challenged. "That's more than I get from you."

"Well, now that we're on the subject of respect, how about what you've done to me? Huh? How do you explain *that*, Ms. Masters? Not many women could take a perfectly healthy man and give him a peptic ulcer in such a short time." He heatedly slammed the ball against the wall again.

"Well, you took a perfectly innocent woman and gave her the hives!" she fired back.

He paused, a slow grin spreading across his handsome face. "I thought you said you didn't know what caused them."

She shrugged. "I lied—but so did you," she returned defensively.

"CeAnn." His eyes suddenly grew very tender as his gaze met hers. "I'm sorry about our misunderstanding. I thought what I did about you for a variety of reasons, none of them worth a hill of beans. But if you'll stop and think about it, what else could I have thought? You've got a crazy way of talking in riddles sometimes. I know now you were talking about your pets instead of your men, but you have to admit you came on pretty strong in the beginning. And then when I saw that guy sending you flowers . . . well, I was downright jealous and thought the worst. I know I was being a fool, but in view of our rapidly deteriorating health, don't you think you should forgive me and agree to start all over again? I've learned my lesson, believe me. Never again will I jump to such hasty conclusions where you're concerned."

"Why? We weren't getting anywhere," she held out stubbornly. "At least you never indicated we were."

"I know, and I'm sorry, but we *were* getting somewhere. I wish I knew how to make you believe that," he explained patiently.

"I'm sorry, but I just don't think we were. I was running around chasing you and you remained aloof and untouchable the whole time."

"Untouchable?" He cocked his head in disbelief. "Pardon me, but I seem to remember a few times when there was a lot more than touching going on between the two of us."

At the unveiled reference to their fiery love-making, she found herself blushing again.

"All right. You want me to get down on my knees and say it again?" He dropped to his knees in front of her and took her hand. "I love you. I don't know why I've found that so hard to say, but if you'll be patient with me, I'll try to remember to say it more often," he finished solemnly.

"What?" She bent over him, not at all sure she had heard right.

"I said, I love you. And if you can put up with me, I want to marry you. You may deserve better in a man, but I can promise you you'll never find one who will love you more."

"Oh, Steven." She felt her reservations begin to melt like ice cream on a hot summer day. "Are you serious?"

"If you don't mind a sweaty man, come here and I'll do my best to convince you." He held out his arms, and she knelt willingly in front of him. Their mouths eagerly met for a few minutes. He pulled her closer and deepened the kiss to one of uncontrollable passion.

"And another thing," he murmured huskily against her mouth. "You're going to have all the dogs and cats and chickens and skunks and whatever damn animal you want when we get married."

"Honest?" she squealed happily.

"Honest. You're going to have anything you want. I'll personally see to it."

"If I have you, I'll have everything I want," she sighed.

When their lips finally parted many long minutes later, she smiled up at him, love glowing in her eyes. "Of course I'll marry you . . . but are you really satisfied that I'm just plain old CeAnn Masters and not some little vamp out to lure the unsuspecting men of the world into her evil trap?" she demanded, tears welling up in her eyes. "You have to believe me, too, when I say I've been just as shy as you all along. It was only because I was so crazy about you that I acted the way I did."

"I know you haven't been misbehavin' with anyone other than me," he conceded. "But I have to tell you, CeAnn, with me you've been a real corker."

"And that's exactly how I plan to be until we're both too old to misbehave." She grinned and playfully caressed him in the most private of places.

He shook his head tolerantly and squeezed her tightly. "If I didn't like you doing that so much, I'd give you a lecture on the fact that it isn't a very ladylike thing to do." He began to shower her face with adoring kisses. "But I like it too much, so keep it up."

They kissed again amid delighted and happy laughter.

"At least we'll have an interesting story to tell our grandchildren about how Grandpa met Grandma," Steve pointed out as he stood and pulled her to her feet.

"Aw, we'll both be too shy ever to bring the subject up," she chided, glorying in the realization that, deep down, that had been their problem all along. Neither one of them had been truly able to express his love.

"Oh, I bet by then you'll be able to," he said resignedly, his mouth lowering hungrily to meet hers once more.

THRILLING GOTHIC ROMANCE BY THE AUTHOR OF MORE THAN FIVE MILLION BOOKS IN PRINT!

Joan Smith

A Whisper on the Wind

Soon after her glorious marriage to the dashing Fraser Audry, young Rosalie suddenly felt that something was terribly wrong. People she had never met treated her as an old friend and people kept bringing up a past she knew they'd never shared. Her uneasiness turned to desperate fear as she chased phantom clues that led nowhere. Rosalie sought comfort in the arms of her husband, but an ominous whisper on the wind warned her not to trust even her own heart.

2950-2 $3.50 US / $4.50 CAN

KAREN ROBARDS

A SENSUOUS BLOCKBUSTER BY ONE OF THE MOST POPULAR HISTORICAL ROMANCE AUTHORS OF ALL TIME!

When Megan had last seen her guardian — handsome, aristocratic Justin Brant — she had been a rebellious child, and he had seemed a stern authority figure. Now, at seventeen, she was a breathtaking beauty, and beneath her dewy innocence lay the promise of unawakened passion. The first time they met as man and woman, their desire for one another blazed into a white-hot flame, consuming them entirely. But Megan knew that she had given her body and heart to the one man whose bride she could never be!

__2920-0   **\$4.50 US / \$5.50 CAN**